T0182711

"An ode to the artistic and individual truth and an unflinching examination of soft-spoken suburban bigotry; it's a crescendo of Florida hurricanes, first love, and the undeniability of becoming yourself." —Rebecca Rukeyser, author of *The Seaplane on Final Approach*

"Spellbinding and original, *Notes on Her Color* marks the arrival of a significant new voice in contemporary literature." —Tom Drury, author of *Pacific*

"This novel sparkles with rich, lyrical, sensuous prose." —Jacqueline Roy, author of *The Gosling Girl*

"*Notes on Her Color* [is] a magical journey about music and race and queerness and passing and mothers and daughters . . . Read this book. Come find me and we can bond over our shared joy. Weep over what we thought we feared." —Gene Kwak, author of *Go Home, Ricky!*

"A tale of mothers and daughters, of Florida hurricanes and the madness of music. It's about code-switching in ways that you've never considered, and about what it means to be of a place and of a people. Jennifer Neal has written a book drenched in hurt and magic, love and grief." —Sami Shah, author of *Boy of Fire and Earth*

NOTES
ON HER
COLOR

A Novel

Jennifer Neal

CATAPULT NEW YORK

First Catapult edition: 2023
First paperback edition: 2024

Hardcover ISBN: 978-1-64622-119-6
Paperback ISBN: 978-1-64622-221-6

Library of Congress Control Number: 2022950661

Cover design by Jaya Miceli
Cover image © Shutterstock / C Design Studio
Book design by Laura Berry

Catapult
New York, NY
books.catapult.co

Printed in the United States of America

1 3 5 7 9 10 8 6 4 2

For Natasha Lomboy, who showed me that for every love language that exists, there is at least one person in the world who can speak it fluently.

NOTES
ON HER
COLOR

1

MY MOTHER COULD CHANGE THE COLOR OF HER skin. From what I'm told, it was a gift she inherited from her mother, who inherited it from her mother before her, passed down from blood to blood along with diseases, artistic hysteria, and a predilection for loving the wrong men. My great-grandmother was an Aniyunwiya witch and used to change color before sneaking into settlements to gather supplies and conduct trade.

I was told that she could assume the form of the most respectable white governess and handle herself in a way that made others believe the color change was more than just skin-deep with mannerisms, words, posture, and a general air of entitlement that lodged deep within her bones and held them hostage like a duplicitous marionette. That all changed the day she met my great-grandfather outside the general store in Osceola County. It's named for the slaughtered chief whose pronunciation its white residents butchered long after his death.

My great-grandfather was tall, brawny, with large shoulders like coconuts and thick, long legs roped in muscle. He wore only a pair of filthy trousers and sat in the dirt next to a pile of horse manure, bound to a horse cart by a slipknot looped around his bruised neck and shackles around his wrists. As he waited for his master to return, he met eyes with the woman he would eventually marry in a fire ceremony beneath the North Star. My great-grandmother had been the color of fresh milk, but quickly blushed into her natural rust-colored state when she saw his copper-colored eyes. He watched this transformation, all while holding her gaze, and when she stood before him with soft red skin and sharp cheekbones, he just smiled up at her and said, "Well, would you look at that."

My mother also told me the tale of when my grandmother, who had long suspected my grandfather of indiscretions, turned into a deep crimson red the night an unknown light-skinned woman showed up on their front lawn. The woman held a bottle of cheap whiskey in her hand and shouted at the Florida midnight air, demanding that my grandmother release my grandfather. She said that they were in love, and nothing would come between them—not even my grandmother's twenty children. My grandmother emerged from the front door, the screen door swinging shut behind her on its rusted hinges. She walked down the broken porch steps, gripping a shotgun in her weathered hands, as red as new blood. A single shot rang out into the sky, cutting the silence into roaring shards, and then she pointed the gun at the woman on the grass.

"If you ever come back to my house or see my husband again, I'll kill you," she said. The woman stared at my grandmother for some long moments, then dropped her half-full bottle of whiskey on the starved grass and walked away, disappearing into the night.

I wish I knew more about these people, but I only know

what I've been told. There aren't any books dedicated to their memory, or birth certificates to confirm their screaming entrance into this world. The only proof I have that they existed at all is that I am here to ruminate over who they may have been. When I struggled to fall asleep as a young girl, my mother retold the stories of these people time and again, her voice reinventing the chronicles of our predecessors—their smells, shapes, colors, and misfortunes. She constructed whole landscapes out of fragmented memories, and she developed the individual characters needed to occupy them. She was good at that—giving me just enough material to trigger the obsessive corners of my mind, which happily filled in the scaffolding around her words like concrete.

I was obsessed with the idea of being related to a witch. I first envisioned my great-grandmother as a toothless miscreant with green, scaly skin zipping around on a broom, raining plague and curses down upon the surrounding plantations. She salted the earth with the sound of her maniacal laughter in the wake of destruction. But as I grew older and began to peruse the dusty shelves of history books at the library, my great-grandmother became an empathic healer, one who set bones and fought injustice, who gave bold speeches about freedom, and who died defending precious ideals against vicious tyrants and fragile empires.

I didn't know the true manner of her death. My mother never told me. Instead, we martyred her at valiant last stands on sacred land or assassinated her in the driveway of her own home—always dying in the arms of the only man she had ever

loved. In our darker storylines, my great-grandmother was betrayed by the ones she protected, forced into exile in the tropical wilderness of Cuba, or gunned down onstage by faceless
men in long coats with deep pockets—wondering how it had
all gone so wrong. We changed her story often, swapped end-
ings like trading cards. As she took her final breaths, it was
never the bullet or the noose that killed her will to live—it was
always, and inevitably, heartbreak.

My mother sprang from her mother's agony as a woman
determined to design her own with my father, who rose to
the challenge. During his time at law school, my father would
sometimes visit a local church to hear my mother sing. He admired the way she straightened her kinky hair into a wavy coif
that fell across her face, kissing her lashes.

Then one Sunday morning, my mother debuted as the new
soprano in the church choir. She wore an oversize violet robe
with sleeves that swallowed her hands as she moved from side
to side clapping to the rhythm. When their eyes met from
across the room, my mother said that both her voice and her
senses abandoned her—replaced instead with a faint whisper
in her ear that said, "You can heal him." My father waited for
her after the service, introduced himself as "the most broken
man in the world," and she ran away with him three days later
with a promise to fix him. His wedding gift to her was a brand-
new piano that she learned to play, but never truly mastered.
Her gift to him was a failure to keep her word. Ten years later,
they had me—to fix them both. When I cried, she went to the
garage where the old piano was cloaked beneath a tarp, and

played melodies that put me back to sleep, giving me harmonious dreams.

I was named after an angel who could resurrect the dead. But she neglected to mention that scripture clearly states the world needs to end before I could do just that. And whenever I brought up that important detail, she smiled at me and said, "We'll rewrite that chapter some day."

This folklore was necessary. I know that now. Preserving our histories required a degree of invention because we knew so little about the people who made us this way. Not their ages, not their faces . . . not even some of their names. Any knowledge of who they were was lost in the footnotes of history, having decomposed in much the same way that their bodies did under the dirt that buried them. So I borrowed from the lives of the people I read about in history books, slipping them in and out of the skins of my forebears, mixing memory with history, to fill the rot of my family tree—of which I still know so very little. For the sake of whatever lurks beyond the visible realm of this life, I sincerely hope they don't mind. I didn't bother questioning this unique mythology of ours until I was well into creating the one that would save me—and destroy everything else.

D Minor
to
F Major

(Pan awakes, summer marches in)

2

IN THE SPRING OF MY SENIOR YEAR, MY MOTHER decided it was time to teach me how to be white. It was the only color I couldn't perform.

"It's easier this way, trust me," she said. "This world was not built for darker skin."

I preferred the other colors and the variety of warm, balmy feelings they invoked. When my mother passed, her skin was a pale and perfect white, hard, like old age. My father liked her best this way and demanded that she always present herself like this while preparing dinner when he came home from work. There were no dark things allowed in our home—except for whiskey, and him. My father was a six-foot-ten scowl. He adorned the house in white oak and pine and white wax myrtle, a veritable glut of white altars on which she crucified her color on a daily basis. She let them drain from her flesh like gore from a slaughter every time he entered the room.

I came home from school, and my mother took my backpack and set it on a kitchen chair, then gestured for me to follow her into her bedroom. We sat together on the pale white carpet while a church choir sang "To God Be the Glory" from the flickering TV screen. They shuffled rhythmically from one foot to the other in their long purple and white robes embroidered with gold doves across chests that expanded and collapsed with the spirit of holy gospel. I folded my long legs beneath me and turned to her, watching the television's glow illuminate the side of her face.

"First of all, you always have to pick your moments." She went through a list of examples of passing into the wrong skin at the wrong time, and when it was advisable instead to be my natural rich brown color.

Don't pass on forms of mass transportation.

"Do it before, or after, but only if you know that you can pass for the entire trip; otherwise, you'll give the person sitting next to you a heart attack," she said. "Except airplanes—because those require ID. Always match your ID."

Don't pass anywhere I'm not able to change my clothes.

"If you show up to a party as white as buttermilk but come out of the bathroom as black as night wearing the clothes of someone who just disappeared, you'll be arrested for kidnapping—or worse." She gave a soft chuckle that said it was a hard lesson she herself had had to learn, and without instruction.

"And if you're gonna pass white, make sure your hair plays the part." She tugged gently at one of the kinky curls around my ear and watched it spring back into place. "You could be as white as a ghost, but *this* won't ever change. Most people won't question it. They'll just assume you're Italian or Greek—but some will. So keep your hot comb and flat irons ready." She sighed deeply and opened up her palms as if pleading.

"The thing is, you have to learn to read a room better than the people who live there." She searched for the words she had spent my whole life preparing to share with me. I tingled with excitement. "You have to feel out different spaces like they've got blood and bone of their own—and make yourself fit into them like a liver."

Noting my confusion, she tried again.

"If you walk into a room, and don't immediately know how you're supposed to look to get whatever you want out of that room, then walk away. You don't know how dangerous a closed space can get yet, but you will—someday."

Never pass around people I have to see again, no matter how close to them I may feel, no matter how much I want to trust them.

"You'll do that on your wedding night with your husband, and not a second sooner."

Don't drink or take drugs.

"They make passing unpredictable. You lose control. And that's dangerous."

And never, ever pass at school.

"Kids your age only see differences as weakness. It could be a chipped tooth, or a stutter. But this?" She tongued her large crooked teeth. "Never, ever reveal yours."

I nodded and opened my mouth to speak, then closed it as I noticed the choir on the television screen had been replaced by the radiance of Reverend Jeremiah's aggressive tan.

My mother lowered her voice and leaned close enough that I could see myself reflected in her eyes.

"As you already know, there will be times when you can pass into other colors." The corner of her mouth curled upward. I loved it when she smiled because then I could too. "And it can be nice to give someone a little heart attack." She pressed her thumb and index finger together and surveyed the room playfully as if she were in danger of feeling too smug about the prospect.

"Only if walking away isn't an option. But know this . . ." She held a finger up to her eyes, pointing it like a gun. "Passing is exhausting. You do it long enough and you begin to let your guard down. You get lazy. You forget who you are. Then that makes it harder to be in your natural state because you're tired all the time. Passing takes all the good you've got to give to yourself and turns it into something else. No matter how different our blood makes us, there's nothing in this world more unnatural than pretending to be someone you're not."

I immersed myself in her words and bowed my head to indicate that I had absorbed everything she had just told me—even though I felt drunk with information. She took my hands in hers.

"Now, close your eyes and think of something really cold. Colder than the deep end of the swimming pool. Colder than my feet beneath the covers in December." I giggled through my chapped lips until the sudden chill that overcame me cut the laughter from my lungs. "Then squeeze that feeling deep, deep down until it's firm and hard like a rock in the pit of your stomach." When I opened my eyes, we were both as white as sugar. Ice had replaced blood, and I missed the warmth.

I could only pass when she was close by. I spent days at school daydreaming about the colors we would enjoy the moment I came home. The first few times I tried, it was difficult to be white—a color I found dull and tedious. I also lacked the proper concentration, and my skin took on the brief glow of a light bulb when switched off. My mother encouraged me to use a variety of different tokens to help me pass properly: our small Florida neighborhood inhabited by white neighbors in their white houses. Our bathroom made only of white tiles. Our cupboards filled only with white sheets and crockery. My mother was allowed to cook only with white salt and white pepper, which imbued our food with a certain white flavor.

She was determined for me to master this skill, and our imaginations joined forces to create strategies that made whiteness more appealing. But my mind would always wander back to the hidden pockets sewed into the lining of her purse, in which she stored small plastic baggies of ground cayenne pepper, paprika, nutmeg, cinnamon, coriander, cumin, and cardamom—spices that reflected some of the many colors she was capable of adopting herself. She only used them when we were alone. Their scent inspired warmth as red and hot as chili powder, and my skin flushed accordingly. The portable spice market wafted strongly from her handbag on hot days, attracting the neighborhood dogs as she walked down the street. This annoyed our neighbors, who bestowed upon her the title "Queen of the Mutts," and though it irritated her greatly, I couldn't think of a more noble title. Other times, when I wrestled with bad dreams or needed to prepare for a difficult exam, she placed the spices beneath my pillow or sewed them into my nightclothes to soothe my mind, and I would wake up feeling brand-new.

The first time I successfully passed into whiteness for my father, my mother and I walked into the kitchen hand in hand like two petrified porcelain dolls that would shatter with the slightest hint of criticism. My father nodded. His cratered black skin, hard like stone, stretched into a smile. He patted my tight curls before placing his mammoth body at the head of the table and regaled us of the wretchedness of his colleagues at the office; how he worked the jobs of three people, but only made the seven-figure salary of one; how his carnal love of free markets, trickle-down economics, and deregulation made him more shrewd than the rest of them.

"They're all too liberally minded and lazy," he crowed, embarking on an extended tirade about why he had joined the Republican Party: "For their commonsense, fiscally conservative banking policies, of course."

Of course.

Since my father couldn't change the color of his skin, he changed the color of his words, he changed the color of his movements, and he changed the color of his laughter so that its natural bass took on a lighter, more diluted hue. And still, it was not enough. So he decided to be greedier than his fellow party members, to love guns more than them, to hunt and kill more than they did, and to beat his chest about it until he had convinced himself that he loved doing these things as much as they loved watching him perform. My mother and I didn't respond while he spoke about work. We never wanted to. I knew long before I had the words to say so that having white skin meant being silent, and complacent with the way things are. I used to wonder if he hated us because we could assume the physical changes that he could not. But men don't need a reason to hate women—it's just that some are born with a natural talent for it.

I struggled to pass consistently. The onset of summer filled the neighborhood with the kind of wet heat that stoked the madness normally dormant in creatures—normally dormant in me. A tropical storm blew through early in the season, and it knocked down power lines and flooded the swamp next to our school. The murky sludge receded to the bog, reluctant to concede to the sun's boundless gaze. David, one of the more popular and difficult boys in my grade, was seated in the bleachers, yelling flattering obscenities to my classmates as we ran past on the racetrack, paying special attention to the exchange students' exotic features, swollen backsides, and darker skin tones. He positioned himself between two large shrubs that had broken off from a buttonbush during the storm, spreading his legs widely enough to disturb their stunted leaves.

"Hey, chica bonita!" David rolled up a cigarette in his short, stubby fingers and placed it in his mouth. His lips were perpetually coated in fuzz and fat beads of sweat. He leaned back on his elbows, and the wrinkled fabric of his crotch winked at us. "Come on, smile! Oh come on, you'll never get an American husband if you don't show off that pretty face!"

When there was no response, David leaned forward

suddenly, the lilt of his voice corroding. "Then we'll have to send you back across the border for a refund." The cigarette hung out of the corner of his mouth as he puffed. Elena smiled nervously as we passed him on our second lap, then maneuvered her way toward the inside of the group, so that her silhouette was obscured by the throng of bodies bobbing up and down around her. I fell back behind Elena, admiring the way she didn't respond—then again, she didn't speak much English. But she didn't have to, to understand the desperation of teenage boys—a language understood in many tongues, across many borders.

As we completed our third lap, a cottonmouth slithered out from one of the shrubs close to David's stamping feet and bit his ankle. He fell from the bleachers to the ground and we slowed down to see his entire leg darken and swell like a sausage. The snake spat venom in all directions—a final defiant hiss at death. Angry tears leaked from the two puncture wounds on his ankle, forming a smile with their liquid trail. Elena came up behind me, placing her hand on my shoulder and craning her neck to see the puddle of dark urine spreading across David's denim shorts. Her breathing told me she was smirking. But when the groundskeeper appeared with a large shovel and brought it down violently upon the snake, severing its head perfectly from its body, Elena burst into tears that no amount of gentle words would comfort.

Later that evening, my mother cooked rigatoni with a creamy mushroom sauce for dinner, a meal that always made my insides curdle. It was my father's favorite dish, even though it made him heave every time he ate it. When we sat down, I attempted to share the story of David, the snake, and the angry hemotoxic smile on his ankle to my parents.

"What kind of snake?" my father asked.

"A cottonmouth." I described its arrow-shaped head, its thick black body, the way its pink mouth went slack when decapitated, then stiff as a blood clot.

My fascination began to combine with the discomfort in my stomach becoming an explosive force.

"May I be excused?"

His expression locked me to my seat.

I crossed and recrossed my legs, wincing from the pain twisting through my side until it forced me to pass my skin into a menacing dark hue—coal: alien and shiny. I burst into tears, trembling with shame. My mother tried to reach out to comfort me, but my father thwarted her with his enormous hand—glaring at us both. He pushed himself back, scraping the floor with his chair, and hoisted himself from the table.

He grabbed a bottle of scotch from behind the white cupboard next to the stove and retreated behind the closed doors of his study. I stopped crying and fell to the floor, allowing my mother to hold me as I traced the black marks from his chair on the white tiles. The sound of crickets marked the passing time until we realized that my father wasn't coming out. That's when she allowed herself to assume the same hue, and we were two carved statues of ash that had burned in effigy to one another. When the next wave of cramps pushed through me, I ran to the bathroom.

I spent the rest of the night in my bedroom, where I stayed until my father left for work the next morning. As soon as the garage door closed, my mother's flesh called out to me like a subterranean echo and lured me from the other side of the house with a quiet reassurance that others might call by a more malevolent name. On sock-toed feet, I slipped across the polished kitchen tiles, its new black scuff marks, and into my parents' bedroom. I slid beneath the covers and let her pull them back up to my chin.

My mother's skin was sweet and warm, like honey scraped right from the hive during the frenzy of harvest. She wrapped her long, skinny arms around me, burying me in the elastic folds of her neck, still slick from the hair grease that was applied to her scalp the night before and had stained the embroidered pillow shams with a translucent glow. My color harmonized with hers and the rhythm of our breath synchronized into a unique song. Only we knew the words. We didn't dare engage in this ritual when my father was home, as we were overly conscious not to provoke his disdain for our shared symmetry. The height of our cheekbones, the diagonals of our eyes, and the mild slopes of our noses, all the familiar angular aesthetics draped in a smooth, rich mahogany that differentiated the little girl who was birthed from the womb, from the man who was occasionally granted access to it.

I allowed several long moments to pass before I slid my thick legs on top of hers, around hers, between hers, hunting for that rare, perfect nook in her body where I enjoyed the heat radiating from between her large, full breasts without being suffocated by them. Only when I stilled and my breathing was lulled to a nearly indiscernible hum did she open her eyes, two shiny black pieces of volcanic glass, and she whispered, "All better, little angel. All better." Then we giggled together, like we were the same age, with the same knowledge of the world, sharing the same secrets about men and God and each other that had to be guarded between those grease-stained sheets. She removed the stocking cap from my head and sank her thin, bony fingers through the labyrinth of black kinks, separating the twists, a sensation that sent currents of electricity rushing through my limbs until my toes curled as much as my hair. Our flesh heated up as one, and I melted into her like our bodies had never been separated, still bound by the primordial breath that shaped me within her. That's when we were closest—when we shared the same fearsome incandescent glow of a full moon. I asked her why I could only do this with her and not with my own father, to which she shrugged her shoulders and smiled before ushering me out of her bed to go to school.

"It's in the blood, girl. It's in the blood."

3

MY MOTHER HAD ASKED ME TO WEAR SAGE THAT day in hopes of bringing better fortune to the election.

"It's not our election," she said, "but in a way, it is." She squeezed my shoulders before I left the house, waving goodbye as her cotton nightgown flapped in the breeze.

I hadn't been able to get an update in school, so I ran home from the bus stop just as the storm clouds circled overhead, and sprinted through rain that slanted across my back. A baggie of dried Rattlesnake Master stitched onto the waistband of my underwear rubbed furiously against my hip, turning the skin beneath beet red by the time I got home.

When I swung open the door, my mother was the color of the winter solstice sky, darkened and aphotic. She sat in the living room with the curtains drawn shut and all the lights in the house turned off, save for the bright glow of the television washing over her. A tall, thin man with dark skin and gray hair stood surrounded by people waving tiny colorful flags. Dressed in a dark blue suit, he spoke like someone who wore the weight of every person in the crowd, of all their hopes and dreams, and afflictions. As he spoke, his reedy legs shuffled and red dust flew from beneath his feet to baptize the crowd below him—something we too felt in our living room.

"It worked?" My eyes couldn't make sense of the scene on TV, but they made sense of the tears rolling down my mother's cheeks. They made sense of the choked air trapped in her throat as she cupped her neck with both hands—steadying herself with a single word that she repeated over and over again.

"Madiba. Madiba. Madiba."

I went to sit by her, leaning in to her side to find that it was boiling hot. She stood up suddenly, and began to speak in riddles about spirits, being haunted, being cursed, and all the other words that evoked images of ethereal deities locked in conflict, waging war on one another. I couldn't keep up. The myths, the stories, the fables interspersed into glossolalia, taking on a life of their own. I tried to cling on to a familiar word or phrase—but none came. She yanked my arm until I joined her and then began to spin. Her limbs cast shadows onto household items; the decorative white relics that lined the white cupboards, tables, and cabinets morphed into sinister villains, brought to life by my mother's incoherent prophecies of rapture and resistance. I clung to her as she spoke, my skin turning a shade of pale, icy blue. Only then did she seem to register me. She looked down into my eyes. "We have to rejoice, angel! Rejoice!"

She pulled me again by the arm and we ran through the darkness to the piano in the garage.

She ripped off the tarp with a flourish, and I played while

she sang. I couldn't read music, but I could repeat what I heard. She preferred the kind of music that spoke about Jesus and Paul Revere, conflating patriotism with belief and faith with loyalty. The grandiose instrumentals of these songs made the hairs on our necks stand on end.

I played while she sang, but my fingers didn't move quickly enough and she relieved me of my place at the bench, taking over the keys. I danced to the rhythm of her fingers until blisters bit into my toes. She insisted on dancing with me, and we ran back into the house and played one of her Christian-rock tapes over the stereo. She twirled. She dipped low then jumped up high. She vibrated in the middle of the living room floor with unremitting ferocity, shaking from the tips of her fingers to the peeling heels of her feet. Her color went from various shades of warm to various shades of cool, like a brush running out of paint.

"'Give me liberty or give me death,'" she sang in unison with the song as tears glossed her cheekbones, reflecting light from outside, and darkness from deep within. Sweat cascaded down her body. I tried to hug her in my dark brown arms, but it was like trying to embrace a ghost. Her body evaporated, hollowing out from my grasp. I sulked impatiently. There was nothing left to do but wait. My mother was the law that governed the miniature cosmos on our street. When she danced or cried, power surges stripped the block, and when she was happy, sunlight swallowed the dark.

Come back, I pleaded silently, hoping that she would hear my thoughts the way she sometimes could. *Come back to me.*

Only when she was ready did I feel the ghostly touch of her fingers on my back. She sidestepped me, mumbling to herself—continuing the conversation with people I couldn't see. They whispered about the man on the television and the promise of better days to come.

"No, I just . . ." She faltered, allowing someone else to finish her thought. She perked up attentively to something I couldn't hear, then she nodded conspiratorially. "You're right, but she has to figure that out for herself." She sighed resolutely, then turned back to me with wet eyes.

"I never thought this day would come."

I didn't know who she spoke to, but I forced a broken smile anyway.

She laughed to herself and her eyes widened while recounting events that convinced her of some new age—even though everything around us still looked, felt, and sounded exactly the same. We were in the same white house. We lived with the same dark man. We were the same people who curated colors from a palette of abuses and called them beautiful.

A bolt of lightning cracked down the street, and my mother went motionless, staring at the covered window as the rain belted across the glass. I opened the blinds, then went to her side and lifted her arm. It fell back limp. I squeezed her hand, holding on to her fingertips as the warmth drained from them. A loud thunderclap sounded out, jolting her back into the living room. Her hand slipped out of mine and she retreated into her bedroom, looking like the most pallid white corpse ever to have survived the morgue.

I passed the time watching emergency utilities workers climb the power lines outside like two-legged spiders. When the garage door opened, my mother resurrected herself as a flawless white wife. She took her time to open the curtains in every room of the house, observing the spectacle on the other side of the glass with wide vacant eyes, as if she did not recognize her own home, neighborhood, or the items that occupied them. She began setting the table for dinner with wooden movements. Her gaze dropped to my dark complexion and then lifted almost imperceptibly.

"Think of something cold, little angel."

So I did, just as my father walked inside.

She was the first person to show me that the meaning of true joy is the resolve to dance—and that dance is the best way to express unfathomable sadness without a single word. The sky outside the dining room window had turned so blue that it was difficult to recall a time when it had ever been any different.

4

AFTER THE SATURDAY MORNING TELEVISION CHURCH
service, my mother and I piled into her Dodge sedan and went
in search of what she called "the ultimate bargain." On the way
there, she enjoyed convincing me that she was the ultimate
bargain hunter, one with an expert eye. I allowed myself to
be persuaded, for these moments suggested a degree of pre-
dictability that was otherwise nonexistent. Some days she was
fixated on a white "Chinese" vase from the outlet mall off the
edge of I-4 near Apopka. On this day, it was a Persian rug
shop run by Bulgarians in someone's farming shed near Lake
Mary.

"This one was made by my grandmother in the old country," said a man with olive skin and sparkling eyes, while convincing my mother it was worth two thousand dollars.

"What's the material?"

"Only the finest threads, made from virgin sheep in the
most beautiful land in the world." That's all it took. The dusty
rug was rolled up and shoved into the car with one end sticking out the trunk and into traffic. Riding in the back seat, I
clung on to one end of the rug while my mother fixed her eyes
to the road, raving about her taste in fine antiquities.

"Did you see the look on his face when I only offered him fifteen hundred?" she shouted over the rolled-down windows and radio. "He didn't think that I know how the game works . . . but I *know*." She laughed while swerving in traffic to keep the rug from swiping any other cars, and I smiled back silently, gripping the armrest. It was easy to be happy when she was happy, because she breathed life into everything around her, and made it sing.

When I woke up the next day, I shuffled into her room for our morning ritual, but she wasn't there. I drifted through the empty house, and I found her in the guest bedroom on her hands and knees examining a single loose thread, gold and glittering beneath the slanting sunlight that poured in through the window. Her skin was cold and creamy.

"He tricked me," she said, her words as flat as the dull edge of a knife. "This rug is fake." Her nightgown was thin, and I saw her body parts dangling loosely through the pilling cotton. She rolled it up and shoved it against the wall. "Get dressed. We're going back." She shifted around in her gown and turned into the rich honey color I had sought out that morning.

We climbed into the car and made the long drive back to Lake Mary. My mother drove like a woman possessed, with five dollars of gas in the tank and fifteen hundred dollars of Bulgarian rug sticking out of the trunk. But when we arrived at the makeshift shop on the far-flung edge of Central Florida, the farming shed was boarded up, and a FOR SALE sign mocked us from the mailbox. My father laughed at her antics at dinnertime, insulting her between bites of white fish and cauliflower.

"You spent fifteen hundred dollars on a piece of crap." He chortled, as if she had done it for his personal amusement. "How did you ever get to be so gullible?" Then, turning his attention from her to me, he said, "Gabrielle, don't be like your mother. Me? I can smell a scam artist from a mile away." His belly shook as he laughed; it too was in on the joke.

It's difficult to imagine that someone of my father's size was ever a child. I used to try to plot out his life by points of time: born in the year when *I Love Lucy* first debuted on American TV, lusting clumsily after a girl when Kennedy was shot, and attending college when the Vietnam War ravaged a tiny sliver of land on the other side of the world. But I didn't know any of this for sure. He appeared only as an entity whose existence stretched back to the dawn of civilization. His annoyance, gristle, and harsh opinions seeped through walls of time, and I often pictured him telling Jesus Christ to pick himself up by the bootstraps and off of that crucifix. Perhaps I adopted this idea for its seductive qualities: I wanted to believe all the myths of self-creation by which my father styled himself so that I too could justify my unusual ability, one where I emerged daily in some newly baptized flesh that wiped clean the sins of the day before.

The rug was thrown in the trash. Besides being expensive, and apparently worthless, it didn't fit the color palette of our home. But my mother wouldn't forget the humiliation that spread around the dinner table, that we felt in the wet chill of her white skin.

She hunted for the Bulgarian rug vendor all over Central Florida. She checked newspapers, pulled down flyers, and spoke to every antiques dealer in the yellow pages, until one Friday afternoon, she managed to locate him. Another dealer confirmed that he had set up shop in Kissimmee for his next round of scams. A look of satisfaction clung to her face when she hung up the phone.

"Wanna play a game, angel?" Her eyes glinted.

When I woke up early the next morning, I could already smell the hot comb on the stove. I sat down at the kitchen table and yawned. The comb hissed and spat as she pulled it through my hair like a loom, melting the flesh around my ears. She slicked back my edges with Blue Magic until my hair fit into a smooth tight bun that made my temples throb. My blue cotton dress with the polka dots was already laid out for me. She slipped on a lavender silk blouse, knee-length skirt, high heels, and a string of pearls that glittered like teeth. "The game is called 'paper bag.'" She held my hand as we looked into the mirror side by side and smiled. "Remember, colder than cookies and cream." I nodded and, concentrating with the intensity of all my unspoken emotions, we passed into a different version of ourselves—fair, white, and clean. Before opening the garage door to pull out into the driveway, she covered herself in an overcoat, baseball cap, and sunglasses, while I lay down in the back seat of the car. Then we sped out of the neighborhood.

The makeshift shop had moved to a bald patch of land nestled deep within an orange grove. A goat milk candy factory sat toward the back of the lot, and the distant aroma of scorched licorice and rotting fruit hung in the air as we stepped out of the car. The same man who had taken our fifteen hundred dollars approached us in a slow jog, his hairy belly poking out from the bottom of his shirt. His face was pinched up close, and it smiled upon seeing my mother. It was a look of blissful ignorance.

"Good day, ma'am! How can I help you?"

"I'm looking for something for the study," my mother replied. It was a voice that belonged on a television program in a different country.

"Yes, of course," he replied. He slicked his thinning hair back and gestured toward the assortment of rugs leaning against a massive wooden slat for support. "We have a large selection."

My mother took her time examining each rug. She rubbed the fabric between her fingers, then she rubbed her fingers against each other, inspecting imaginary dust and frowning in disgust before moving on to the next one. Her head normally hung between her rounded shoulders, but I watched her transform into something else. She kicked up her heels like a show pony and stood with a steel-rod spine that stretched taller than seemed possible. She interrogated the salesman, and raised her voice at the tall tales of his grandmother and the old country. She stopped in front of a rug that was an exact replica of the one she had bought and thrown away.

"How much for this one?" she asked. The man rubbed his hand on the back of his neck and puckered his lips.

"For you? Fifty bucks." He smiled widely, revealing several dark spots of missing teeth. My entire body tensed. My mother didn't say a word at first. She considered the carpet once more and noticed a loose thread in the exact same spot the other one had been. She zeroed in on it and clenched her jaw, then reached out and pulled it gently. The patterning unraveled without much effort, so she intensified the tug until a large patch of the carpet turned threadbare in her hands. The pile of material floated through her fingers to the ground, so fine that it was no longer visible once it hit the dirt.

"Fifty bucks for this hatchet job?" she scoffed. I recognized my father's voice through her words. "You must think I'm an idiot. I wouldn't pay a cent for this crap." Then she turned on her knockoff heel and strode back to the car with me jogging behind her, already afraid of the car ride home. We peeled out of the orange grove lot kicking up a cloud of red dust behind us, while the salesman watched with his hands on his wide hips. She didn't say a word on the drive. When I turned on the radio, a song came on where two women proudly proclaimed that they liked to touch themselves, and she switched it back off. When we were safely back inside the garage, she turned to me and shoved her index finger into my chest, pinning me against the passenger-side door.

"Don't you *ever* try to do that yourself."

Her hands shook as she unbuckled her seat belt and went into the house. It took me several minutes to follow.

The moment I was inside, my father pushed me back out the door again to attend another local university tour. At the last parent-teacher conference, which only my mother attended, my guidance counselor seemed disappointed that I wouldn't be heading straight to college. The rest of my classmates had already applied. But my father wanted me to stay home for a year. He said he wanted me to learn basic life skills that weren't taught in college which, if our home was any indication, were mostly about learning how to clean up after a man. He took charge of my future, citing his law degree as the mitigating factor that granted him authority to make decisions on my behalf. Whereas my mother's high school diploma, which he had grown expert at introducing into casual conversation, was always reserved as ammunition in an otherwise busy routine to humiliate her when it suited him.

The University of Florida was decorated in orange and blue, like the inside of a wacky chocolate factory. We were greeted by a perky blond pre-med student with a smile so insistent it made my face hurt. With her ripe-peach tan and a constellation of freckles, Kelsey could have been a spokesmodel for acne cream. We walked in a group with other parents and their teenagers, and yet my father still wrapped his hand around my neck as if I might wander off and crash into something. When we went to the medical school, his grip constricted in excitement. I tried to edge myself closer to Kelsey, but he reeled me back every time. A group of medical students greeted the tour and told us what they were working on, which rare diseases they were researching, and how fresh their cadavers were. My father nearly strangled me. The conversation I shared with his closing fist was the longest we had shared in a while.

Kelsey handed out brochures with small plush alligators attached as parting gifts at the end of the tour. I thanked her quietly, but she stopped me before I could make my getaway.

"Did you enjoy the tour?" I nodded my head, the tenor of her voice attaching itself to something inside me.

"I know it seems silly." Her tone was suddenly more remote, peeking out at me through a small hole in an otherwise extroverted personality. "But when I visited I really fell in love with the campus. There's a lot to do and everyone is very welcoming." A lock of hair fell across her collarbone.

"Do you know what you want to study?" She inched close enough for me to smell the lemon juice in her hair.

"Not really . . ." I tried to smooth a curly tuft of hair behind my ear, but it ballooned back out, blooming around my burning ears.

"She'll be pre-med." My father reintroduced himself by placing his hand on my neck once more, pulling me back to him. Kelsey looked from my father to me then back to him. She smiled again, this time from the center of her mouth, making it tighter.

"Well, it's very competitive," she added flatly. "But it's a great program. I would recommend playing up your extracurricular activities to give you the best chance of getting in." She tied her hair back in a final gesture and put her hands on her hips, turning back to face me, lowering her voice. "If you have any questions, please don't hesitate to reach out. My phone number is in the brochure." She smiled at me with her whole mouth, and winked.

"IT JUST MAKES sense." My father got started when we hit the turnpike on our way home.

His enthusiasm only heightened the more distance we put between us and the university. I scoured the passenger door with an irritated fingernail, obscuring its shiny finish. My mother's sedan smelled like grapefruit. In the winter, it smelled like a fresh citrus harvest, but by summer it smelled like fruit rotting in the sun at the bottom of a boot. But my father's SUV smelled like bleach and dish soap—the way a space does when it's used to collect human waste.

"And you *should* be a doctor. You're good at science."

I nodded.

"Then you can come home and take care of me if I need you." I nodded.

"What will you study for your language requirement?" I opened my mouth but he interjected before I could answer.

"You should learn Japanese. Reggie's kids learned Japanese at *their* school, and now they're working in commodities and making a shitload of cash. They send their father on trips around the world. He can't stop yakking about it at work." I nodded as my father disregarded my last four years of intensive French, weaving in and out of congested lanes of traffic. He pushed tiny vehicles aside with his car's tremendous aluminum grille only to pull up next to a police cruiser at a traffic light. Suddenly, he went quiet, turned down the radio's volume, and placed both of his large hands on the steering wheel, the leather covering squeaking as his grip tightened. I rubbed my neck in solidarity. The police officer seemed to glance over at my father, then at me, and back to him. In his dark sunglasses, I saw the flawless finish of my father's white Ford SUV. I wished I could pass white just then. I wanted to get pulled over.

But officer, I've been abducted and my mother is looking for me!

The light turned green, and the police cruiser raced ahead with its siren on.

I wiped down my face, feeling my father exhale as he turned the volume on the radio back up.

"Although Spanish probably makes more sense since you're staying in Florida."

I searched for the police car ahead of us, but it was gone. Conversation, the kind where two people engage with each other and create a unique story that describes that moment, was never my father's thing. But he enjoyed having an audience. I kept nodding in the passenger seat, thinking of Kelsey's freckles as the car drove us farther away from the university.

Arriving in the suburbs, we passed a group of homeless men huddled inside a bus stop to shield themselves from the heat. My father crept past slowly with his high-beam lights turned on, illuminating the terror on their weathered faces before pulling away again. It was important to make an impression, because he didn't like to linger.

"Gabrielle, do you think there's any excuse for someone

to be homeless?" There was a vigor in his tone that sped the words up, so that he could get them out as quickly as possible, assemble them like building blocks, then stand on top to make himself taller.

I shrugged, feeling terrible for them.

"I don't know."

"That's the wrong answer. There is *no* excuse," he said through knitted brows and peak enthusiasm. "None whatsoever. Some of these people just can't help but feel sorry for themselves."

I fidgeted half-heartedly, watching their faces shrink into the landscape behind us.

"If you work hard and apply yourself, there's no reason why you can't succeed in America," he continued. "That's why it's the greatest country on earth."

I sniffled to acknowledge this comment. I knew better than to respond. It wasn't a conversation. It was a performance.

"It doesn't matter what you have to do. If you work harder than everyone else, if you sacrifice more than everyone else, if you discipline yourself more than other people can, and you dress respectably." He stuttered and licked his lips to regain his composure. "And you don't give them a reason to think any less of you, or distrust you, or disrespect you, then you can have what they have."

As we pulled into our neighborhood, the streetlamps switched on, washing over my father, turning his skin light and then dark again.

"But . . ." I bit down on my tongue.

He waited.

"Go on, say it." I didn't, and this only irritated him more, clipping the corner of a street as we turned onto our block. "I don't want you winding up tongue-tied like your mother." I hesitated.

". . . If I work harder than everyone else, then why can't I have more than them?"

A grimace marred his face as we turned onto our street.

"What a terrible question," he replied—his tone affected. "You shouldn't be so greedy."

The house was filled with smoke when we returned. Through an open window I saw my mother standing on a chair fanning a dish towel against the ceiling while the smoke detector blared and flashed. She'd burned a chicken in the oven, leaving a lightly blackened skin that made my father recoil. He threw it into the garbage, "For the coons," he said, and made a drink in his white plastic cup—the logo it once wore peeled and cracking like dry skin. He ordered out from a local Italian restaurant.

"How hard is it to cook a chicken?"

My mother and I didn't respond. She used the side of her fork to mash down the pasta.

"There's a knife sitting right there next to you."

She stared at it, considering its various uses—as a utensil, or perhaps as a weapon. She picked it up.

"So you *do* know how to use a knife?"

She paused, letting the brunt of the question land, then silently continued cutting her food into tiny pieces.

"You're ridiculous, Tallulah." Laughing to himself, he finally accepted that she wouldn't respond. Then he looked at me for corroboration, his eyes cutting shapes out of me. I sneered at her.

"Utterly ridiculous."

He stood, satisfied.

When the table was cleared and my father's snores drowned out the crickets outside, I went to my mother and hugged her from behind as she dried the plates. She turned to face me, placing her soapy hands gently on my shoulders. "I understand why you did it . . . but you should also understand when I do it back." She dropped her arms and went back to the dishes, her promise still haunting the space between us. Though the dishwater had turned cold, my skin burned darkly where her hands had been.

5

AT SCHOOL, I SPENT SO MUCH TIME EXPLORING THE
crevices of my mind that I had trouble understanding basic com-
munication on the ground. I couldn't read expressions or voice
tonality, and found it difficult to look into people's faces for too
long, opting instead to watch their body parts, which seemed
so much less capable of lying than their mouths. I liked watching Jacob in particular, who had a unique ability to convince
the most introverted students to arm wrestle in the courtyard
during lunch, beneath statuettes of philanthropists who looked
on from their bird shit–covered perches. One such match had
led to his suspension, and he had become more careful since—
only challenging people during off periods when nearly no one
else was around. His most impressive conquest was Karl, the
president of the literary society who cast aside his sophistication
upon a summons from Jacob. I learned a valuable lesson that
afternoon as I watched the spectacle unfold from the shade of a
palm tree: when the thirst for recognition surmounts dignity, it
sounds like tendons snapping in ninety-seven-degree heat. Karl
hobbled to the nurse's office, and Jacob seized his prize money
from Kraig. I watched unseen from that ambiguous dimension just outside of Jacob's line of sight before making myself

known. I emerged from the darkness, swatting at a cloud of mosquitoes screaming in my ear. Jacob paused while cramming the crumpled bills in sagging jeans, and they both turned to me to see that the shadow had an unruly face.

Kraig whispered something to Jacob, wiping the frown from his face. They walked toward me and Kraig snatched a five-dollar bill from Jacob, handing it to me. It was smudged with damp circles of grit.

"She's cool," he said to Jacob. "She won't tell anyone." Kraig leaned in to cue my response. I stuffed the crisp bill into my pocket, and this satisfied them both. Kraig lingered just long enough to trigger a wave of colorful internal changes that I was grateful could not be outwardly reflected.

Kraig seemed different. And I had suspected it had to do with the large gap between his teeth—that was his difference. He had bowl-cut blond hair and light blue eyes, and while he did what he wanted to do much of the time, he also did what he was told. What he wanted was to design buildings. I saw him in the library flipping through books with photos of large, asymmetrical structures surrounded by moats of crystal-blue water.

But around his friends, Kraig bragged about the size of his average penis with his average friends—and to anyone else who would listen. To his teammates. To his coach. To his girlfriend Haylee, and her friends. As finals approached, and the summer break taunted us from beyond the edges of the school's property, I heard them even more.

"How do you know it's bigger than everyone else's?" she teased him as we filed out of a classroom into the hallway.

He scooped his books into his backpack, one still covered in plastic wrap. Kraig blushed and pulled her close as I tried to dodge their bodies. But my knee grazed the back of Kraig's thigh, and his eyes found mine.

"Because we checked."

Those three words haunted me for the rest of the day. And I spent all of English and Biology trying to figure them out. I manufactured various scenarios that made sense. Maybe boys just had an inherent understanding of each other's penises, like competing predators in the wild. Maybe they sniffed it out of each other like the German shepherds they use on TV to search suspicious cars.

Fourth period ended, and lunch began. I sat in the gym bleachers, several rows behind Haylee, listening as she recounted Kraig's comments to her friends.

"So, they just whip it out? In front of each other?" Vicky seemed dubious, which might have been more difficult for the others to see. She was too dark for her opinion to matter.

"Well think about it—how else would they know? And is it any more strange than when we look at each other's breasts?" I gulped at the thought of lining up in a row of teenage girls while we compared the size, shape, and weight of our chests. My eyes wandered from Haylee to Vicky, taking note of the way their tank tops hugged their torsos.

Kraig and his friends flooded into the gym bouncing a basketball among themselves. As I watched them play, I imagined Kraig and his friends taking turns holding their penises out at one another's houses while one measured the growth with a ruler, jotting down the numbers in a Captain Planet Trapper Keeper that monitored progress from week to week. David would be the worst at this exercise. He was short with early signs of facial hair that cast a constant shadow on his rounded jawline. I imagined him taking too long and making cryptic sounds of approval or disappointment with every measure, often sticking his finger between the boys' gelatinous, pale buttocks for encouragement in case they went soft in his hands. I imagined Kraig going soft, and David stroking his penis with a surgical focus to revive him, the flaccid shaft flopping around in David's hand like raw chicken skin, accompanied by curt sounds of support at the results. *Keep going, keep going . . . there you go, champ!* he would say, holding on for an extended moment before releasing, and Kraig would exhale a long sigh of relief, knowing that he would live to brag another day.

It just made sense.

The game devolved into cursing and insults before David stood and limped off. I grew bored and headed to the band room, where I often tinkered around with the instruments, playing brief melodies my mother had taught me—expounding upon them, transposing their notes into different chord progressions reminiscent of an era I hadn't lived through. Pushing into the band room's large double doors, I caught the distorted reflection of two people in the wide brass surface of a tuba hanging from the wall, their melting figures circling the bell like a drain.

David cradled Elena's bronze toes in his hands while his tongue darted in and out over her bright red nail polish.

When she saw me watching them, Elena yanked her foot away, sending David tumbling onto the floor. She gathered her things and ran past me and out the door. I caught the rage in David's eyes.

"What the fuck are you doing?" I backed away from the door as he approached me, the fuzz on his upper lip sweating furiously. "You're Haylee's friend . . ." He thought I was Vicky, who was both half a foot shorter and ten shades darker than me. It wasn't the first time someone had confused us. We were the only two nonwhite students in our English class. Once, a teacher had given me her exam results, which had a much lower grade than mine. When I quietly passed it over to Vicky, she reluctantly handed me my own. Her eyes were red and swollen from failure.

I didn't correct David.

"Wait, you're the girl . . . you're in Elena's gym class." This time I nodded.

"Not a word to your friends about this . . ." His words were encased within a mixture of fear, frenzy, and desire—excited by the malice in his own voice. But he pulled back at the word *friends*, seemingly amused by the novelty that I had any. Rather than finish his threat, he just shoved me against the door on his way out.

I settled at the piano and began to play, my fingers discharging a rush of adrenaline in a pattern of shaky trills and melodies. The familiar hallway traffic and laughter washed over me, before Elena entered the room again, the door snaking closed behind her, confining us in a separate world.

"I hear you're good at keeping secrets," she said, her accent cloaking the anxious words with cunning.

"Can you pass this on to Haylee?" She placed a pink note folded like a crane onto C-sharp, its wings adding elegance to its narrow balancing act. She didn't wait for me to answer. I did as she asked.

Haylee expressed her joy over the note to Vicky, who told anyone who would listen about David's sweaty armpits, the smell of his oozing, snake-bitten leg, still wrapped in heavy gauze. The Caribbean students couldn't get enough, and I absorbed their stories as they ricocheted across campus. Other exchange students came forward to share similar stories in a series of notes. Fatima, a sophomore exchange student from Ghana, said that David liked it when she wore green toenail polish. Abuya from Nairobi said he preferred electric blue.

After that, my skills in secret-keeping became highly sought after, and I often spent my free time delivering them in the form of notes from one anxious pair of hands to another. Our school had once been a women's prison and I sometimes passed remnants of barbed wire on the track or the barred windows outside the cafeteria along the way to my note's recipient, instilling a sense of purpose in my messaging service. A central watchtower that was once used as a lookout for escapees had become a bird sanctuary, but whenever I passed beneath and looked up at the wad of nests and shit spilling onto the brick, I still felt chosen for a dangerous mission. I never read the notes—but they spoke to me anyway. I learned the meaning of red ink, and green. I learned the heavy-handed script of anger, when my fingers could trace the lettering of the insults through the paper without reading a single word.

Not long after, Kraig asked me to pass a note to Haylee between classes, creased and blotted with smudged green ink. I did so without question. When Haylee asked me to relay a sharp, vocal retort to Kraig—without a note—I did so in turn. Class emptied and a thunderstorm uncurled in the sky. Wind dipped low into the courtyard, turning umbrellas inside out and tipping over abandoned water bottles. Beneath the watchtower, past the gymnasium tagged in fresh obscenities, I made my way into the Science corridor, turned frigid by the preserved fetal pigs delivered to the Biology lab for dissection. A thin cold mist hovered just beneath the door of the room where they were kept.

"Really?" Kraig asked. I had just taken my Algebra II final, and my brain had confused the intended message with different polymath equations. "She said to fuck off?" I shrugged, tucking a dark kink behind my ear. The message danced around in my brain as a distressed mathematical alphabet that consisted only of A, B, C, and X. She could have said *Fuck off*, but when I stopped it could also have been *Fuck yourself* or *Get fucked*, or even just a lazy *Fuck you*. It was an unmistakable glut of fuckups, until Kraig had an epiphany of his own.

"Are you sure she didn't say 'Let's fuck'?" A thick blond eyebrow perked up at the suggestion, unsouring his disposition. "Or 'Fuck me'?" He straightened his back and placed the Algebra book into his locker. Various pictures of topless women winked back at me, along with grunge music posters, a surplus of rubber bands, and a fetid smell. I was bewildered by this attempt to rewrite the abuse as a display of cunning feminine wiles; an obstacle to overcome in love; a rejection that he rejected himself, and replaced with a sanitized interpretation that spoke only of her desire for him.

"So that's how she wants to play it, huh?" A smirk tugged at his narrow lips, pulling them into an invisible slit in the middle of his face. *Gee Kraig, I don't think it's a game.* "All right then. Have it your way, babe."

He considered me for a minute.

"I knew you were all right."

David and Sam came up behind him. David glowered at me, harder than usual, and I left before he could complete his earlier threat. They slapped each other on the back, arms, and ass, and shouted devious things about each other's moms in a display of masculinity not yet earned, but somehow owned.

Sam observed meekly. Most of the time, I barely registered his presence. I suspected Jacob, Kraig, and David liked him for that reason. When Jacob was breaking arms, Sam cheered him on. When David was heckling us, Sam laughed at his insults. Sam was skinny, with a negligent physique and a face that was easy to forget when you shut your eyes and tried to recall its shape. He liked F. Scott Fitzgerald and recited passages from T. S. Eliot. He played the acoustic guitar, wore a knotted hemp necklace around his scrawny neck, and wanted to study finance. He prided himself on his objectivity, the ability to understand both sides of an argument equally, and from him I learned about the virtues of many misunderstood historical figures—from Nathan Bedford Forrest's interest in real estate to Hitler's love of painting.

The boys and their shouting pulled Kraig away from me and farther down the hall. Each raucous comment added momentum to the speed at which they moved—boy encircling boy as caged animals often do right before they attempt to eat one another, or fuck—or measure dicks. I shuddered next to Kraig's locker, retracing my interaction with Haylee to figure out if I had inadvertently rewritten her message. I didn't feel that I was someone to macerate words. But perhaps I could calcify them instead, until even the softest commentary felt callous, familiar—like home. When Haylee asked me to pass on her response, she had done so through narrow eyes and lips pressed into a thin line, while Vicky and Amanda both stood behind. Vicky's dark face was barely visible in the dimmed hallway, but Amanda's pale squalor pulsed.

Everything I learned about Haylee and her friends, I learned by listening in on their conversations during lunch. I learned that Amanda took Polaroids of herself in her underwear and sent them to boys when she wanted them to pay her attention. I learned that Vicky lived in a government housing complex and was bused two hours across town from a neighborhood my parents always took care to drive around whenever we were in the vicinity. I learned that Haylee had lost her virginity to the gym teacher, but told Kraig that he was her first. I learned that Mr. Stephens liked to scream his own name when he came, and he enjoyed fucking her in the ass, because it made her seem like a virgin every time. But the most interesting thing

I learned about Haylee and her friends was the slander they spread about one another.

Does Amanda ever use conditioner? Her hair looks like it died in a drought!

I bet Haylee's asshole looks like a fishing net. Do you think his wife knows?

Did you hear that Vicky's father lost his appeal? Yep, that was his last one. Well, that's what you get for dealing pot. He should've just gotten a job like everyone else.

It didn't take anything for them to throw each other under a variety of passing buses. They did it to alleviate boredom. They did it for sport. But when push came to shove, they rallied around one another like a pack of wolves, not out of love or respect, but to emphasize the imaginary line that distinguished them from the rest of *us*. And that was all they had.

AFTER SPEAKING WITH Kraig, I made my way across the campus to the toilets in the Literary Arts wing. The janitors there used air freshener instead of matches and sawdust to cut through the odor of shit and vomit. Rain began to thump on the bathroom windows, rattling the paper towel dispenser, which jostled against the dark green tiles. The door to the bathroom swung open and a pair of clumsy shoes stumbled their way into the stall next to me, slamming the door shut behind them. With a body firmly anchored against our shared stall wall, I guessed that four feet were actually involved, and the fevered shadows devouring each other on the scuffed floor next to an ambiguously dark stain confirmed this.

"Fuck *me*, huh?" a voice growled, deep and comical in its posturing.

"Come on, you know I didn't mean it like that," Haylee crooned in a whisper, punctuated with skittish giggles. "I just wanted to see if you really cared. That's all . . ."

A storm intensified outside as the sky opened up and sheets of rain began to belt down onto the building; the space between cracks of thunder filled with the raspy lyrics of their incoherent lovemaking.

They didn't hear me as I exited the stall. I skirted out on shaky ankles and the school day ended. My mother was waiting to pick me up outside. She normally did when it rained, and I was grateful to avoid taking the bus home in a storm that was picking up more speed, more branches, more reptiles. Wind and rain bent the palm trees into unnatural angles while large flat leaves snapped and chased me to the parking lot where she waited with the windshield wipers moving frantically, clearing the rain just long enough for me to see the vexed expression on her face through the glass before it was drowned out all over again.

The next day, Kraig broke up with Haylee, and began to date Amanda instead. I delivered Amanda's notes detailing this turn of events to various people in red ink and whimsical cursive. The last one I gave out was to Haylee, who was the last to know. Her neck bore a slight bruise that formed the shape of a smile.

6

I BUMPED INTO KRAIG AS I WAS RUNNING LATE FOR a final exam on Roman history, distracted by thoughts of Lucretia. He was waiting by the classroom—holding the door open for me. When the class ended and I handed in my exam, there he was—holding the door open yet again. His loose blond hair swooped across his left eye, which I noticed was darker and bluer than his right.

"Don't mind me," Kraig said. "I've just been waiting for you for the past hour."

"Oh," I replied. "I hope you didn't get into any trouble." The words were clumsy as they fell, landing unnaturally between us. My mind went down the list of reasons as to why he had spoken to me at all, and somehow landed on *This handsome but unfamiliar stranger will murder you when you least expect it.* In trying to follow up with something else, I attempted to read the glossary of meaning behind his eyes, in the writhing of his lips, in the angry red topography of his pimples, twitching as if they had their own opinions. He shuffled his feet and looked down, then gestured once again toward the open door before walking through it himself. I pressed myself against the wall as I snaked past, willing my skin to thicken, since it could not pass. My skin didn't protect me, so I had to protect it—from everyone outside my home, as well as everyone inside it.

I completed my next final early, and spent the rest of my time fantasizing about slipping into broom closets as my darkened self and reemerging light and glowing, a sudden burst of sunshine that peeks out between the dark, pregnant clouds—surprising Kraig in the hallway, in the cafeteria, in the courtyard. I would sneak into more of his classes, and he would invite me over for dinner to eat at a table among a family that didn't belong to me. I would speak with calm breath in my lungs, and pretend that I could slip on a new life as easily as I could slip on a new skin.

Later that night I took a long bath. When the heat from the water had loosened and wrinkled my skin into the color of virgin earth, I stretched outward in every direction with a relief that flooded my veins with desire. I squeezed my eyes shut and tightly pursed my lips while I filled myself with impatient fingers. When I raised my head, I thought only of the color of Kraig's left eye and how it matched the new cerulean glow of my skin.

——

Haylee and I had been friends once—until I had the misfortune of learning about sex in her home. We were thirteen when we built a fort in her backyard with printed bedsheets and an old camping tent during Halloween, the celebration of which was forbidden in my house. My mother used to let me dress up as an angel with a tinsel halo and aluminum wings to go trick-or-treating before being escorted back home with five or six mini candy bars, an apple, and a travel-size tube of toothpaste in my pillowcase. But that ended as my mother became more fixated on stories of Satanic worship in cemeteries, spiritual possession, and cyanide-laced sweets from the same neighbors who operated the school crosswalk every morning as volunteers. As Haylee and I took turns telling each other scary stories, my mother's tales would replay in my mind. I knew Haylee had invited the wrong member of my family to participate.

We positioned our fort next to a giant pile of dry wood covered in spiderwebs, and the chill crept in from outside. Her ten-year-old sister Liz joined us, carrying a large teddy bear and showing off a small bottle of peppermint schnapps. They took turns passing the bottle back and forth, but when Haylee extended the smudged and half-empty container to me, I declined. The decision was as reflexive as blinking.

"You'll never get laid with that attitude," Haylee said in a surly, pompous drawl.

"Get what . . . ?"

"Get *laid*." She rolled her eyes, already glistening with inhibition. I stared back at her blankly, waiting for further elaboration, chewing absentmindedly on marshmallows.

In a moment of inspiration, Haylee grabbed Liz's teddy bear. With a sharp stick that she had used to roast marshmallows earlier that evening, she proceeded to violently defile the stitching between its fluffy legs until plumes of white cotton jumped out. In the glow of the flashlight, I unraveled quickly, screaming. I ran out of the tent and into the neighboring woods, wandering through the mud until I lost my way and sat on a decaying log. Soon, I was found by flashlights held by Haylee's parents—and my mother—who took me home that same night.

The following school day, I went to the library and looked up *sex* in a dictionary. I was redirected to the entry "sexual intercourse," which read as follows:

> *Noun*
> Noun: sexual intercourse
> Sexual contact between individuals involving
> penetration, especially the insertion of a man's
> erect penis into a woman's vagina, typically
> culminating in orgasm and the ejaculation of
> semen.

It was the first time I remember ever feeling betrayed by my own body.

After that night, Haylee stopped acknowledging our friendship. I approached her in the lunchroom. She shoved her sweater in the seat next to her, while her friends stifled laughter, transposing my shame into a sound. Confusion distorted my face before tears could, and when my lip began to tremble, Haylee clutched her hand to her chest and began to scream. Her friends collapsed in hysterics, and I ran away as fast as I could. My seat in the cafeteria moved farther and farther away from her as the school year wore on, until I could only glimpse her changing body from a distance. When she emerged the following school year with brand-new teeth, an underwire bra, and clear milky skin, I had convinced myself that she had always been this stranger—as illusory to my life as I was to hers.

7

KRAIG AND I WERE PUT TOGETHER ON OUR FINAL
English class assignment. We were meant to summarize *Heart
of Darkness* in front of the class on the last day of school. I
wrote the report over the course of finals week, and we agreed
to meet up in the library on the day of our presentation to go
over it. Content to let me speak for the entire ten minutes of
our presentation, he didn't bother to read the report, instead
using the time to talk about what college life would look like.

"Where are you going?"

"I haven't decided yet." I smiled, biting off the eraser of
my pencil from nerves. I was trying to think of the most effective way to finish a sentence about the madness of Kurtz
without saying *madness*, because our teacher Mrs. Cohen had
said repeatedly how she found the word trite and overused. But
Kraig's attention didn't help. "I'm taking a year off." I flipped
through an open thesaurus and went back to the paper, inspired by *hysteria, mania*, and *delirium*.

"Oh, like Europe?" Kraig leaned in closely. "Sam is doing
something like that. Like, going to Prague, Paris, and Berlin
for the summer. I'm trying to convince my parents to let me
go with him." Kraig twisted a piece of paper between his long

fingers, distorting the spire of a particularly beautiful hand-drawn cathedral. "Where are you headed?" He picked a piece of lint off my shirt. I twitched.

"Um . . ." My hand started to scratch out a pair of new sentences, but I couldn't think of any new words. "I'm staying here for a year. Taking some . . . time . . ." The judgment on his face bit my sentence in half.

"*Here?*" What a bewildered word. I blushed inwardly, and went back to the paper, my palms suddenly greasy.

"Do you want to read what I have?" I pointed with my chin. Kraig's expression flattened again, restoring his trademark expression of disinterest. The bell rang and we walked out of the library together.

"I trust you." He winked as he stretched his arms, gathering his books. "Besides, I already got into UF." His satisfied expression said that he was happy to wait for me this time—the thought that he enjoyed it made me blush. I remembered Kelsey's freckled shoulder beneath the orange-and-blue school banners in the student union. I wondered if they would meet, and if the wary transition to adulthood would turn them into friends, lovers, or foes.

"So, what does Conrad mean when he writes that 'All Europe contributed to the making of Kurtz,' Gabrielle?" Mrs. Cohen examined me from her desk after I read the paper out loud. A fan blew hot air just behind her in the corner of the class, causing her dirty-blond hair to fly around her thin, pointed face. Gray roots had begun to sprout at her hairline. I collected my thoughts for a response, but felt something inside of me break—screwed loose, hardened shut, floating around inside my belly. I felt the blood slip out of my body. Kraig stopped his doodling to look up at me, his eyes a question mark. Everyone else was drifting to sleep, or had already been lulled there by their own apathy.

"He's talking about responsibility," I blurted out, walking quickly back to my seat. A sharp pain twisted in a part of my stomach that didn't even feel like part of my stomach, and I coiled in my chair, shrinking into a warm sensation that began to press against the back of my shorts. I finished my thought from there, barely audible: "He's talking about the legacy of empires." Mrs. Cohen rubbed her mouth thoughtfully before responding, but the bell began to blare over the classroom speaker.

"I guess that's a good place to leave it," she concluded, throwing up her hands in resignation as everyone began to pile out of the room. "Have fun in college!" She paused. "Or whatever you plan on doing!" Mrs. Cohen approached my desk when the classroom emptied. I reached down to my seat and when I lifted my fingertips, they were red with blood. She certified the shock on my face and laughed, her silver fillings smiling back at me.

"I envy you," she said. "I got my period when I was thirteen, and what I wouldn't give to have had a few more years of clean lacy underwear."

Mrs. Cohen handed me her sweater. After stuffing fistfuls

of tissues into my pants, I shuffled through the empty hallways clutching the garment around my waist with white-knuckled fear. My shoes tapped loudly against the linoleum floor, past everyone dumping their notebooks into the garbage. I went home on a city bus.

When I walked through the door, my mother turned into a deep burgundy, rich and aromatic like a sun-ripened vine of grapes. She already knew. The denim of my shorts, once wet and sticky, had hardened like cardboard under the Florida sun. I smelt like a fistful of pennies. I scratched myself with the stain's sharpened edges while detangling the shorts from my bloodstained skin using just the tips of my fingers. My mother had no such delicate sensibilities. She hosed my clothes down in the backyard still in her nightgown and stocking cap with one hand on her hip. The blood ran from the edges of the cloth before sinking into the dirt and staining the grass like a murder had just taken place there.

After walking past an endless selection of tampons, my mother selected the thickest pads in the entire drugstore. They were placed right next to the overnight diapers for senior citizens and bulged from their plastic packaging the way that cotton does from a violated stuffed animal. Old white women in sweaters smiled at each other across the plastic, while young teenage girls in yellow bikinis frolicked on the covers of the tampon boxes farther down. When I inquired about less conspicuous options, my mother clicked her tongue and replied, "When you get married, that's when you've earned the right to hide your shame." I trailed behind her with my head held low, my skin the color of white pearls, hers the color of melted butter. My insides continued to fold over themselves, but she refused to buy painkillers for the cramps. "Ain't no daughter of mine doing drugs," she seethed, equal parts proud and something else. A cashier whose face bore deep scarring from aggressive acne nodded in approval. She bagged the items with care.

"You're lucky to have such an involved mother," she said, her voice thickened by the rolls of fat around her neck. "One day, you'll miss this."

I snatched the white plastic bag and waited by the car.

"I got mine late too," she said. "It's always bad in the beginning, but it'll get easier."

THE PAIN BECAME worse with each passing day. The blood didn't bother me—but I couldn't eat. I couldn't stand. I couldn't sleep, speak, or walk in a straight line. It was as if my blood had been drained and mainlined with the pure current of pain. My color started oscillating between unnatural colors that threatened to split my skin wide open. I went from shades of deep golden yellow to the color of the sea. It didn't matter where I was, or how far away I was from my mother.

One day, I rode my bicycle to a gas station to buy a can of grapefruit soda and a bag of chocolate kisses that I found myself craving. But I had to lock myself in the bathroom stall for hours while my skin contracted and expanded. I coiled like a snake until the attendant came knocking on the door.

"Do you want me to call someone for you, gal?" The

Southern drawl in his voice disguised his irritation over my monopolization of the one toilet stall not covered in shit.

When my mother eventually picked me up, she told me that it was beginning, and that I needed to learn how to control my passing once and for all.

Afraid of what the heat might do again, and who might see me, my mother stopped allowing me to leave the house. I had to skip graduation, and the school mailed my diploma to me in an envelope decorated in stamps that read *Class of '94*.

She tried multiple remedies to help me stabilize my skin: juice cleanses, grapefruit diets, even a dial-in exorcism from Reverend Jeremiah who heard the complaints of her "moody daughter" over the phone, and told my mother to turn the air conditioner down to arctic. Not content with that, she drew a cold bath, dumping several trays of ice into the tub before submerging me beneath the water.

"Demons are like bedbugs," he shouted over the phone as I wailed from beneath the frigid surface. Bubbles distorted my mother's face into fractals of light as she repeated his words, interspersed with emphatic gibberish that they called the voice of God. "They hate the cold." She held my arms crossed against my chest until my lips turned blue.

And it worked. The cooler I was, the less I passed. For this service, a near case of hypothermia, and an exorbitant electricity bill that later sent my father into a rage for six straight days, the Reverend charged my mother three hundred dollars.

With my period came other developments. My breasts grew bigger, pointier, and hung lower. My belly grew rounder, protruding slightly above the zipper of my jeans. I hovered around my mother, who made no secret of the pride she felt in her own naked body—which she felt compelled to put on full display in the heat, sticking herself to each room in the house with a sort of juvenile satisfaction. I compared mine to hers, wondering how she was able to maintain such perfect, buoyant beauties while mine resembled the teats of a cow. I wondered about Vicky's breasts, and Haylee's. I wondered about Kelsey's. My mother laughed when I compared my body with hers, took my face between her bony hands, smoothed away my hair, and told me there was nothing wrong with my peculiar, prickly breasts.

I elongated practically overnight, and sprouted to an impressive height with large, slender hands—the only discernible sign that I was my father's daughter as well as my mother's.

8

I WAS GETTING READY TO WATCH THE FIREWORKS with Matthew, the boy with red hair and freckles who lived at the far end of the street. He didn't have the luxury of attending college either, given that he was allergic to eggs, peanuts, wheat, strawberries, and sunlight. But his parents let him out of the house on the Fourth of July so he could pretend to be normal for a day. At dusk, he emerged from his house slathered in sunscreen as thick as afterbirth, regaling anyone who would listen with the latest results from his various medical exams and blood tests.

I heard the doorbell ring, but couldn't make out the exchange. My father answered the door, and shortly after walked into my room without knocking.

"Is Matthew here?"

The fireworks crackled outside as bright colors illuminated the curtains on my bedroom window with shades of red, white, and blue. My father extended himself diagonally across my bed, the metal coils protesting beneath his weight. His bare feet dangled off the edge—cracked and peeling from the fungus that coated his heels. Every time I saw them I was reminded of when I was little—when I used to hack at them with a nail file while he watched television. It was attention he took as a sign of daughterly devotion—even though I only did it to see him bleed.

His eyes scanned my body for the easiest place to begin.

"All that *denim* . . ." he said, scratching the stubble on his chin. "That's what you want to wear?"

I didn't respond, and focused on containing my hair in a tight ponytail using a neon scrunchy. Loose tendrils kept unraveling from the edges like question marks.

"Stand up straight."

I was. If I stood any straighter my torso would have detached.

I picked up my detangling brush and went to work with several bobby pins sticking out from between my lips, in search of that perfect, smooth silhouette.

"Your face looks kind of oily today."

I brushed and brushed, and licked and brushed.

"Have you learned to pluck your eyebrows yet?"

The skin around my hairline turned red at the roots.

Each provocation was a cut. He didn't stop until he had burrowed so deep that he kicked against bone. My mother walked past holding a stack of folded towels, and she stopped in the doorframe as the conversation floated out into the hallway, her gaze shifting uncomfortably around the walls and on the floor, refusing to meet mine. I silently willed for her interruption, but it never came. My mother was a woman of her word. She kept walking as my father reorganized his insults like the pieces on a chessboard. The next time I took my hand

away from my scalp, a thick lock of hair fell into my palm—
black and curly with egg-white roots. It took a second for me
to register the place it had come from. I touched a bald spot
directly above my ear, and studied the blood on my fingertips.

"Okay." My voice was too soft even for prayer. "I'll stay
home."

"Come here." He beckoned me toward the bed. I sat beside
him, gripping the lock in my hand, curling my fingers around
it. "You're so beautiful. Do you know that?"

I didn't say anything. He furrowed his brow and scratched
himself, attempting to solicit a response.

"Don't you know how beautiful I think you are?"

The loose lock of hair burned in my hand, turning the skin
around it scarlet.

He unanchored himself from my bed, stopping just before
walking through the doorway to open his arms. I walked to
him, and let them wrap around me.

Think of something cold.

My skin color quickened into a smooth pearlescent hue,
and I welcomed the cool, clean feeling of being completely
numb. He smiled.

"I love you," he said.

I tried not to react. Reacting only would have made it
worse. My father didn't love us, but I am certain that he did
need us. He often used one word when he meant the other,
and we used to confuse them as the same thing. But there was
something off about the way he used the word *love*, which sat
awkwardly on his tongue, jagged and misshapen like a shard of

glass. If he said it too comfortably, he'd hurt himself. If he said it too enjoyably, he'd hurt himself. Nothing frightened him more than the threat of his own suffering. So he used the word like a weapon instead, so that he could hurt others.

I said the words back as convincingly as I needed to for him to let me go. When I shut the door behind him, I stripped the bed of its sheets and piled them on the floor. Then investigated myself in front of the mirror again and removed the scrunchy that held my hair back. It inflated around my face, covering my bushy eyebrows, oily skin, and brand-new bald spot.

9

SEVERAL HURRICANES THAT WERE MEANT FOR US were rerouted to the Keys instead, flooding homes, fishing stores, restaurants, and scuba diving shops. Bleak faces appeared on TV to list all the items they had lost, and a hotline was set up for donations from around the country. After Hurricane Frederick, reports poured in over the radio, and my father made himself available to residents in the affected area so that he could convince several prominent business owners to file lawsuits against the state for damages. Most people fled from hurricanes—but my father sued them.

I knew he was really gone when my mother's voice filled the house the way a pleasant smell expanded from the oven—and it finally felt like summer. But even with his absence, I went to her less and less to pass our colors. Our morning ritual was affected by my new moving parts, my new unreadable thoughts. We tried recovering our intimacy, but every attempt pulled us farther apart. The last time I tried, she turned her back on me and her shoulder blades presented as steel-plated armor.

"I'm resting," she said flatly.

Then, reading my mind, she grayed her skin to the color of

a rotten egg. The memory of who we used to be to each other bristled at the thought of trying to re-create a ritual that no longer made sense. We watched television in different rooms and ate our breakfasts at different times. I cleaned my dishes when she was in the toilet, setting them on the wet rack before disappearing into an empty room, so that she could reemerge to put them away once they had dried.

But when she sang, I always went to her—no matter where in the house she was. My skin would pass into colors like refracted light bursting through a prism. When I heard her voice floating through the hallways, I would follow it outside, and then sit in the dirt pulling lovebugs apart by their tails and letting them go while my mother weeded the grass around the hibiscus bush. The bugs circled around one another several times before finding their way back to one another for a second, third, and fourth round. She grabbed fistfuls of pennywort and shoved them into a large black plastic bag while an aria floated from her sweaty mouth, over the fence, to the clamor of cries and pool splashes on the other side that quieted as the children, their parents, their animals, and their fleas stopped to listen. Her knobbed fingers wrapped around knots of dogged green plants and yanked them out by their thick white roots. Strong things weren't allowed to grow on our property.

"Why can't I sing like you?"

I followed her inside where the radio flooded us with music as she changed the bedspread in a guest bedroom that had never been used. The accumulated dust floated up into the air and hovered in a fog.

"We've been through this before," she said, coughing through the filth.

It didn't matter how many times she showed me how to stand, or how many times she placed her hands on my stomach and told me to breathe from my gut first and my chest last. My voice had the grating depth of a grown man's. My mother's voice could make any word sound like an invitation.

"It's just not for everyone." She folded down the soiled bed linen and placed her hand gently on my chin, smudging it with dust, before walking past me out into the hallway.

As we migrated from room to room, the songs on the radio changed and I tried imitating synthetic pop vocals from London. Then the sultry croon of a woman who made herself available anytime, and anyplace. I tried the lush screams of a wounded man from Seattle with a sandpaper smile who had killed himself just before summer—howling in unison with the radio until my throat felt raw like orange pulp.

"You don't even sound human." My mother cackled. But her laughter was soon replaced with pity, and she only sucked at the corner of her mouth when I reached for a note beyond my grasp. I plopped down on my bed, and she switched radio stations to drown out my sulking.

I was watching a banana spider weave a web outside the window when a low bass note spilled out of the speakers that I had never heard before. The sound went up, down, and side to side. Notes that made me pass into electric mint and amber. My skin shifted to the melody with reptilian ease. My mother stood in my bedroom doorway holding a bundle of folded towels in her hands, watching me with a strange countenance.

The piece ended—replaced by the voice of a mild-mannered DJ. But before he could finish his monologue, the house began to shake. My mother was gone and the crystal ballerina figurines that she had arranged and then rearranged on my dresser danced across the white surface until I skirted them away from the edge. The sounds of chaotic instruments built up to a sharp point, until an invisible string was pulled to release a symphonic harmony.

I ran out of my bedroom and into the white of the living room where my mother sat with a portfolio of grimy records scattered before her. We were both the color of finely polished copper plates—two smooth, smiling echoes.

"Look at you . . ." The words caught in her throat, and I saw the skin soften around her wet eyes. She took my face between her hands, and pulled her head close, resting her forehead against mine. We hummed to the music together. A soprano, and an alto, synchronized both in sound and flesh. I curled into the side of her body, a chipped piece of marble reunited with her statue.

We didn't hear the sound of his voice, but his authority flexed like a muscle until I felt it squeeze my neck. We sat up quickly, but he lingered in the kitchen with an unreadable expression. My skin cooled back into a soft white with rosy-pink cheeks. My mother registered my alarm but did not greet it; instead, she casually pulled the needle off the record player, stood up, smoothed her blouse and pants, passed back to white, and then went into the kitchen. I heard the sound of cupboard doors opening and closing. Vegetables and meat arranged themselves neatly on the kitchen counter like prisoners before a firing squad. I retrieved his white plastic cup from the cupboard, and his fingers shook as he took it.

It was so humid that I felt an extra pound weighing every drop of sweat. My father switched on the evening news, muting the sound, searching for updates on the floods that had swarmed the state from the Everglades to the Keys. He slumped back into the chair, fanning himself. The news displayed piles of dark bodies splayed out on the ground in asymmetrical patterns. The dirt beneath them was stained red—it was difficult to determine if it was the color of the earth or the broad brushstrokes of death.

She stopped chopping to view the events unfolding on the television. There was an illustration of Africa with a red mark over a small country in the central part of the continent. She clenched her jaw. My mother knew how to possess her own suffering. She understood its shape, taste, and smell as if it had slithered out from between her legs—but she couldn't stomach the suffering of others. If I had been closer, she would have reached for my hand and squeezed. She would have tried to comfort me. She would have told me that everything was going to be okay.

On the muted television, a woman with dark skin and yellow fingernails rocked back and forth on a stoop shaking the body of a limp child in her arms, caressing the violet ribbons in her hair while tears and spit fell from her dark, toothless mouth. The dirt beneath her was as dark as shadow. At the bottom of the screen, the words *Families turned against each other* appeared in white and red.

My father unmuted the volume, and we caught a news commentator with blond hair and blue eyes halfway through a sentence.

". . . up to one million deaths. But an exact toll is still needed."

———

The next day, I came home and the piano had been moved from the garage into the dining room. It appeared self-conscious, awkward, a beautiful auburn stain in its sterile, white environment. I opened the lid to say hello, and it greeted me with a mothy book smell. Its keys seemed to smile up at me as I pushed them down in a clumsy way, filling the house with random, discordant sounds.

My mother came up behind me, wrapping her white arms around my waist. I felt the cold seep into my belly, but I glowed like pollen.

"I never did get a handle on this." She sighed, using her fingers to tap out a quick melody on the highest notes of the black keys. They sounded like wind chimes. "I guess I'm a singer at heart. But I think . . ." She trailed off and squeezed my shoulders. "Maybe this could be your trumpet?"

"But it's a piano—not a trumpet?" I squinted an eye at her, squeezing her arms around me playfully.

"Okay, so Gabriel had a trumpet. But Gabri*elle* can play

a piano, or whatever you want. Just, put it in your story." She winked.

Heavy steps entered the room. My father held his peeling white plastic cup as both he and the liquid swirled dangerously close to the edge of spilling over. He placed a pillow beneath his arm as he lay on the floor, waiting for something to happen. She released me, and my shoulders felt weighed down. We both passed fully white again, and I reached toward the keys, wondering if I was their accessory or if they were mine. She left the room soundlessly, a scent of ginger lingering behind her that only I could smell.

"It's been sitting out in the garage for ten years," he began. "When I was younger, I always wanted to learn to play. And then your mama promised to learn, but she never did." The words came between slurps of booze that invoked the Southern drawl he normally disguised. "That lady at UF said you needed some extracurricular activities."

"Kelsey." The pattern of freckles on her shoulder was vivid in my mind.

"Right—her. Anyway, if you can dedicate yourself to mastering an instrument then you can dedicate yourself to being a doctor. Admissions boards love that stuff."

I began to fiddle with the keys. I didn't know how to read music, but I could play what I heard, which was usually whatever my mother was singing. But that was in the garage. No longer outcast, the white keys looked different without shadows.

"You know, my mother worked three jobs, but she still

couldn't afford to buy an instrument." A chill passed between the piano and me. "She said that I didn't have time to be messing around with no white people music." The ice cubes in his cup rattled loudly—normally an indication for me to refill it, but my feet were tethered.

"But you will."

I nodded. I would have done the same if I were speaking to a rogue wave. The wetness from his eyes leaked down to the rest of his face in thin, reflective streams.

"Being what you are . . ."

A grimace lurked beneath his smile. Neither he nor my mother seemed capable of whole smiles; only fractured expressions of happiness. He stretched his long arm out in my direction and shook the cup in his hand, the sound of ice replacing the words he wouldn't say. I took the cup from him to refill.

It was not that my father previously lacked interest in my activities, but that they had previously lacked the ability to interest him. Once I began to demonstrate that I could help him to reimagine the injustices of a past that could not be rewritten, I felt myself becoming an extension of it. I sank into it comfortably, feeling some small amount of relief knowing that I could fix it. I could fix them both.

10

I WAS DREAMING OF MY GRANDMOTHER'S SHOTGUN when a hand jostled me awake in what felt like the middle of the night. My eyes stung as they flew open, trip-wired from the inertia of waiting for something to go wrong. My father's eyes stared back at me—two dark, smoky barrels cocked within firing range as he knelt beside my bed.

"Get dressed." I flushed into a pearlescent white, and he sneered in response. "Don't patronize me."

His shadow stretched across my bedroom into the opposite corner as he pulled himself upright. He wore penny loafers that displayed his ashen ankles and khaki shorts that bunched between his skinny legs. I wondered how so much of one man could sit above the waist. It seemed there was simply too much of him. Too much skin, too much bone, too much muscle.

"We're going for a drive." The round white clock next to my bed read 6:38. In the living room, my mother was perched on the sofa in her natural state, her knuckles stiff and tense. She wore her white nightgown and satin cap, and I realized that wherever we were going she wouldn't be joining us. I stretched into the color of tanned leather to match her. She waved goodbye as the garage door closed, and the last thing I saw was her bare feet on the hard surface flashing yellow like warning signs.

WE CRUISED DOWN State Road 50 and passed a mattress store that had been going out of business for the past three years—suddenly resurrected in red and gold balloons with a large sign that read GRAND OPENING.

"I want you to know that I love your mother." His face was obscured by a pair of dark sunglasses so that I couldn't see him lying. "She means well, but she doesn't know how the world works. And she doesn't know how to commit to anything. I don't want you to be like her. That's why you need to learn a hobby."

I acted as if I agreed, and maybe I convinced myself that I did. I couldn't fix her if I couldn't acknowledge that something was wrong.

"Learning an instrument would look great on your college application. And that discipline will take you far in life."

He segued into my final GPA and my school performance.

"The bottom line is, you studied hard. It demonstrates a high degree of . . ." He trailed off, scratching the salty stubble on his chin. "Self-concordance."

Satisfied with this answer, he stopped speaking as we pulled up to a stoplight where a man with sun-weathered skin was selling bags of grapefruit through open car windows. I tried to roll down the window as he approached, but the child lock was on.

"We can get fruit from the store," my father muttered. I gave the man an apologetic smile, and he held up a grapefruit, tapping on the window. A thick scar above his lip gave him the appearance of a man with two smiles instead of one.

"Gratis para la chica bonita!" My face beamed, but my father was already pulling back into traffic, nearly crashing into another car from the intersecting lane.

"But it's not all about grades, you know. If you want to succeed in life, you have to be willing to take risks too. You have to learn how to enjoy hobbies that other people enjoy," he continued. "That's why I want you to try new things."

We pulled up to a flattened stucco building sandwiched between a McDonald's and a Taco Bell. It was a perfect square—compressed, confined, and constricted from the sounds of children screaming in ball pits next door.

"We're here!" He put the car into park. The sight of the firing range made me begin to sweat.

A stocky man with a thick gray beard wearing army fatigues and a red baseball cap greeted us from behind a glass display counter.

"How can I help you folks today?" He spoke as if half of his mouth was full of peanut butter, and homed in on me before clearing his throat to address my father directly. A tag with a smiley-face sticker on his shirt said that his name was Randy. "Looking for anything in particular?"

My father's broad hand swooped in from the side like a hook to shake hands. "My name's Robert. My daughter just graduated, and we're here to buy her first firearm." He smiled, his voice changing to a bright and friendly color—two consummate salesmen.

Randy's face eased slightly, and he tugged at the bill of his baseball cap. "Well, all right then. That's what I like to hear!"

The shop was much bigger than it appeared on the outside. Racks of gun supplies draped in camouflage netting covered the main floor. Rifles hung in a geometry-like honeycomb, buttressed by the stuffed heads of dead animals with hollow eyes.

When Randy leaned over the display case, I saw the gun holster attached to his hip. A stuffed grizzly bear loomed behind him with a hunting rifle nestled in its armpit and a sign attached to its belly that read FROM MY COLD DEAD CLAWS.

"I reckon a Taurus. Even a dummy could use it." Randy was peering over the counter to examine my hands. He leaned back and opened the display case, rolling out a small red velvet blanket and placing a jet-black handgun on top.

"Don't be fooled by the size, gal, this one packs a mean punch." His hairy hands gripped the gun and demonstrated the different parts and components. "I'd say this is the best carry gun on the market. It comes with two twelve-round magazines with a yellow follower." He turned it over several times, stroking the frame with his finger. "It has a manual safety, but it's easy to activate here." He flicked it with his thumb back and forth several times. "So during a draw . . ." He placed it next to his hip, and lifted it quickly, pointing the weapon to all four corners of the building. "You can turn it off easily."

He walked around the display and slid the gun into my

palm, then molded his hands around mine. He turned me so
that we pointed toward the taxidermy bear—at the furry spot
where its heart used to be. The tip of my finger began to os-
cillate in and out of black when he placed it on the trigger
beneath his own, and I felt him suck air into his lungs right
before we pulled it together, killing the bear for a second time.

"Thatta girl."

My father grunted.

The bell above the front door jingled and a skinny woman
with curly blond hair entered. She was accompanied by a slight
person around my age. I hardly recognized Sam. He always
looked pale, but in the shadow of this woman, he was near
transparent.

"Oh hey there, Cynthia!" Randy retrieved two pairs of
protective goggles and earmuffs from a bucket decorated in
stickers designed like bullet holes. Cynthia followed Randy.
"Same equipment as always?" She tugged on Sam's arm, and
he took a smooth black case out of her other hand, placing
it on the floor to open. "Oh no need, I trust you. How many
targets?"

"Let's start with two." Randy ripped two paper targets
shaped like men from a large pad.

Cynthia and Sam entered the firing range while I wandered over to the rifles, drawn to a familiar long black barrel.

"Don't touch those, gal." Randy walked over with my father tailing him, still holding the handgun. "If you want to
hold one of the long-barreled firearms, let me know. I'll take
it down for you." I pointed to the shotgun pinned against the

wall above me and felt eyes from around the room tracing the direction of my finger.

"Little lady, you've got good taste." Randy lifted the gun down from the wall, positioning it in his hands with the butt end nestled in his armpit. "The Mossberg Maverick 88 12-gauge shotgun. The best budget home defense system money can buy—this is what Cynthia's firing off over there." He jerked his head back toward the bulletproof glass that sealed up the firing range. The shotgun echoed. Each shell was gaseous, filling the space around us with aggression. "Eighteen-and-a-half-inch barrel, lightweight, with a five-round mag plus one in the chamber," he began. "You could take out a lotta thugs with this here piece if you loaded it with the right shells." He lifted the gun and aimed. "It could take out a hundred animals as big as gorillas."

"A colleague of mine has the same model and loves it," my father replied, rubbing his dry hands together. Like most successful men, my father didn't enjoy movie theaters or fine dining but took pride in an extensive collection of guns and knives, each more silver and expensive than the last—bored with the pleasures enjoyed by lower classes.

Randy lowered the rifle and grinned through a cluster of yellow teeth and angry gums. "I'll tell you what. They're great for firing off a little bit of steam at the end of the day." Gunfire popped in the back of the building, and he handed the rifle to my father, who aimed in the same direction and squeezed one of his eyes shut. Randy crossed his arms proudly across his chest while his eyes drifted over my body. "I'll tell ya, Robert, you're one of the good ones. Is there anything else you want to see?"

"I think we'll take these two."

As Randy began to fumble around with paperwork and IDs, my belly glowed what felt like a dark green—the color of sick. I walked over to the clear bulletproof glass where I saw people in camouflage jackets and neon-orange vests. Men, women, and older people in T-shirts with military insignias, all shooting from their divided booths into the distance. Sam held a handgun not too dissimilar from the one Randy had shown us, firing on shaky feet barely parted. His clothes were too big for him and rattled around his limbs. Sam couldn't pick up the shotgun properly. He tried to put the butt into his shoulder, but it had nothing to grip against. Each time the gun fired his thin arms kicked back like hinges. Smoke swirled around his head. Cynthia leaned back against the glass laughing.

The sound of gunshots startled me when he opened the door, and I felt my face quickly pulse from brown to black to red and brown again. I turned away from the glass, until I stabilized. As he came to my side, Sam's face was blank, and bored—but alert. I couldn't tell if he saw me pass. We stood like that for a while, with gunshots punctuating the seconds as they passed.

"Didn't see you at graduation." He was looking at my face in the reflection of the bulletproof glass. This comment surprised me, and I wondered if he had mistaken me for Vicky.

"Were you sick or something?"

"Yeah, I had the stomach flu pretty bad." It wasn't much

of an exaggeration. But I didn't know why I needed him to
believe me.

"I really enjoyed your English presentation."

"Mine?" I sounded afraid of myself, and cleared my throat.
"My presentation?"

He nodded. *"Heart of Darkness,* right?"

He knew who I was. Was this what people did when the
classroom politics were no longer relevant? Speak to each other
like human beings?

I nodded. A man dressed in army fatigues walked through
the door into the firing range, where he opened his case and
pulled out a gun as large as a bazooka. He set it on the wooden
platform in his booth and started firing at a dummy at the far
end. The sound made the glass shake, and my hands, which
were pressed against the window, turned a leafy green. I
promptly hid them behind my back. Sam's eyes were still on
me, not even a fraction wider than they had been before. His
mouth dropped open, and then shut again just as quickly.

I wanted to get away, but my feet froze. I couldn't move my
body until my father called my name. He had finished with
Randy, and even though he was just a few feet away at the
counter, the sound of his voice could have summoned me from
across the other side of the world. Sam's eyes followed us out of
the store. By the time we were back in the car, target shooting
had resumed.

11

WHEN I GREW TIRED OF SUCKING ON ICE CUBES AND wearing wet rags on my forehead to treat my PMS and passing spells, my mother brought home a tub of chocolate ice cream. We ate it together in front of the fan in the piano parlor, dipping our spoons into the melting slush. We passed the carton back and forth between us until we got to the bottom, licking it clean until it appeared brand-new. My color thanked her by being still.

"We had to finish it before your father came home, otherwise he would have thrown it out." She crumpled the paper tub and threw it into the neighbor's garbage bin. I felt sick but happy, even while planted on the toilet only minutes later.

A few days before my period was meant to start again, I cycled to the local ice cream store to pick up something colorful, cold, and sweet. Vicky was behind the counter, wearing a striped apron and matching hat that sat awkwardly on her relaxed hair. Her natural roots peeked out from her hairline, looking confused.

She didn't acknowledge me at first, leaning against the glass sneeze guard, resting her elbows across the top. She pushed herself up slowly, annoyed. Sweat glossed her forehead.

"Well, what'll it be?"

"A cup, please." With one hand she grabbed a small white cup, and with the other, rinsed the ice cream scoop in the sink. I pointed to the chocolate, and then to the blood orange. The color combination alone made me swallow hard. While I was counting out the dollar bill and coins in my hand, the door opened and a rush of warm, wet air rushed into the shop. I heard them before I saw them: Kraig, David, Jacob, and Sam, bouncing a basketball among them. The bravado was unmistakable. Vicky perked up immediately and threw my change into the cash register before leaning across the counter, pushing her small breasts forward. They circled in as I moved away, swallowing her up.

Jacob and David asked Vicky for samples of all thirty-one flavors before finally deciding on which ones they wanted. Sam and Kraig made their way toward my table at the far end of the shop, beneath an air-conditioning vent that kissed the back of my neck.

"Hey, there she is."

Kraig approached as I was licking the edges of the ice cream cup, and I bit down on the curled paper lip. I nervously wiped the spit from my mouth, and then the sweat from my forehead. Kraig still had the large gap between his teeth, but it was complemented by gold stubble on his chin, a fuller mouth, and a harder jaw that tensed when he walked. A life in transition. The end of school had meant the end of softness, and I wondered briefly if I was doing it right—growing up and older.

I mixed both flavors in my cup before sticking the spoon in my mouth, letting it melt so I wouldn't have to talk.

"You weren't at graduation," Kraig said. Sam stayed quiet. I wondered who had noticed first—him or Sam? Who had told the other? Who cared first?

I shrugged and pulled the spoon out of my mouth. "I was sick."

Sam was attentive but quiet. Sweat started falling down my neck, and from beneath my breasts, sticking to the skin of my stomach. Vicky squealed from the front, where Jacob was playing with the soda pump, spraying Vicky behind the counter. David was bored and went to the front door, shouting impatiently to the rest of his friends.

"You coming or what?"

Kraig rolled his eyes and waved his hand in a way that made David stop there, their respect for this social order like the behavior of grown men.

"Well, see you around." He turned, bouncing the basketball a few times on the floor before following David, with a quick wave at Vicky on his way out. Jacob left next. Sam was the last one out, ambling through the open glass door.

———

Kraig played basketball in the park three times a week, and I began to adjust my walks home to catch him squatting low, legs wide, shirt off. I'd circle around the block and double back on the opposite side of the street so he wouldn't see me return. I followed him from a distance when he went home, down the hill behind a narrow divide of undeveloped residential property where he lived in a house that looked not dissimilar from mine.

Eventually, I chose a seat close to his friends in the bleachers, and listened in on the conversations he had with his friends about the girls he slept with on the weekends. Sometimes, he brought remnants of these affairs to the court—a used condom, oily and bloated from use, or the shriveled butt of a cigarette marked with bright pink lipstick. He didn't care who saw. He wanted everyone to know what he was capable of.

Once, Kraig passed around a pair of panties, which he claimed had belonged to Elena. They fingered the unraveled blue lace with quiet awe, inhaling the lingering residue and describing it like a catalog of observations that might lead to a critical discovery.

"It smells like my toaster after burning strawberry Pop-Tarts," said Jacob.

"It smells like mayo crust," said Sam.

David glowered.

I enjoyed watching them. The only thing more fascinating than my own awkward body was learning how boys my age interpreted it. They were collectively enthralled with the souvenirs from Kraig's sexual exploits, fascinated by the milky stains. But for some reason, the lingerie also distorted their ideas of what it covered. The concept of a vagina made sense to Jacob, David, and Sam. It was a hole where babies and blood came out, or things went in—fingers, penises, theoretically even inanimate objects like fruit and loose change. All of which gave me the distinct impression that they were all lying. David talked about revues in Thailand where naked women inserted all of the above, before launching them back into a crowd of drunken, exhilarated tourists who caught the sticky items in their hands and shouted violently.

I compared their words to my body parts, but there was a disparity between what they said and what I had. I moved closer to their conversations—as if I could learn more about myself by surrendering to their expectations. How to be beautiful, how to be desirable, how to be feminine. I needed someone to tell me how.

David sat on the bench with paper and pencil to create interpretations of vaginas. I sat behind him. When the sun went behind the clouds, I could see the drawings clearly. It appeared as if he had pooled fragments from Kraig's stories into a blurry hypothesis; the results were nearly always illustrations of large, black circles girdled by bloody fangs, or bat wings. Drawings that made me cross my legs, press my knees together, and squirm—wanting to swallow the thing that seemed to be the architect of endless confusion for them.

Kraig looked over David's shoulder at the drawings and laughed, ripping them out of the notebook. I felt my body relax again.

"Bro, not even close!" He laughed until the others had no choice but to join in, and I laughed too. Kraig heard me and smirked. I focused back on the sun, toiling with nothing in particular. I still felt his eyes when I left.

I was pumping liquid cheese onto a paper carton of nachos at a 7-Eleven on the way home when I ran into Kraig again.

He waved to me as he tore open a package of Twizzlers with his teeth before paying for them. The attendant scanned the opened plastic, then examined my nachos.

"How many pumps of cheese are on these?" His face was sunburnt, and he narrowed his patchy eyebrows at me.

"One, just one," I said.

"Looks like two to me." Small beads of sweat had formed where a mustache would have been.

"It's just one," I repeated flatly. He sized me up before scanning my items. On our way out, Kraig ran to join me.

"You live this way too, or . . . ?"

"Yeah, just by the Thurmond developments."

"Yeah?" He pulled a red licorice rope from the plastic bag. "Me too. I think I've seen you around there."

I nodded, and we walked side by side with silence itching between us.

He reached into his pocket and presented a note folded in the shape of an envelope with a pull tab. I scanned the area around us and found his friends lingering in the background. I hesitated before taking it, and it slipped from his hand to mine.

I decided to read it then and there. Kraig shifted from one foot to the other, and I could tell that he had expected me to be too embarrassed to do that. It amused me to make him a little uncomfortable. I unfolded the paper beneath the sun and found several dried magnolias along with a sketch of La Sagrada Familia drawn in bright red ink in my fingertips. My tailbone itched silver beneath the sweaty shirt clinging to it.

"Well . . ." He ran a hand back through his hair. "Do you like it?" He seemed interested in a drainage ditch, averting his eyes to the sludge that leaked from it.

"Yes." I paused before adding, "It's very beautiful." And it was, but more importantly, that sounded like the right thing to say. I didn't want to make my pleasure obvious.

"Thanks." He coughed even though it was a mild day. A cool breeze kissed my cheeks, and the skin between my breasts melted into the color of orange embers. We began to walk again.

"I don't really draw." I didn't know what else to say. The words became less assured as they left my lips, as if someone else was speaking them.

"If you want, I could teach you . . . how to draw, I mean."

My eyebrows furled.

"I love to draw." The sunlight brushed his cheeks, turning them pink, and he smiled.

"I noticed . . ."

I remembered the concentration on David's face as he sketched out body parts. Kraig's friends were still close enough to see us, but far enough away to only make out their golden silhouettes.

"Oh hey, that other stuff that Dave does, I'm not into it." He stopped walking again. I waved Kraig's drawing in front of my face to indicate my indifference.

"You two seem . . . different," I began. "From each other, I mean." I kicked some loose pebbles as I continued to stroll down the sidewalk.

A car passed, and the driver leaned almost completely out the window to gawk at us as we tried not to look at each other. "I know . . . he's stupid, I know that. But he's a good guy. I mean, you gotta know him, I guess, but those drawings are dumb."

I nodded approvingly, even though it didn't feel true. He held out the bag of Twizzlers. I took a piece, twirling the sticky red rope between my fingertips and sucking on the end.

"So . . . do you want to learn?" I bit on the end of the rope, the plastic taste sticking to my tongue. "Want me to teach you how to draw?" We rounded the corner of my street, and I stopped before I risked seeing anyone who might know my parents.

"Sure." The response came suddenly when I spotted my mother in the driveway, watering plants in her nightgown while the neighbor's dog chased the stream from the hose, yapping and drooling around her feet. She laughed while it chased her around the yard.

"Okay, cool, so maybe we can meet at the park tomorrow around lunch?" I waved vigorously as I broke into a loose jog to get away from him. My mother stopped laughing when my neighbor called the dog back from his porch. But she was still smiling when I walked into her arms, and I was beaming in Kraig's direction when she let go.

12

"I WAS BEGINNING TO THINK YOU WOULDN'T COME."
Kraig wore a polo shirt and khaki pants, his face pink from the
sun, browning slowly from the outside in.

"You didn't say what time." Lunch in my house wasn't a real
meal. It could be as early as twelve o'clock or as late as four, if it
happened at all. The only meals that counted were the ones we
suffered together.

We headed to a local café that served stale pastries and
scalding tea that burned my gums. I tongued at loose flaps of
skin that blistered behind my teeth while Kraig explained focal points and perspective. He began drawing, his hair covered
his face, and I marveled at his straight, blond strands of hair.
He didn't seem real.

"All of your perspectives have to go back to this point on
the horizon. That's your focal point. It informs the rest of your
angles." He turned the notebook around and pushed it toward
me. I mirrored his technique on the opposite page and he
seemed pleased. This time, I didn't look away from his blue
eyes; I held on to them.

When we parted a few hours later, he handed me the book
and told me to keep it.

"Draw something for me in there and bring it next time."
He paused. "Or write something. Whatever inspires you."

"Okay. I will." I gave him a full smile, unable to recognize
this new kind of life.

I felt like an adult, as if I could just decide to be anywhere I
wanted at any time, and with him. Of all people—him. When
I brought the journal back to Kraig a few days later, he read my
notes and looked at the drawings of my mother and the piano.
Sketches that had been crossed out, redrawn, erased over and
over again.

"You drew all eighty-eight keys?"

"Well, I tried to."

He traced his fingers over the thick graphite line of the
piano's upper panel. "It looks really good."

I felt my face flushing.

He took the journal home and brought it back with notes
that described how much he admired architectural designs
that manifested all the things he was incapable of expressing
but nonetheless felt with tremendous depth—sadness, frustration, a vague understanding of spaces and the people who
filled them, the latter being something that confused him
more times than not.

I read these notes at home, curled up on the couch while
sitting next to an open window. I burrowed into his thoughts
on architecture, college, and basketball—finding that I could
be interested in these things if they mattered to him. My
mother came inside from weeding in the garden.

"What are you smiling at?" I didn't realize she had been

staring at me. Plucked from my thoughts, I peered at her and frowned.

"Nothing."

"Nothing, huh? What are you reading?"

"It's my journal. Just thinking about things."

"You should be practicing the piano. You don't want to end up like me."

I didn't respond, and she seemed to interpret my silence as permission to continue.

"Just . . ." She sighed. "It's better to wrap yourself up in a thing instead of a person. People will let you down. Music won't."

Her skin passed chili-powder orange. Mine did the same.

"Stop it." I stood up and retreated to my bedroom. Her eyes followed me the entire way, and even after gently closing the door, I could still feel them on the other side.

———

"Luis Barragán is my favorite." We sat with a book of Mexican architecture between us, and he flipped it open to a double-page spread of a yellow hallway flooded with light. "I want to go there to study abroad. To see it for myself, you know?" I could see him in Mexico, learning Spanish, drawing buildings, and building new ones. I could see myself standing in the yellow light, swimming and blending into it. When I attached myself to that fantasy, the nightmare fell away—its cold cadavers and white lab coats. He picked up his pencil, opened our sketchbook, and began to talk about how to shade. While he did, I noticed the promising script of a new note. The muscles in his throat rippled when he sucked on a cup of ice cubes while speaking about dimension.

I cycled home quickly with the journal, bursting into a bright rosy shade of pink the moment I rushed through the front door.

His latest entry detailed that he was fond of traditions, not just artistic ones, but social conventions as well. He didn't understand people who moved from place to place with the confidence that they belonged in one and not the other, and told me that when his older brother left for college it was the saddest day of his life. Kraig wrote about how he was confused by people who had one favorite song on Monday, and a different favorite song on Tuesday. He hated those people—he found them disingenuous and distanced himself from them. Kraig couldn't comprehend the idea of being so self-possessed that the idiosyncrasies of other people didn't throw everything he knew—which was to say, everything his father told him—into an erratic, terrifying frenzy. It seemed, to me, like a handicap that he would warp, obscure, and disguise over and over again, to distort his thought processes into convincing fictions in which he was misunderstood, and everyone else was just hysterical. Reading this made me feel chosen.

We all have our part to play, right? That's what I hate. When girls try to be boys, or boys try to be girls. Dad says we should just be ourselves. He scribbled this final sign-off beneath a drawing of his family sitting around the dinner table, eating together.

The next time I saw him, I listened to him detail how he

was preparing for college. I licked pastry crumbs off my finger-tips as he spoke. It hadn't been particularly great, but the nov-elty of eating something dark and brown always made foods more delicious than they really were. I luxuriated in Kraig's generous attentions, his inner thoughts, and musings—which made the pastry taste even sweeter.

Then, one day, he pulled out a different sketchbook, flipping through the pages to a drawing of me. I leaned closer, flooded with memories of a school year that had only just passed but felt long gone. Up until that moment, I hadn't realized that I had been involved in the undercurrent of life at school at all. He slid the notebook over.

"Turn the page." He rested his chin in his hands, support-ing the hopeful expression written across his face. I flipped one page, and there was a picture of me studying for finals in the library, drawn in light gray shades of graphite. On the next page was a sketch of me several shades darker in a floral-print red dress, eating a banana while I watched him and his friends play basketball from the bleachers. Finally, there was a draw-ing of me with a black Sharpie giving a presentation on *Heart of Darkness* on the last day of English class. I felt the heat com-ing on, and my spine tickled with silver. I reached into my cup for another ice cube and began to suck on it, concentrating on the shape and temperature as I cooled back down again.

———

I was standing outside in the street, waiting for the shuttle to land while cars parked along the curb. Neighbors laid out blankets on their hoods, holding makeshift picnics. I kept my eyes trained on the sky, staring just off-center of the dimming August sun, clouds as thin as thread weaving around each other like needles through fabric. The sonic boom always shook the trees and set the dogs off, pulsing through the neighborhood like hunger.

Kraig walked up to me, slowly coalescing into a solid shape as I shielded my eyes from the sun. We had been meeting up for several weeks, but my skin told me that this time would be different. David, Sam, and Jacob hung back playing with firecrackers.

"I've seen the shuttle land six times. My cousin flew it once," he began. We both moved to the side to allow a long silver sedan to pass by, the driver shaking his head in disapproval.

"Did you know that the space shuttle travels around Earth at a speed of 17,500 miles per hour?"

I shook my head, distracted by the light beams darting through my parted fingers.

"Did you know that the gross lift-off weight of the space shuttle is 4.5 million pounds?"

People in the distance began to clap and yell. A man standing on the hood of a red Mustang held up an American flag and waved it from side to side. Others quickly followed suit—each more eager than the last to demonstrate their patriotism. My mother was sitting on our front porch, watching us. I stepped slowly away from Kraig, but he stepped closer again.

"So, I'm leaving soon." I didn't want to, but this made me face him.

"Next week. We drive to Gainesville." My blood went cold. I knew the moment was approaching, but I didn't want our meetings to end. I had convinced myself that we could keep our correspondence going even after he left. The shame I felt for being so naive forced me to look away.

"Maybe we can, like, celebrate before I go? You know, go out once. Maybe tonight?"

My skin burned hot, and large violet sunspots danced around the blurry shadow where his face used to be.

"I dunno. I need to ask my parents . . ." I figured my mother was my best shot, but even then I wasn't sure.

"Well, I'll be at the Classic tonight. I'll be out front at eight, so I hope to see you there." The dark gap between his front teeth widened as he smiled. I opened my mouth to respond, but he was already too far away, rejoining his friends, who slapped him on the back and shook his hand like he had returned from a journey to a dangerous, exotic land.

I attempted to call out to Kraig, terrified about what would happen to me when I told my parents about what I didn't agree to do. But just as I decided to approach the group, the shuttle barreled over us with a thundering objection. My protest fell silent to the awe of 4.5 million pounds traveling at 17,500 miles per hour into the Earth's atmosphere.

MY MOTHER ASSUMED her scariest color, bluish-black like vintage velvet, before dropping me off at the box office.

"What movie are you seeing?"

I shrugged, not even caring—tapping my finger impatiently on the armrest.

"Get something cold." Her grip twisted against the warm leather of the steering wheel. "Like a soda with extra ice."

"Sure." My tapping turned to scratching. "That's a good idea."

"And don't let him . . ." My finger went flat against the armrest. "Just . . . don't," she muttered.

I bowed my head, in case she wanted to whisper anything else more ominous. She didn't. Her taillights disappeared into the shadows as she drove away.

Kraig wore his oversize starter jacket and acid-washed jeans. We walked in together in perfect unison but never touching. He paid for my movie ticket, and I paid for the popcorn and drinks. For an hour, plus previews, we sat next to each other with erect posture, staring straight ahead, unwilling, or perhaps incapable, of uttering a word out loud. In my mind, a complete conversation had already taken place, where our words and voices were replaced with subtle gestures, shifts in chairs, and awkward coughs.

During an especially scary moment in the movie, when some blonde went into some dark space that everyone knew would result in her immediate exsanguination, Kraig grabbed my hand and I felt every cell of my body turn into a bright orange flame that he must have also felt. He released me, and, and my skin returned, pore by pore from the top of my head down to the tips of my toes, reveling in the shock plastered on Kraig's face while I transformed to my previous state of warm cocoa. It seemed like the appropriate color for the re-lief flooding my veins. I lifted my soda for a sip, allowing the fizz to settle me. His mouth parted into a question, or per-haps an accusation—I didn't give myself a chance to find out. I leaned forward and kissed him, darting my tongue into the gap between his two front teeth until he opened his mouth and granted me access. When I pulled back a moment later, it was his color that had changed—and it took him a lot longer to return to normal.

I CAME HOME by bus. When I walked into the living room, my mother was a creamy, pale eggshell. Curled up into the corner of the couch with both hands tucked between her legs, she receded into the spectral depths of the room, scarcely illu-minated by the television's glow. My father was passed out on the hard, white floor, one hand tucked beneath his large, taut belly, the other crammed into his sagging pants. He snored louder than the evangelists shouting fire and brimstone on the television.

The skin beneath my mother's eyes seemed anchored with weight, sagging heavily in oily folds around her cheeks. I imagined Kraig arriving home, wondering if his family was like the neighbors we hardly ever saw. If he had a meticulously attended lawn, had friends over on weekends, and played Mo-nopoly with his family on Sunday nights. Knowing the tem-plate of his life seemed unfair, and yet the anonymity of ours wasn't negotiable.

As I approached the couch, my mother transformed into a metallic gray. She looked as hard and as polished as the barrel of a gun. Her cold fingers coiled around my forearms to anchor me in place. I could never predict when she would suddenly feel strong and fearsome. It seemed as if the mornings of honey skin and fleshy nooks were just dreams, and this was the reality.

My mother examined each of my fingers. Then, she took off my hard, black boots and examined each of my toes, as if they would tell her something that my lips could not. She undid the buttons of my dress and squeezed my small, pointy breasts until I winced, then stuck her hand under my dress, searching between my shaky legs, and prodded harshly. I watched her eyes deepen into a shade of black that I am positive exists on no color spectrum. Satisfied, she removed her hand, wiping her fingers on her nightgown, stood up, and lightened once again.

"Brush your teeth and go to bed." Her voice was barely a whisper.

Returning to the couch behind my father, she pulled a blanket over her legs and turned the television to a new channel where an old white man with thick gray hair and a heavily embroidered suit was calling for donations in exchange for miracles.

13

A FEW DAYS BEFORE KRAIG LEFT, I AGREED TO MEET him at his house instead of the café. His place smelled like pumpkin pie, cinnamon cake, and other delicious aromas that stimulate images of food that white people don't know how to prepare themselves. A small, nervous dog with large, weepy eyes barked from behind the glass of the front door when we entered and followed us into the kitchen, jumping from its own neuroticism.

Kraig's house was filled with pictures—all over the fireplace, the kitchen counter, the spice rack that didn't have any spices, as well as the hallway that led to Kraig's room. It was a collective portrait of a family that was, for all intents and purposes, happy and loving. There were pictures of Kraig on the toilet as a baby, pictures of his parents at their wedding mashing cake onto each other's sepia-toned faces, pictures of his siblings at baseball practices and ballet recitals, and a bronze cast of baby feet that was the same color as my mother when she sang me "Happy Birthday" every year—my favorite turn of hue because I could see myself smiling back in her reflection.

The door shut abruptly behind us when we entered Kraig's room, and David emerged from the corner, large damp stains spread beneath his arms. The stubble on his chin hinted at the beard to come, and tender, fat pimples had formed into an aggressive composition around his jaw. Jacob and Sam materialized from the closet, eyeing each other in that way young men do when they're clueless. Kraig and Jacob probed each other silently for instruction on the horrible things they only thought about doing on their own. My stomach moaned in discomfort; I felt the drop of contents moving from side to side like a lever, pushing the cramp farther and farther down.

"Can I use your bathroom?" I asked the room, knowing that the people within it weren't listening.

"Grab her arms." The order trembled in David's mouth. Kraig clutched my arms, and I felt the fear seeping through his fingers into my skin, a catalyst going straight to my guts. I remembered my mother's grip and questioned Kraig's convictions. His neck hung low, and I tried to meet his gaze, but he didn't see me. I felt bonded to him through the visibility of my skin, and the invisibility of the person it contained. Jacob tried to push me onto Kraig's bed, but I was still, angling my head slowly to peer into each of their faces.

"What are you guys doing?" I stared at them, and they gawked at each other as if they didn't even know.

David helped Kraig try to force me onto the bed. Sam stood closest and the mole above his eyebrow quivered. David and Kraig kept pulling on me and pulling. I giggled.

"What are you guys doing?" I laughed, but the sound was small, and I was the only one who heard it.

They managed to get me down and Sam fumbled with the

loose bra strap that fell down my shoulder. The bed was covered with prints of surfboards, and stains cemented with dust. My stomach sank farther, swelling until it spread through my hips. Pinned beneath Sam, I noticed the posters on Kraig's walls, including athletes in various celebratory stances, and a 1754 map of the American colonies. A large U.S. flag hung on the wall behind the headboard. Sam moved close enough for me to see the sweat on the top of his fuzzy lip. David, Kraig, and Jacob closed in from the other sides.

"Is she gonna do it?" he asked Kraig, who glanced at me nervously and shrugged, still pinning my forearms against the bed.

"Well, go on. Do it. Change. That's all we want to see, I promise." Sam softened *promise*, while Kraig tightened his grip.

I thought about that day at the shooting range and my heart sank. I imagined my shiny new gun.

"Change what?" I asked.

"I saw you do it," Kraig said, keeping his eyes down. "In the movies. I saw you."

"Just show us how you change color like that and we'll let you go."

"I don't know what you're talking about." I tried to stay firm, but my voice evaporated. I didn't want the others to see me like that. It was for him, and him alone. David rolled his eyes and sneered.

"You guys are full of shit. I knew it." Sam and Kraig bristled at this. I had the hierarchy all wrong.

"Gabs, we don't want to hurt you. Just do it once, and we'll let you go." Jacob adjusted his crotch, the closest attempt at addressing the tension in the room.

I could feel myself sinking into the floor, beneath it, going underground—entombed by the darkness.

"Like, what brings it on?" Kraig asked. "Was it because we kissed?" Jacob and David both jeered at that admission.

"You kissed that?" They laughed and made monkey sounds, scratching beneath their arms. Jacob grabbed my chin and pulled my head toward him. He smelled like dirty laundry, cut grass, and burnt toast. I yanked it away hard, the muscles in my jaw turning to stone.

"So she just needs another kiss," Jacob suggested. "Any volunteers?" Kraig was silent.

I probed them with my eyes one by one, not saying a word. I itched but I remained still, ordering every muscle in every limb to obey the silent undercurrent in my belly as it began to crest. Sam bent down and lifted up my dress, and I kneed him away. He laughed as he found his balance and stood back up.

The others shifted around, digging their toes into the green shag carpet while the dog yapped on the other side of the door. After a moment of silence, one that later defined this memory as an instant of conviction more than planning, Sam took off his baseball cap, wiped the sweat from his brow with the back of his pale forearm, and grabbed my face again. Before I could pull it away, he pressed his lips to mine, pressing hard against my nose and cheeks. I felt a sharp pain in my neck as I used my head to shove him back as hard as I could. He laughed synthetically and stepped back.

"I guess I'm no Prince Charming." He waited silently for someone else to step forward, then threw up his arms. I began to shake, sneering at him. I pulled my arms back. Kraig, surprised, released me before gripping me once more. I kneed Sam again, again, again. My breath became heavier, but he just kept laughing.

"Fine. We all agreed that mine is the biggest now, so it'll be easier for the rest of you when I'm done." He undid his pants, and I saw the bones of his narrow hips dance to the sound of his clinking belt buckle. Kraig, Jacob, and David closed in once more—tightening their grip on my arms.

Kraig's eyes were cast so far down that they bent inward. He was mesmerized by the pallid feet shuffling on the pale carpet. I focused on Sam as his face descended—my face as hard as bone.

I felt the warm sensation before I saw or smelled it. My stomach released and loose pellets of wet shit sprayed all over Sam's face before he could lower himself onto me, dripping onto the bedspread. The smell came second, and that was what caused Kraig, Jacob, and David to release me all at once. I slowly hoisted myself by my elbows, taking care not to break eye contact with Sam. My hands slipped in the mess, the sound of slop underlining every move as I stood. I spread my legs wide and squatted to finish vacating my bowels until there was nothing left but gas. Then I stood up again, clenched my fists, and, with every cell of my body, willed myself into polished black like volcanic glass, darker than burnt ash or mined coal; darker than that pit of myself where I keep questions that

I know not to ask; a black so menacing that it exceeded the depths of its own darkness, and demanded that white brighten just a little bit more to maintain the balance of neutrals in the color spectrum.

I summoned every molecule of air into my lungs until the fibers that held them in place felt like they would stretch and snap into bloody tendrils. Then I opened my mouth into a large, round shape, and I screamed.

The high-pitched cry carried over their frightened faces, suddenly leached of their white color, over the sound of the yapping, nervous dog, and over the sound of the lawn mower down the street. I screamed until the glass of the mounted photographs shook in their frames. I screamed to disturb their images of the happy, loving family behind the glass. When I opened my eyes and stopped screaming, the boys were on the floor, snailed into tight little balls and holding their ears with their hands as blood wept through their fingers, slow and deliberate like warm caramel. I stepped down from the bed, wiped my shit-covered shoes on the carpet, passed back into my normal color, and walked out of the house leaving viscous brown footprints in my wake, thinking of how proud my mother would have been if she could have heard me. The dog was nowhere to be found.

———

My mother didn't examine me when I came home. She only looked at me from over the stove where she kneaded bread dough, her skin glowing red and her veins throbbing through her flesh. Her thin papery hands were covered in fine white flour. "Now you know the only thing you have that a white boy could ever want," she said. She added milk to the mixture and proceeded to beat the dough in the large metal bowl as if it had said something unpleasant, and true.

I took a long bath, scrubbing beneath every fingernail, and spreading folds of my body to let the filth wash away. I extracted waste out from behind my knees and between my toes. Outside, my mother hosed my soiled clothes down on the grass, watching all the mess run from the cloth of my skirt and socks into the flower bed of blossoming white magnolias, which had grown thick and lush feeding off the remnants of my humiliation.

My father came home from work with a dark cloud shadowing his darker face. We sat flanking him during dinner in our crystalline-white skin. He lowered his head over his plate and scooped large portions of food into his mouth.

"I found you a piano teacher," he said when he finished. "It's not right for you to be home all day doing nothing," he added, staring at my mother. I didn't say anything. There was nothing to say. It wasn't a conversation. He might as well have said that the sky was blue. "You start next week."

I asked my mother a question with my eyes: *What about Black boys?*

She responded with a polished expression, cold and bright like silver. When I went to bed that night, I found a small bag of lavender beneath my pillow, and I cried into it until the scent of magnolia blossoms woke me up in the morning.

A Major

(What the flowers in the meadow tell me)

14

CALEB WORE COLORFUL BOW TIES AND SPONTA-
neously broke out into Broadway songs. He was from Bos-
ton and breezed in and out of lessons like a cool Northeastern
wind. My father found him from a radio ad. When he wasn't
giving piano lessons, he was on tour with a band playing im-
provised jazz, which seemed nothing short of extraordinary.
He instinctively knew which fingers went where to complete a
melody—as if he had a rotating jukebox of scores in his head
trussed to his fingertips. He didn't read sheet music, so he
didn't teach me either. Instead, he marveled at my perfect pitch
and taught me how to understand the mathematics of music
by listening. With him, I discovered the innate connectivity
of harmonies where one hand always sought to complete the
other.

"It's the most perfect relationship you'll ever have," he said.
"What happens between you and this instrument is sacred."

No part of Caleb surrendered to boundaries or restrictions,
such that even his hairy belly bristled against the shirt buttons
trying to contain it. I knew without ever asking that this per-
sona had formed from the need to adapt—not from a desire to.

It was exhausting to keep my color in check during our

classes. Sometimes I felt a toe slip into a red, or a metallic blue, but most of the time I made do with intense concentration and a glass of ice water. I took lessons for a month before my father told me that Caleb had moved to New York for a permanent slot at an exclusive jazz club. He had left me in the middle of my introduction to Mozart's sonatas, and I sulked for three days. When I mentioned at the dinner table that I would miss him, my father brushed it off, saying, "I never really liked him anyway. He was too queer."

The fork scraped the inside of my mouth. I flinched more from my father's words than the blood and then, too aware of the silence, I began to chew even louder.

I MET DOMINIQUE the Saturday after Caleb left, and my father liked her even less. She pulled into our driveway and, because of my father's oversize SUV, was partially parked on the grass. He saw the spoiler anchored to the back of her car and the giant dent in the passenger-side door before he saw her. We slowly took in Dominique's dark skin, the color of burnt molasses, kinky hair framing her face.

"How long have you been giving piano lessons?" he asked. The four of us sat in the living room, my mother pouring sparkling water from a jug into our glasses while the piano served as a fifth witness. It was obvious by the way he kept glancing toward the window that my father wanted Dominique to leave before the neighbors saw her car parked in our driveway.

"Oh, well, technically—you would be my first student."

She spoke while searching for an empty pouch in her bag, slipping a book inside—its green cover bent and dog-eared from being forced into many other pockets before. She smiled through cherry-red lips. "I'm hoping to save enough money to go to school next year. " She sat upright but spoke casually, unintimidated by my father. While uncrossing then recrossing her legs, an ankle bracelet of sunflowers dangled just below the slender ankle bone. "Piano actually isn't my first instrument. I play the drums." She smiled and thanked my mother when handed a glass of water.

"The drums?" The list of things to disapprove of just became longer by one.

"I *love* jazz. It's like, the only pure American art form, because, you know, it tells the story of who *we* are, how we got here." My father instantly prickled.

"Who are your favorite jazz musicians?" I inserted myself before the conversation turned catastrophic.

"Oh gosh, Elvin Jones. Tootie Heath. Rashied Ali. The more experimental the better. I've always wanted to learn to play tenor sax like Sonny Rollins, but you know, maybe one day." She shrugged. I swallowed a shade of crimson deep into my belly.

"Do you sing too?"

Dominique shrugged, either missing the sarcasm in his voice or choosing to overlook it. She laughed, shaking her entire body, affecting the air around her with a scent of chili and ginger.

"I'm not a singer, but if I were I'd want to be just like Cesária Évora." I pretended to know the name.

"I love Cesária Évora," my mother said. "I don't know what she's saying, but her voice . . ." Her face brightened and she began to hum a tune that Dominique recognized, and she snapped her fingers until my father turned to glare at his wife, shutting the light out on her face.

My father stood to indicate that the interview had concluded. "Well, thanks for coming in, but we want Gabrielle to receive a classical music education before she starts pre-med next year." I tried to come up with another question, stuttering from panic. My eyes roamed over Dominique's frame and settled on her red velvet shoes, which would take her to the questionable car parked in our driveway, and then pull away and leave forever.

"Oh, well, that's no problem." Dominique held my father's stare. "I love classical music."

She stood, and though her short stature fell well below his, she seemed to match his height, lifting her curved nose to see his face, before turning her back on him. Dominique approached the piano and adjusted the stool so that her elbows sat in a perfect L-shaped position when her fingers touched the keys. "But it's no jazz."

My father approached the piano in protest, either to her statement or her continued presence, but when Dominique began to play, the room fell silent.

My father softened and suggested that we take our lessons to her house instead.

"We'll start with one lesson a week and go from there."

On the days when the sun was too harsh, I took the bus—
but most of the time I cycled to Dominique's house. I enjoyed
simulating the ritual of leaving home, the sound of the spokes
clicking as I turned on different street corners, pretending that
each lesson was also a final farewell to the white house and
its secrets. Dominique lived across town, where all the houses
sank into the earth. Flower gardens were replaced with iron-
barred windows and steep curbs that scraped the bottom of
cars whenever they pulled up. My heart was racing by the time
I reached the front door, but she opened it before I could press
the bell.

"You made it!" This time she didn't wear lipstick, and I
fixated on the way the dark hue of her skin bled into her lips,
cushioning their bright pink center. "Did you have any trouble
finding me?" I shook my head as she led me into the parlor
that completely mismatched the house's dilapidated exterior.
Inside, there were abstract paintings, shelves piled high with
books in different languages. Several small children consumed
with sleek rolls of fat, each of whom she affectionately referred
to as her "cousin," were playing with an old, gray-haired golden
retriever near the piano.

"Come on, now. Auntie's gotta work." The children's large
brown eyes stared at me through tight braids decorated with
colored beads that fell over their round foreheads. Two of them
looked like twins. One pulled on Dominique's pant leg, and she
bent down to hear. She smiled at me, then turned back to them.

"Why don't you go over and tell her that?" She kept staring at me, then pulled herself up between Dominique's legs. Dominique rolled her eyes and unhooked the girl's hands, turning her and the other one around. She ushered the children through a swinging door, unleashing the smells of a kitchen.

"Those are your nieces?" I mentally recalculated her age.

"Oh them? Cousins, nieces, whatever." She smiled and shrugged. "It takes a village, right? Anyway, for the next hour, they're Mom's problem." She walked over to the dog to stroke its head. "Come on, Foxy." The dog stood and followed Dominique over to the sofa before collapsing once again on the floor and closing her milky silver eyes, immediately drifting off to sleep. Dominique plopped onto the sofa and leaned back.

"Whenever you're ready." She propped her elbow up and rested her head on her hand.

I was confused by her question, urging her to elaborate.

"You want me to play?"

Her smile widened.

"It's the best way for me to get to know your level. Where do we start? What do you need? You've seen me play, now I need to see you—make sense?"

It did—the kind of sense that made me squirm, and question my repertoire, my outfit, my body odor, and a series of other choices, which, at that point, all felt poor. I dropped my backpack and sat on the piano bench. It was a beautiful antique Bösendorfer made of polished cherrywood with flowers and vines etched into it. It belonged in the house of some Viennese lord, not in Eatonville. I rubbed my hands together, then onto the top of my shorts. Caleb's words rang in my ears: *Play as if you have nothing to prove to anyone.* It was the first piece that came to my head: "The Turkish March," which seemed like an unusual title for a piece, mostly because I had associated it with elevator music and pharmaceutical commercials.

I was stunned to hear my music played on a proper piano, not one that had been sitting in the garage for years. It had character, and depth, with a timbre that indicated it was proud of its voice. I played what I remembered, fumbling a few times as I struggled to adjust to the weight of the keys. They had teeth and grip, but my fingers shook with sweat. I stopped at what I imagined to be the second page, wiped my hands on my shorts, then turned back to Dominique, swallowing hard. Her smile was even wider. It reached the corners of her eyes, lifting them.

"Oh honey, you're not gonna like this at all." I felt the color drain from my stomach and the skin blanch pale yellow, then orange, then brown again. I reached into my backpack and pulled out a thermos of ice water and took a long sip.

She launched herself up, giving Foxy a start as she moved about.

"You know music, and that's a great start. You have perfect pitch?"

I shrugged.

"That's what they tell me."

"But you don't know how to read music?"

I shook my head. "I learned pitch from my mother. She's a singer."

Dominique's face elongated. She was impressed.

"Right! We'll start with a strict repertoire of scales, fingering exercises, and theory." She pulled down a book of exercises from the bookshelf and put it on the piano.

"This will feel . . ." She bit her lip, letting it slip out of her teeth slowly. "A little remedial at first, but it's really important to get the right foundation. So, let's start with C, G, D major, and D minor. Do you have a metronome?" I shook my head. "Right." She rummaged through a plastic box on one of the lower shelves until she found one. "You'll need to add batteries, but it works like a charm." She pulled a pencil out and circled several pages in the book.

"Start with 4/4 timing, then move to 2/4 timing. That's twice the speed." She sat next to me on the bench but I slid over before we had a chance to touch. "It goes like this." I watched her fingers move. The delicate bones shifted beneath the dark skin as she demonstrated the first time signature, and then the other. Then she motioned for me to do the same. As I did, she took her pencil and put it underneath my hand so that it pricked into the meat of my palm. I pulled my palms away and narrowed my eyes at her. She laughed.

"You should watch out for this. Keep your hands rounded at all times. Right now, you've got spaghetti fingers." She took my right hand and placed it next to hers on the keys.

"Round enough to hold tennis balls," she said. "This way, when we get to more complicated fingering, you'll be able to move more quickly." I nodded and went back to the exercise.

"This is ridiculous," I spat out. "I'm playing Mozart, and

you want me to . . ." I opened one of the books, flipping to one of the circled pages. "You want me to play 'My Friendly Dog'?" My entire posture slumped.

"I know it's boring now, but trust me—technique is everything. And it's not a piece, really, it's a scale exercise." She was unbothered by my annoyance, accustomed to it apparently. "You get that down, and we can get to the fun stuff sooner." She winked and leaned into my side playfully.

"But since this isn't exactly your first rodeo, and you have some experience, let's also give you an invention. Maybe number four?" She looked at me as if I knew what that meant, standing up and retrieving another book from her shelf. "Be right back." She disappeared through the swinging door, and I exhaled for the first time that afternoon. I wanted to cry and scream and laugh all at once. I lifted my arms overhead and felt the bones in my shoulders crack as my skin flexed to a deep, rich violet before recuperating just as I heard her approaching again. When she came back, she handed me two xeroxed sheets of music.

"This is my favorite one, and it only has one flat, so it won't throw you too much. Just pay attention to the *fingering*." She bared her teeth as she pointed emphatically with the pen to the tiny numbers written above the notes. Then she put her hands onto the keys and began to play the most beautiful thing I had ever heard. Her fingers occasionally slowed down during trickier sequences to demonstrate how her fingers maneuvered over each other to find the right keys at the right times, like a needle pulling thread. "Do not. Ignore. The fingering." When she was finished, she faced me. "So, what will you pay attention to?"

"Um . . ." I bit my lip and scrunched my nose. "The melody?" She shoved me, and I held back a pleased expression.

"First of all, there's more than one, but we'll get to polyphony later. For now—fingering. Got it?" She leaned in close and narrowed her eyes while a smile scratched at her lips, and I nodded.

"Got it."

MY MOTHER WAS sitting at our piano when I got back home, numbly fiddling with the keys and a disharmonious melody that I didn't recognize. Evidently, my father wasn't home yet. She immediately stopped and rushed toward me.

"Well, how did it go?" She grabbed my shoulders, making my skin turn a cool lavender that made me feel drugged.

"I think it went okay." She silently urged me to continue, but there was a synthetic quality to her curiosity, and uncertainty in her grip.

"I think she's really good. Strict, but good." I opened my books and showed her the sheet music, summarizing the lesson.

"Ah! This is where it starts." She clapped her hands and pressed them against my cheeks. "I remember this one, the invention. I started to learn it when I was younger, but then I met your father." She sucked on her teeth. "Well, it doesn't matter. Now, you can pick up where I left off. Oh, I can't wait to hear you play it!" She put her hand at the small of my back and we walked into the kitchen together, where I heard the good Reverend's voice billowing out from the TV nearby.

My mother stopped for a moment, regarding the enthusiastic rants coming from the TV, then went back to preparing dinner. "I think I'm going to start going back to church." She poured some chopped onions and garlic into a pot, filling the room with a crisp, warm aroma. "I want to sing again. You've inspired me. I wanna pick up where I left off. Who knows? Maybe one day we can perform together."

I swooped behind her, wrapping my arms around her waist. She placed her hands on mine, and we stayed like this for a while. The familiarity of this embrace made me pass into warm indigo, and she did the same, and we reveled in the harmony between us once more. I let go and leaned against the counter as she continued to cook.

"I wasn't sure about Dominique at first. She seems kinda uppity, to be honest." My mother opened the cupboard and took out two cans of white cannellini beans, then started draining their juices in the sink. "But as long as she does her job, I don't really care how she dresses. Or smells." She dumped the beans into a colander and rinsed them beneath the tap before adding them to the garlic and onions. The sizzling intensified. "Strict teachers are the best teachers. If she's hard on you it means she wants you to do well. Like we do."

I sat at the kitchen table, leafing through the books. There was an air to Dominique that indicated she thought being strict would earn her more respect than being talented—even though she was clearly both. It was that anxious need to prove herself that told me she couldn't be more than a few years older and was therefore amenable to lively distractions—whether people or things. I was glad to have caught her at that moment, before she managed to secure a place for herself among people who were actually impressive—an ambition I understood, even if I didn't share it. But the idea of impressing her gnawed at me, and I wanted to do my best to become one of those people as well—if only to preserve my place in her life.

That's when *Play as if you have nothing to prove to anyone* became *Play as if you have everything to prove and everybody hates you.*

I understood that too.

15

SOMETHING WAS BURNING IN DOMINIQUE'S KITCHEN when I arrived for my next lesson. A plume of peppery smoke coiled through the piano parlor and outside when she opened the door to greet me.

"You're early," she said while fanning the smoke away from her face, coughing. Her hair was tied up in a colorful silk scarf and through the back I saw the thick two-strand twists that filled it up like a pillowcase.

"I don't think so." I walked into the parlor. It felt like I had interrupted something I wasn't meant to see, and I moved through the room feeling that any abrupt gestures might make her feel judged. The clock that hung on the wall above the piano read 4:59 p.m. Our lesson began at 5:00 p.m.

"You're right—sorry. I'm just on my own time." She moved the piano stool and stood on top of it, fanning the smoke away from the smoke alarm with a kitchen towel as she spoke. "Have you ever had curry goat before?"

"Not really . . ." She wore a loose green top that fell off her shoulder.

"Not really?" She stopped fanning the smoke alarm. The swelling above her eyelid indicated her eyebrows had been recently plucked, tamed into two smooth arches. "Have you ever had curry goat or not?"

I shook my head.

"Right." She fanned the detector again, the kitchen towel a soiled flag covered in dark oily splotches. "Well, you're about to, because I'm starving."

Dominique's mother, Niyala, came into the parlor through the swinging door, wearing a fitted dark green dress that bunched around her curvy hips. She was trailed by Foxy who nuzzled at her ankles, waiting for a happy accident to fall from above. It was easy to see that Niyala was Dominique's mother. They had the same hooked nose, the same eyes that crinkled in the corners when they laughed. She spoke as if everyone else was wrong, and that she was the only one who realized it.

"It's ready! Hey child." She acknowledged me with a loud suck of her bright teeth. "How are you?" She didn't wait for me to respond. "C'mon now before it gets cold!" And she vanished into the kitchen, followed by Foxy. I watched them walk away through another swinging door that broke up images of colorful paintings, large brass pots, and carved wooden statues on the other side.

"Yes!" The alarm stopped beeping, and Dominique jumped down from the stool, waddling as she moved it back to the piano, accentuating the muscles that made up her stocky legs. She gestured in the direction of the kitchen with a playful jerk of her head.

"Come on, then." I followed her through the swinging door.

The kitchen had an orange glow. The room was made of peeling wooden parquet, bronze-flecked countertops, and coppertone laminate cupboards.

"Have a seat!" Dominique took two bowls from the cupboard and scooped in the stew with a ladle. She smiled and placed the dish in front of me.

"Curry goat, fried green plantains, and rice and peas." She shuffled playfully and shifted her hips from side to side as she named the food. My stomach grumbled, and my feet blushed red at the sound of Dominique's laugh.

"Hungry?"

"Yeah, I guess so. I didn't eat much today." I turned the food over in my bowl, marveling at the colors, the thin slices of garlic, the tiny diced red chilies that winked from the undersides of meat.

"Well, don't be shy. There's more up there if you want it." She unfolded a napkin and placed it in the middle of the table between us. "You can put your bones there." She shoved a spoonful of curry into her mouth. Her fingers fished out a large round bone that she sucked on loudly, working her lips like fine machine parts until there was nothing left but pale yellow enamel. "I tried to make roti, but you saw how that turned out . . ." She grimaced.

"That's what you get for trying on that Trini mess!" her mother shouted from the other end of the house. Dominique laughed.

"There's plenty of roti in Kingston, Mama!" Niyala entered again, this time wearing a loose cotton dress. Nobody in that house obeyed the laws of color coordination. She reached into the cupboard and retrieved another bowl.

"Pfffft!" She sucked her teeth. "And you can find rice and peas in Daytona Beach, but that doesn't mean it's any good." The conversation didn't have room for disagreement. "Pizza Hut is a block away, but you won't catch any dignified Italian cook working in the kitchen, will you?"

Dominique rolled her eyes dramatically. "And *here* we go! You know, Ma, people are allowed to learn from different cultures." Niyala held her bowl and a dish towel in her hands when she bent down to kiss her daughter on the forehead with a loud smack. I noticed a small, dark scar cut through one of her eyebrows.

"Of course they are, my love. But keep that learning authentic. Don't sully the beauty of those cultures with a whitewashed interpretation for people who don't give a shit." She kissed Dominique's forehead again and again, peppering it with her lips until she was fanned away. "You're young and allowed to disagree, but I'm right, and that's the end of it. Anyway, I'll leave you two alone to talk about how wrong you think I am. Gabrielle, my child, a pleasure to finally meet you." She looked at her daughter, then flashed a row of perfect teeth toward me, and I couldn't help but smile back. "Have a good lesson." Foxy sat perched on the other side of the door, waiting patiently for a bone that Niyala provided to the delight of a tail that moved so frantically it nearly knocked over a potted plant. She vanished in that place where moms go to provide the illusion of privacy.

"Don't mind her," Dominique began. "She wants to give everyone who enters her house a lesson on something— cultural appropriation, institutional racism, radical feminism— something, anything."

"No, it's okay." I genuinely meant it.

"I'm just glad she didn't start with her lecture on sex positivity."

"I like her. She's funny."

"You mean funny ha-ha, or funny bizarre?" Dominique leaned back in her chair, tilted her head, and studied me, her thick lips curled with bemusement.

"I mean . . . what's the difference?"

She laughed and shrugged before picking up her fork again and digging back into the stew.

I ate quickly, mimicking Dominique as she sucked loudly on the bones. She finished before me and watched while I scraped the very last of the thick brown paste from my bowl with the back of my pinkie finger. Then my eyes landed on the diamond ring on her left hand. My spoon slowly dropped, and I swallowed a burp that seared the back of my throat.

"So, uh . . ." The words burned on my tongue. I hadn't noticed the ring before, but that oversight only reiterated its cunning.

Dominique looked at the ring as if aware of it for the first time.

"Oh! Yeah, I forgot." She put her finger into her mouth and slid the ring off. "Fifteen bucks at the Abbie Elizabeth Boutique if you're interested."

I pursed my lips, and she laughed.

"I took on another student and his dad is divorced and a little too involved in his education and it's just . . . easier this way." I lifted my eyebrows. "You look surprised."

"I mean, a little." My hands turned my bowl over, and I stared at the pieces of star anise piled neatly on one side. "You seem like the kind of person who wouldn't have a problem telling someone to back off." Dominique's face softened and she opened her palm as if about to make a case for this form of conflict resolution.

But she decided not to, clicking her tongue instead. There was that sound again. I decided that I wanted to learn all its iterations: the way it sounded out of joy, in frustration, in dis-agreement, in amusement, and in satisfaction. One sound that was also its own specific language.

I wondered if she played different roles too, disappearing into them through portals shaped like gold bands. Even before I had the words myself, I knew that people vanished into those rings, and reemerged as shadows of their former selves.

"Wait, why do I feel so weird right now?" She blurted her words out. "You're the kid here. Aren't you boy crazy or some-thing? Go on. Tell me all about the guys on your side of town and which one you're planning to marry. Or has your dad al-ready picked out an aspiring investment banker for you?"

The skin around my hips slipped ever so slightly into a lime green, and I resented her more deeply in that moment than I thought possible. For giving me a seat at her table, and then putting a price on the plate. I pictured my father's hand-picked suitor, his erect posture, sandy-blond hair, and clearly articulated vowels bereft of any Southern timbre. His circle of socially respectable friends whose unspoken names afflicted me with memories of quiet grief and rage. The images rushed into the kitchen, turning it cold.

"No." My response was ice. "I've never really thought about it. Marriage or anything like that. I've never really thought that far in advance, to be honest. It seems, just, so far away." I scraped at the bottom of my empty bowl. Dominique watched my hands, and I watched hers.

"My mom got married when she was sixteen, but you know—she was pregnant with me, and didn't have much of a choice." Dominique toyed with a bay leaf in her bowl, twirling it between her fingers then sucking on the shriveled edge. "Kingston can be a very hard place for young single moms, ya know?"

I tried to picture a young Niyala, bossing everyone around, and that continuity settled me. Most things complied with the laws of time, but every now and then you encounter someone who resists.

Her eyes hardened, she took in another breath, and with her exhale she added, "I don't wanna be some man's wife." She continued to inspect the bowl as she spoke, this small act rendering her younger, less confident.

"What do you want to be?" This time I cocked my head, my eyes wandering over, around, and in between her eyes, controlling the urge to look directly into them.

She contemplated the question, but laughed and pointed her fork at my empty bowl. "Damn, you really were hungry, huh?"

I had devoured the food, but the chili continued to tingle in my throat. "Oh yeah . . . I guess." I blushed internally and shrugged my shoulders.

"So you liked it, huh?"

I bowed my head slightly and used my hands to gesture toward the empty bowl with a response that said, *Obviously.*

"Well, if you have such a good appetite, why in the hell are you so skinny?"

I opened my mouth to respond, but words didn't come out. I didn't know what to say, unfamiliar with that particular slight, confused by its meaning.

"I'm . . . not . . ." Since getting my period, I had developed an extra layer of fat that consumed my angular muscles. It was why I was always sweating. I was tall and lanky. My waist was narrow, but I had thighs so thick they disconnected my butt from my heels when I sat on them.

"You want some more?"

I did, but I also wanted to get started with my lesson. I had been coming along in my practice, and I wanted to show her my progress. I hated fingering. I loved the invention. Somewhere in between the two emotions, I had found complete devotion to a new skill.

"All right, all right. I know you're a woman who likes to get down to business." She picked a bone out of her mouth, wiped her hands on a napkin, then leaned in close enough that I could smell the chili on her breath. "I'm ready to be impressed now."

We went back into the parlor and took our positions at the piano, followed by her senile dog who collapsed beneath the bench, nipple-side up, belly full of scraps. Dominique reached for the book of inventions, then she put it down and picked up my book on theory, opening to the scales.

"Okay, let's start with D minor."

I played the scales without any trouble. She was right. They were easy. They were boring. I made a show of it as I played each one, rolling my eyes, smirking, shrugging, pretending to fall asleep and snore as I went along.

"Okay, okay, I get it." She bowed her head dramatically and picked up the sheet music for the invention. I didn't get far before she interrupted me.

"Where's the tempo? You're all over the place." She walked to the shelf, retrieved a digital metronome, and set the timer to 3/8, placing it next to the music. "Again."

The device taunted me with its electronic clicks and danced all around me as my hands fumbled. It pointed out every off beat, every torpid finger, every difficult transition. I tried to catch the tempo, but it fled. I felt exposed. My mind understood the music's progression, but my fingers struggled. My skin maintained the same color, but at times I felt myself bursting and popping from frustration. I was certain that if my blood were examined closely, the cells would have been dividing uncontrollably like a cancer.

"What's the matter? You know this key. It's D minor. You *just* played it for me."

I pulled my hands back, wiped them on the top of my skirt, then tried again. This time, it was worse, and I accidentally changed the time signature of the piece halfway through.

"What was that?"

I leaned over and pulled my thermos out, taking a long sip of ice water, already feeling my toes blacken.

"Again." Her voice was stone, no longer warmed by spice.

I played again, this time rushing through the first page, overtaking the tempo, and ignoring all the dynamics on the page. She leaned back, ironing out the wrinkles on her forehead with her fingertips. I pressed my hands between my knees, willing them to stop shaking before they passed.

"It's a dramatic narrative," Dominique began slowly, her voice low and thick. "It has a resigned melancholic opening that gives way to a noble chorale that offers a haunting recovery from despair." I blinked, unsure of what to say. She started to describe what sounded more like a tragic love story than a piece of music, but she stumbled over her words, untying then retying her thick black hair in frustration. She seemed to be describing some iteration of sadness, an emotion she seemed uncomfortable recognizing, settling instead on a graceless rant. I tried to play the opening bars again and the bones in my wrist shifted beneath my skin when I stumbled to correct the fingering.

"I just . . . I think this is going a bit fast. I've only been playing this for a few days."

"Seven days."

"Right . . . seven."

An awkward silence sat between us. She scratched just below her eyebrow and reclined.

"Well, maybe you should practice more."

It was a light insult, but it stung.

"I practice." My voice sounded muffled. "I practice a lot."

"Look, we're out of time for now. But why don't you just keep practicing, and we'll pick this back up next week?" Sunlight poured through the window into the dim parlor. I hesitated for a moment, then grabbed my things and ushered myself out of her house before she had a chance to escort me herself.

When I arrived back home, I went around opening and slamming cupboard doors until my father woke up angry from his afternoon nap. Disoriented, he yelled at the TV screen in a frenzy, believing it to be the source of disruption. I sat down at the piano, concentrating obsessively on the diagonal notes stacked against one another. I positioned my fingers onto the keys, and I played them over and over again, until my fingernails began to bleed.

16

I BEGAN TAKING A LONGER ROUTE TO MY LESSONS AT Dominique's house. I biked down a side street that wasn't mine, but could have been, that wrapped around and eventually led me to the street that guided me across town. The next week, I took two more side streets and biked through a park before meandering back. And then one afternoon, on my way home, I found myself winding through a neighborhood that was not mine, but could have been, until I stood across the street from a house that could have been mine, but wasn't.

My skin was dark, and I didn't linger near the house for more than a few moments, trying to memorize one or two details before cycling off again—the bicycle on his front lawn, the raised flag on the mailbox, the surfboard bedspread. A woman with loose skin hanging off her arms eyed me from her front porch as she swept leaves that weren't there. When I returned the next day, creamy and white, I compared those memorized details with the new ones in front of me—to see that the bicycle was leaning *against* the garage, the flag on the mailbox was turned down, and the front door of the house opened to let Haylee walk out. She hopped down the porch steps in a pink sundress that kept moving around her when she stopped. She turned and faced Kraig who, shirtless, held her hand, pressing his lips to her knuckles before letting go. He was home.

It began to rain and as I mounted my bicycle on shaky legs, the same woman from the day before ran out of her house flailing her arms, pale skin slapping her in the face.

"Come inside! You'll catch your death!"

I pedaled away as quickly as I could.

I was soaking wet when I arrived home, walking through the front door at the exact moment that my mother was taking off my father's tailored silk jacket. He turned to me and opened his arms with an expectant look upon his face—waiting for me to convey the admiration and enthusiasm of a new bride. His wife tethered herself to the colossal spread of his shadow.

"Is that how you greet me now?"

He pulled me into his large arms, clutching me until I passed darkly, my skin black as coal. He released me, an air of disgust shading his face. I was relieved.

I didn't sleep in my bed that night. I lay down in it, but every time sleep threatened to take hold, I jumped back up, feeling darkness closing in. There was too much negative space, too much emptiness waiting to be filled. I placed my pillow and bedspread on the floor and, sensing that this too was an uncomfortable level of exposure, slithered beneath the bed. Only as I stared up at the tightly coiled metal parts of my box spring, after sneezing through multiple clumps of dust and hair, did I allow my eyelids to become heavy and pull me into the undertow of sleep.

I had nightmares that placed Sam's pallid jawline on a continuous loop as he pulled my face toward his. Just before he could, the pale white skin around his lips peeled away and revealed a darker face with wide nostrils and dimpled chestnut skin, where plump drops of sweat trickled down onto my lips and into my eyes. Kraig, Jacob, and David stood with their backs turned, looking out and away. But I couldn't move, paralyzed by the look on Sam's face that seemed to command the breath in my lungs, reverse the blood flow in my veins, the alignment of cells in my skin. I reached out for Kraig. His body turned toward me, but his head remained fixed, his neck unnaturally twisted in the opposite direction.

I woke covered in sweat, my heartbeat obscene—my skin as black as deep space. That was when I stopped being able to sleep altogether and entered a permanent, disoriented state of dreaming.

17

MY FATHER WAS MOWING THE LAWN WITH THE REST
of our neighbors when I came home. A mechanical symphony
of men taking pride in the curation of their gardens which,
much like their children, were weeded, watered, and nour-
ished by their wives the other six days of the week. I was attempting a scale where my hands felt like they were playing
from two different sheets of music, but every time my fingers
began to ascend the keys, the lawn mower knocked against my
train of thought. I saw my father on the other side of the window, a makeshift gray sweatband tied around his head and his
shorts bunched up between his skinny legs, laboring over the
push handle. Sweat ran down his cheeks in a clear stream that
rinsed the color from his face altogether, reflecting the harsh
glare from what was said to be the last warm day of the year.

I could feel the heat of him when he came back inside. My
mother was in the kitchen, skin as white as milk, snacking on
sunflower seeds and watching Reverend Jeremiah on the television. He spoke passionately in his plum-colored suit, aroused
by his own fevered sermon. My father entered the kitchen and
opened the white cupboard where he stored his whiskey, only
to remember that he had finished it the night before. He stood

in front of the bare shelf. My mother and I froze in our places. It wasn't that we encouraged him to drink, but we appreciated the way it dulled him into a harmless man snoring loudly on the floor.

He sat at the table and lifted his soiled white T-shirt to wipe his face, exposing the drum of his belly. "When is dinner gonna be ready?"

"It won't take long." My mother's words came out slowly, carefully. But she knew as well as I did that it wouldn't make a difference.

She edged her way to the fridge and removed containers of chicken and white asparagus, placing the first onto a cutting board and the second into the sink to wash off the black soil.

My mother stopped what she was doing, knife in one hand and plate in the other. She looked at him, inert and unemotional. He scoffed and leaned back in his chair, a sneer pulling at the corner of his dark mouth.

My mother lifted the plate she was holding high above her head, engulfing her angular face in its circular shadow. Then her arms lowered it back onto the counter. She passed into the color of lush cherrywood, and my skin instinctively followed suit. She pulled her car keys from her pocket, and walked out of the kitchen into the garage. I listened anxiously as the door opened and her car pulled out into the street before the door closed again behind her. The noise of the engine was replaced with the discordant harmony of the other lawn mowers still at work.

My father called my name, and I walked into the kitchen.

"Bring me some ice water." He pulled his shirt up to wipe his forehead again. I retrieved the white plastic cup, filling it. He told me to sit down. We sat awkwardly for a while, and I stared at the pile of sunflower-seed shells on the damp paper towel in front of me. I tried to be hard like her, unresponsive like her, to turn myself off like her—but I couldn't. The heat embedded itself beneath my skin, stoking the claret to a boiling state. He told me to stand up, so I did, and he grabbed at my dark arms, at my dark shoulders, at my dark chin, twisting me this way and that, turning me in the glare of the sun streaming through the kitchen window. His grip was barbed and rough like sandpaper, but everywhere he touched, I felt myself feel nothing. He devoured feeling.

He grunted after his inspection, pushed away from the table and went to his office, closing himself off behind the two doors that clicked behind him.

Once I was sure he wasn't coming back out, I went to the bathroom and stared into the mirror, fixating on the places he had grabbed and prodded. I wanted to break something. I wanted to pick up the small, jagged pieces of their aftermath, and use them on my skin until I had carved myself into pieces so small that they could melt away. Blackness came, and I tried to fight it off. I imagined something cold and hard sitting in the pit of my stomach, then stretching out like an electric current to all my limbs. It didn't work. It was still difficult to change my color completely without my mother nearby—but the humidity assisted the transition.

I thought about white things. I thought about the color of

an egg's shell. I thought about the color of our house, and the color of my teeth clenching against each other. When I opened my eyes, my skin was the same.

I closed my eyes again and slowed my breath, waiting for something to come to mind. A slot machine of images passed through the space behind my eyelids. Avocado on toast. Apple cider vinegar. Sea salt. Dessert hummus. Mount Everest. When all the slots landed on Kraig's gap-toothed smile, a chill broke out over my body—a rash of memory.

I opened my eyes and extended my arms in front of me. I could practically see through the translucent skin to the veins pumping blood underneath. When I walked out of the house to the nearest bus stop, I swung my milky-white arms back and forth like a pair of trophies.

———

The shopping center was quiet on the outside, but when I opened the door, I was greeted by the wild roar of heat—money, breath, conversations—the stubborn ego of everything inside. I walked from one end of the mall to the other holding my head high, with my shoulders pushed back, trying to feel comfortable, but staying close to the exit signs. The shape of my posture distorted other things—it didn't make me taller, but other people suddenly became smaller, in size and in stature.

I felt diseased with anger.

I had walked past the Abbie Elizabeth Boutique a number of times with my mother. Hungry teenage models sometimes posed in the windows, and I watched small children put up funny, distorted faces, stick out their tongues, and cross their eyes to make the girls laugh. I gazed through the window for a long time, taking stock of the wall of accessories pinned behind a rack of autumn-colored dresses while unaware shoppers passed me by. My eyes landed on a ring, one that looked similar to Dominique's, being handled by a young woman whose cool expression seemed to notice everything else except me, watching her. I didn't plan on going inside until I saw a young Black woman with skin like dusk. She lifted ring after ring, staring for long moments before replacing them.

The store was laid out like a French parlor with plush sofas and ornate coffee tables. A woman whose name tag read *Charmagne* rushed up to me the moment I walked through the door.

"Hello! Welcome, welcome!" Her anxious voice was disguised with warmth. "Are you shopping for anything special?" I shook my head, licking my lips, swallowing hard, and straightening my posture for the dozenth time, so worried about appearing demure that I bent myself backward. "Well, let's get you started. Can you tell me what kind of fit you're looking for?" She was shorter than me and moved around the store with an exhausted gait that made her appear older.

I could only stare, but that seemed to be enough. Charmagne blushed through her peeling tan skin as she guided me toward the dressing room. The other woman peeked out of hers, wearing only a black bra.

"I'm waiting over here too, you know." She disappeared

behind the curtain, but Charmagne ignored her, and the woman ignored me.

"I'll be right back, miss." She avoided my eyes when she spoke and turned on a wobbly heel that clicked against the floor.

My dressing room was the size of a small office, cast in an unforgiving light that highlighted every blemish. I placed my bag on the floor, next to a side table in the corner, where a crystal jar of water infused with fruit sat next to a small glass, casting colorful reflections on the mirror-covered walls.

"Miss—are you ready?"

I opened the curtain. Charmagne held a dozen dresses in different colors. She breathed heavily as she talked me through them.

"With your complexion, you have a lot of options, depending on the colors you prefer. I'm guessing your size is around ten, but let me know if I'm off base." She stepped into my dressing room and hung them on a hook above one of the mirrors. When she reached up, the burnt skin on her shoulders flaked off and floated to the carpet. "This fuchsia dress with the A-shape cut is a gorgeous silhouette on a curvy figure." She pointed at my hips and winked, showing off a pale blue eyeshadow. "This black dress with gold trim would also suit your skin tone, but it's a different material than the first one. It's a satin-silk, and it feels luxurious. You'll never want to take it off."

"I can go through them myself," I cut in impatiently, bristling in my skin.

"Of course." She stopped, blinking back a scream. "I'll be

out here if you need anything." She stopped on her heel and retreated. The Black woman snapped in her direction, but Charmagne kept on walking.

I took my time trying on the dresses. I fingered the material and noticed how my skin responded—puckering when
touched by satin, chills when kissed by lace. They draped over
my body like membranes, but the dress made from black-and-
gold satin made me feel like a god. The price tag read $399.99.
I didn't have any money, and my father was the gatekeeper
over the family's finances. Asking for four hundred dollars
would be the quickest way to start a fight that I wouldn't win.

I began to panic. I wanted the black-and-gold dress. I suddenly wanted it more than I wanted anything else. I didn't
recognize that desire in myself, and it unsettled me. My skin
contracted tightly with dread, and sweat began to pool beneath my arms. The dress should have been easy to fold and
collapse in my backpack because the material was delicate and
soft, but my hands were damp and clumsy. The zipper on my
bag didn't work. I had trouble getting all the material inside.
Even then, I couldn't stop shaking. The golden trim smiled up
with embroidered teeth, fading as I pulled the zipper closed.
I dressed myself quickly, then mixed the dresses together on
the lounge chair so that the one I took wasn't easily noticed. I
waited inside the dressing room until I heard the other woman
leave hers, then followed her back into the storefront, hoping
that Charmagne wouldn't come to collect the dresses too early
and notice that one of them was missing.

On the floor, the Black woman began to thumb through

the dresses closer to the window. Her manicured fingernails moved like long needles from one garment to the next. Charmagne approached her to ask if she needed help, but she just shook her head.

"Now you wanna help me?" She rolled her eyes and turned her back to Charmagne who continued to lurk as she browsed. Charmagne reorganized racks that the Black woman touched as she moved farther into the store. She kept an eye on the woman's backpack, the same make and size as my own, which never left her shoulder.

"A-HEM!" a woman shouted from the cash register, waving her credit card in the air. Charmagne hurried over with flushed cheeks.

When the Black woman grew bored of the gowns, she moved closer to the exit, stopping once or twice, it seemed, to reconsider the items leading closer to the door. A customer appeared behind me with a branded garment bag folded over her arm. Her tightened smile pushed me out of her way before her shoulder had a chance. The three of us maneuvered toward the metal detectors framing the entrance. The woman with the garment bag walked through first, and kept going, her long auburn hair swinging behind her. I took a deep breath then negotiated my way through the door with the Black woman at my side, timing our exit. A loud siren went off behind me, but I kept walking behind the woman, who stopped and turned to catch the aftermath. I craned my neck up high and kept my shoulders pushed back until a cramp the color of silver tickled a piece of flesh over my heart.

"EXCUSE ME!" Charmagne called out behind me. A thick sweat formed in my armpits, its smell spilling out around me, but I didn't stop. I didn't slow down, and I didn't speed up. I walked confidently like I was owed by everyone around me, like I owned all of their possessions, like I owned them all. The Black woman behind me stopped and turned; her eyes wide with terror. "Excuse me, girl, could you open your backpack for me? What did you take?"

"I . . . I didn't take anything." Her voice was shaky and bewildered.

"Just show me now and I won't call the cops," Charmagne shouted, already dialing three numbers on the store phone.

"I swear! I didn't take anything! Here, look through my bag."

Charmagne took and unzipped the backpack, dumping its contents onto the linoleum floor, kicking around books, lipsticks, combs, pads, and toiletries while people watched, their stares becoming more accusatory by the moment.

"Oh God, another one!" an older woman hissed behind me. Her arms were crossed over her chest and she held a large drink in her hand, the straw marked by bright pink lipstick. "They just can't help themselves, can they?"

I continued to walk, quickening my steps until I rounded the corner and was through the double doors. I didn't stop until I heard my feet pounding against the concrete of the parking lot like an erratic heartbeat, just as the police pulled up from the opposite side of the street.

18

I HUNG THE DRESS IN MY CLOSET, AND OCCASION-
ally brought it out to admire when I was alone. When I turned
the black-and-gold fabric in my hands beneath the sunlight,
its reflection warmed my face. The woven gold trim was thick,
and ropy, and it banded around my chest in a coarse embrace.
I began to fantasize about all the potential rewards there were
to enjoy for being so brazen. I imagined slipping it on at fancy
parties, feeling sophisticated and wealthy. Then I imagined
seeing the Black woman from the store at the exact same parties wearing an orange jumpsuit that matched her beautiful
nails, and I felt filthy and ashamed. But when I slipped the
dress on and looked into the mirror, I couldn't see myself. I
vanished into the fabric, where the images from Kraig's house
were quickly forgotten, replaced with the smooth, silky comforts of darkness.

But when I returned the dress to my closet, where it disappeared among all my regular clothing, the memories came
flooding back. And the nightmares woke me up in the middle
of the night. I would then slip back under my bed, clutching
the dress, interlacing it between my fingers until the gravity of
sleep dragged me under.

My mother was spending more time at church. She usually left after dinner, and I would watch her sing on TV, glowing in a way that only I could see. It made me proud. She was the only one of the choralists with an unlabored smile when her mouth stretched open to sing. And with my father being away from home more often, the additional evenings my mother spent singing at church didn't mean they saw each other any less. But this intensified their arguments whenever they were in the same room. I tried to make myself scarce when this happened, but usually ended up involved in one way or another. Normally, my father would find her in the kitchen and take up one of their regular quarrels—about money, or seasoning, or the amount of starch she had used in his ironed shirts. While he was at work, my mother brooded about these arguments. I watched her win in the kitchen as she punched into meat that didn't punch back. I watched her lose when my father returned. It had been years since he had given her a new cause to fight. Most of the time, he just stepped into the residue of conflict that followed us around the house like a bloodstain. No matter how many days went by between fights, it never seemed to wash out.

I partially blamed the heat, and began to leave small cups full of ice around the house for my mother before leaving for Dominique's house—but they remained untouched, having melted by the time I came home from lessons.

"There you are!" I tried to slip out of my bedroom, hoping to quickly grab my piano books before retreating to Dominique's house—but my mother thwarted me in the living room.

"I just need my books." I tried to negotiate around her, but my mother moved quickly, ushering me in the other direction.

"I have lessons." My words were more of a plea than a statement.

"You've been hiding in there all afternoon." Her hands pressed into my lower back, and I felt the skin beneath her fingers blush. "Your father just got back from Tallahassee. Come into the living room and say hello."

I was already exhausted from their screams, having tried to mute them with the harmonies of various waltzes and preludes. None proved a match for their feuding. I tried to dig my heels in and twist away, but the tone of my mother's voice told me that wasn't an option. She opened her mouth to say more, but stopped short.

"Tell him about your day, and then you can go."

She wiped her hands against her lap, where small grease stains dampened her white shorts.

"I'm already running late." I grabbed her hands and pressed them between mine, enveloping her with the cold sheen of sweat coating my palms.

"I'm not done talking to you, Tallulah." My father's voice triggered a familiar leak in my gut, abating slightly when I realized he wasn't speaking to me. "Get back in here."

She closed her mouth and took my backpack away, placing it near the living room. This seemed like a kind gesture, until I realized I was defenseless. I passed my color, while hers remained natural, and we walked into the living room together.

Kraig was sitting on the couch with his head slouched

between his shoulders, and every part of him that I could see looked angry—even the blood dripping out of his ears. My color briefly flushed dark maroon and then white. I closed my eyes tightly while the blood accelerated in the dark. I opened them again, the hallucination rapidly blinking away. I recognized the shape of my father's head again, reigniting the terror, and my shoes scuffed the pale surface of the white floorboards. My mother pulled me harder and as I rounded the sofa, I saw his back, then his ashen elbows balancing on his knees, then his dark round belly sticking out from the taut cotton of his T-shirt.

My father's attentions recalibrated through the booze to focus on me. Kraig was gone, but I still felt him, and my stomach turned. My father picked up the remote control to mute the television. This was his favorite way to argue: he'd have two things going on at once so that he never had to focus on one or the other. My eyes fluttered hard several more times to make sure it was his face admonishing me.

"I was just—"

He cut me off before I could make an excuse for whatever imagined offense I had committed.

"You've been spending too much time at that church, and you're never home anymore."

His tone was tense, sedated in my presence. His eyes were yellow instead of bloodshot.

"Who's looking after our daughter?"

"Robert, she's a high school graduate getting ready to go to college. She can put herself to bed."

"And who's preparing her for that transition, Tallulah?" Irritation pickled his face. "I work hard all day so you can stay at home and be a mother to our daughter. You need to be teaching her how to conduct herself when she's gone. She's not supposed to be running wild out there. She needs you to guide her, to show her how to stand up for herself, and speak up, and be confident so that she'll be ready to leave home."

I looked at my bag, mocking me from the doorway to the living room.

"Once she's studying medicine, she won't be able to call on you day and night. You should be here"—he stuck his index finger into the white sofa cushion—"preparing her now. Gabrielle, don't you want your mother to spend more time at home?" I sucked on air. My father's frown urged me to respond. I felt my mother twitch through the grip on my shoulders, but my father's glare was uncompromising. Beneath it, I didn't feel like someone on the precipice of adulthood. I felt small and inconvenient, scraped off from somewhere I wasn't wanted.

I murmured assent, and the shame of my response knocked the wind out of me. The whiteness drained from my skin leaving only the outline of veins, as translucent as a water glass. My father read my face and then my mother's, an ugly, satisfied grin stretching his mouth wide.

"See? There you go."

My mother's grip went limp, and I tried to think of some way to take back what I had just done. She moved to position herself directly behind my father. She opened her mouth to scream and began to slap my father on his broad back. Her arms were slight, and her hands were oil slick as they rolled off his torso. I wanted to believe that she didn't really mean him any harm, because I didn't want to believe she was really that weak. Her body heaved as she shook, taking in dramatic gulps of air through her mouth that came out as whimpers. He didn't move until she was finished. It took a minute before the cries turned to sniffles, the sniffles turned to coughs, and the coughs went silent. Her grief became self-aware and ate itself.

When she went into the bedroom and closed the door, my father turned the volume up on the TV again. He stretched his arm out and shook his empty white cup at me. I went to refill it.

19

MY MOTHER WAS THE COLOR OF LEMON SKIN THE first time she tried to kill herself. The house was still, but it wasn't empty. Empty spaces feel safe. A record of "Arabesques" was trickling from the speakers in the living room, a sound that pushed me away instead of drawing me closer. All the doors in the house were open except for one—a tender sliver of light from the bathroom. When I pushed it open, she sat up in the tub, her head resting against the white tiles and angled toward the door, a slight smile punctuating the heat-wrinkled flesh of her cheeks, and a white towel wrapped around her head. One arm hung over the edge of the tub, paler than the rest—sickly yellow. The water was black with blood, leaking from the incision that started from her wrist and climbed all the way up to the soft pit of her elbow. A bloodied kitchen knife was on the floor, and an orange bottle of pills had spilled out next to it in a colorful pattern. Black, red, yellow, orange, and white—the analogous gore of autumn.

But in the bath, my mother and everything around her was still. There were none of the usual noises that accompany silence—the subtle shift of air coming through the vent, the shuffle of my feet against the tile, the creaking faucet expanding with the flush of warm water. Death was the absence of sound and silence. Death devours everything.

The record skipping was my cue to move. It was the climax on the last page—*poco a poco dim*. I probably did some things that didn't make sense, like pick up the pill bottle or shut the door behind me—as if people were breaking it down to join us. But I ended up in the bath, my hands hooked beneath her armpits, trying to pull her out of a tub that sucked her back in, claiming its grim prize.

With each attempt to extract her body, my breathing became more erratic, until panic broke me. I felt the vibrations in my throat, and the dull ache at the back of my mouth that turned angry and raw, but I didn't hear a single thing. I don't know if it was the kind of scream that delivered me from Kraig's house, or the kind of scream that feels like relief when exhaustion has endured for too long.

They're not the same. Don't you dare think that they sound the same.

I removed the towel from her head and stroked her matted damp hair, still wrapped in large pink rollers. I began to remove them, one by one, *poco a poco dim*—separating the curls with my fingers like the teeth of a fine comb. Her hair was shiny, dusted with flecks of gray, and thinning at her temples. But as I sank my fingers in farther, I found waves of heat rising off her scalp.

She wasn't dead.

Sick surged in my throat. The room sped up as the realization settled in—slowly at first, then frantically. The pills on the floor shifted. The air through the vent quickened. The water in the bath warmed, and my mother's face flushed from lemon to amber. I stepped out, taking care to place her head gently onto the edge of the tub, watching the faint rhythm of air enter and escape her throat. Grabbing a stack of white towels, I tied them around her arm and squeezed the knots so hard between my hands, my knuckles, wrists, and forearms that they glowed white from the force. A sound escaped her cracked lips, strained and slight, forced out by the pressure I had pushed into the wound. I latched on to that breath by the fist and held tight before it could slither away, then I ran into the kitchen.

My father was in the living room with the curtains drawn shut. The sound of "Arabesque No. 2" floated through the air, and the notes fell to the armchair where he sat, his fingers gripping the cushions—covered in blood. His eyes fixed across the room on the blank wall, narrowed and pointed like arrowheads.

"She's not dead." I rushed to pick up the phone, slipping on the white wooden floor, nearly cracking my head against the kitchen counter as I stumbled. I expected him to be by my side, but he slowly uncrossed his legs, stood, and approached the record player to remove the needle, a series of deliberate, concise movements—none of which acknowledged what I had said. I shrieked at him:

"SHE'S NOT DEAD!"

He removed the record, replacing it with another, and the only sound I heard was the opening and closing of fine paper sleeves, a needle catching vinyl, a backbiting orchestra pounding through the speakers.

He sat there listening until the ambulance arrived.

20

THE HOSPITAL SMELLED LIKE DISH SOAP AND bleach, the only odors strong enough to disguise the smells of blood and death. Strangers curled around each other in huddled groups along the hallway, bracing for signs, predictions, or miracles. I didn't know the answers to most of the questions I was asked, and the ones I did know—I lied about.

Yes, she's generally quite happy.

Yes, I would say our home life is normal.

No, she has not been under any undue stress. She's a stay-at-home mom. What does she have to be stressed about?

My father wrapped his fingers around the back of my neck like a collar and tapped on my throat with encrypted warnings.

No, he's wonderful.

Yes, a little hysterical I guess.

I'm very close to both of them.

I knew exactly how to lie. I didn't need to be told how to survive.

The doctor had bags beneath his eyes. He was tall and blond—genuinely blond. I could tell by the golden stubble on his chin, which he scratched between exasperated sighs. He said words that conjured images of chemicals sliding around dangerously inside my mother's skull. After he exhausted himself and left us alone, my father was quick to invalidate everything that the doctor had said, insisting that it was best simply to keep our private lives to ourselves to save the doctors and nurses the trouble of misunderstanding the way our household worked.

"They're doctors, Gabrielle. They should be more focused on mending broken bones than broken minds. And besides, she's fine," he muttered under his breath. "She's always been this way."

We stood in the doorway to her room, while nurses and doctors moved around her bed, weaving in and out of the piles of bloodied rags filling the metal basin placed between them. I mentally checked off attendants as they carried gauze and metal instruments around the room:

Blood, nurse, blood, doctor, blood, Mom—*bingo*.

"It's in the blood," my father said. His grip tightened until I could feel my heart beating into his palm. Blackness began to flood my vision.

"Your grandmother and great-grandmother had it too."

———

They lost my mother six times, and six times they brought her back to life. She was playing a game—a silly, morbid, agonizing game that mocked us from the dim space that exists somewhere between life and death. She hid in the cobwebbed corners of her mind, and the doctors searched without any map, any light, any hint to help them; only a twitch here, a spasm there, a violent seizure that wrinkled everyone's face with confusion. It was just a game. The doctors all but cheered when the machine they used to jump-start her heart shouted triumphantly every time it brought her back from the brink of death. I secretly braced myself for her color to pass after every victory—and she never did. Even on the precipice of mortality, she was teaching me how to control my color.

I went to the sitting room alone and waited for someone in bloody scrubs to deliver the news of her death, and maybe hand me a pamphlet for bereavement counseling. I felt the urge to pass flooding my body like a narcotic, but I resisted, focusing on the people around me: the man with a cold compress placed on his nose; the little girl whose arm was swollen with bee venom; the elderly woman in the wheelchair who claimed an entire cocktail of ailments, but who quieted down whenever a nurse stopped to chat or brought her a cup of water.

I landed on a group across the room. There were three of them, a woman and two men, with dark skin that shone like glass beneath the hospital lights. The woman had a head full of thick black curls and swollen hips that bulged at the seams of her skirt. Her fingers toiled at a string of pearls around her delicate neck, and she minimized herself in the shadows of her companions—though who supported who was difficult to tell.

She could have been an aunt, or a sister, or somebody's mistress—but I knew that she was a mother. Fatherhood is an act of addition—children are the tool used to create the ideal life they didn't have before. But motherhood is a subtraction: mothers are required to surrender all that they have to someone they might not even like—every limb, every bone, every loving word and drop of spit, until there is nothing left but an empty skin. And even this too must be surrendered. The woman's posture told me that her body still remembered how it felt to be held ransom for nine months so that men could feel proud.

A young doctor with wired eyes came bursting through the double doors in freshly laundered scrubs. He tucked black tufts of hair behind his ears as he approached the three of them. The woman smoothed the front of her skirt in nervous movements, but the moment he spoke, shook his head, then stepped away, her efforts went to waste. The two men turned in to face the mother, each holding one of her arms as she stared at the floor—without blinking, without moving—until a faint drop of saliva spilled out of her lips and hit the tip of her shoe. It was the disorientation of someone who woke up that morning as someone's mother, and would go to sleep as something else.

My father approached from behind just in time to watch a nurse set down a pamphlet and take the woman away, accompanied by the two men at her side. The woman scratched at the skin of her neck and tore the fabric of her blouse, screaming and spitting, until it ripped and exposed the tan lace of her bra and all the accompanying stretch marks underneath. Having given every ounce of who she was to someone who no longer drew breath, she was now reduced to something else—a shadow of her former self that her loved ones would have to learn all over again. One of the men took off his jacket and placed it over her, but she wanted nothing to do with it.

Men don't understand grief. She wanted everyone to see. Why couldn't they understand that the greatest kindness they could afford her was to simply watch?

I acknowledged my father.

"She'll live."

Then he was gone. The woman's screams continued to echo from down the hall until they were gradually replaced by the ringing of telephones.

———

My father went to the kitchen cabinet to pour a drink into his white plastic cup, recently unburdened of its partially peeled logo that had been its hallmark—and he liked it better this way—plain, white, disinfected of color. I packed some of my mother's jewelry, her scarves, an orange tiled blouse from the seventies that still smelled like her, some hair grease, and her handbag filled with secret spices, and placed it by the door to take to the hospital the next day. When I walked into the living room, my father sat on the couch looking at the television, but not watching it. I looked at him, noting all the imperceptible little chips that began to flake away, cracking right in front of me. I didn't have anything planned to say, but felt that something *must* be said before the sun rose, and he apparently felt the same way.

"Who will take care of me now?"

His tiny eyes hardened at the sight of my hickory-colored skin, and he turned back to the blinking screen. "Don't let me *ever* catch you up in my house like that again." It was a rare display of colloquial negligence.

"Okay." Despite the exhaustion, I passed the cold feeling back into my stomach so that I was white once more, and removed the record of the "Arabesques" from the sound system, assuming that that was the extent of our conversation. With my back turned, I heard him clear his throat, and my kneecaps slipped into the color of rust.

"You know, a son is a son until he finds a wife." The ice cubes rolled around in his mouth, clanking against his teeth like marbles.

"But a daughter is a daughter for life."

I gave a slight nod. It wasn't an affirmation; it was a desire for a stealthy retreat. He disappeared from view as I backed away slowly into the hallway that led to my room. I closed the door behind me and tried to lock it as quietly as possible, afraid that the slightest hint of a boundary between us would provoke him to trample it to dust. My skin felt as if it had been pulled into a fine point that could be split wide open.

I'm not sure what happened first—me snapping the record in half, or me passing out on the floor. My skin was the color of blood when I awoke, but not my own. It was her blood, covering my arms and hands and face. I marveled at its depth and hue while clutching the embroidered black-and-gold dress beneath my bed.

C Minor
to
C Major

(What the animals in the forest tell me)

21

WHEN I WOKE UP BENEATH THE BED, SALIVA HAD dried into a thin crust on the side of my face, picking up the dust and muck and giving me the appearance of chin stubble. I didn't leave my room until the next evening, once I was sure my father was gone. The house creaked and murmured as I slipped through its halls toward the bathroom. I had wanted to take a bath, but my limbs stiffened when I saw the state of the tub. The faucet groaned when I twisted the tap, releasing hot water that mixed with the thick pattern of brown spotting and swirled into a dark sludge along the bottom of the tub. Using a soft rag and a bottle of bleach from beneath the sink, I began to scrub. My arms and shoulders ached by the time I finished. Water flows down and out of a faucet, neat and ordered. Blood from a sliced vein goes everywhere, planting a flag and staking its claim.

When I was finished, blood marked my body like war paint. It got between my fingernails, turning thick and black like dirt, and dried into coarse rivulets in my hair as if I had bathed in it. I washed myself off in the sink, then cleaned again until the bathroom was white as bone.

*　*　*

FLOODLIGHTS FROM THE front porch washed over me as I approached Dominique's house, but my finger shook as it hovered over the doorbell. Inside, several people shouted over who had the honor of answering, and Niyala won. She opened the door, and her face brightened when she saw me.

"Goodness, Gabri—! Is that you?" She chuckled, then turned her head back briefly to shout at everyone heading into the kitchen for another bottle of champagne. "What are you doing here so late?" She checked her watch, the hour hand somewhere between eleven and twelve. She wore a fitted yellow dress with large shoulder pads that framed her figure, and the dark skin around her eyes was thick with pearlescent violet makeup.

"What is that . . . ?" She stepped forward to eye me more closely, scattering a swarm of moths to focus on my face. I didn't have to see it myself to imagine what she saw: wild eyes, gaunt cheeks, the feral expression of an animal caught digging in the garbage cans. In my head, a confession poured out, with the tone and volume of a compelling epic, but nothing came, and I stared back like a fish gasping for air as it flops around on a kitchen floor.

"Never mind. Wait here. *Dominique!*" She ushered me inside and closed the door behind me, twisting her neck to yell, then sitting me at the piano.

"Stay right here. Do you need anything?" She didn't wait for me to answer, pushing through the swinging door that led to the kitchen, and yelling for her daughter a second time while steadying herself on loose ankles. Dominique came bursting through the door, laughing and annoyed. She wore a pair of pajamas, but otherwise seemed groomed for a night out, with her hair pressed straight and pulled back into a long ponytail that hung down between her shoulder blades. Her face was smooth and matte with foundation, but it changed when she saw me, striding quickly in my direction, and stopping just short of touch.

"I'll be in here if you need me." Niyala glanced between us before removing herself.

Dominique stared at me. Laughter came from the kitchen, and her breath caught with the promise of words that didn't come. In my impulsivity, I had taken her away from something else. But I needed her in the room. There was no one else.

"I'm sorry . . . I'll . . ."

Dominique held up her hand and disappeared again, leaving me alone with the piano. I leaned over the closed hood to steady myself, unmoored by the sudden heat of the room. She returned trailed by Foxy, and I corrected my posture, feeling heavier after the brief reprieve. Dominique held a wet dish towel. She hesitated before placing it in my open palm.

"You have blood in your hair," she said as if she had only spotted a stray leaf.

I curled my fingers around the towel, hot, soapy, and fragrant, then began running it over my curls while Dominique stepped back with her arms crossed. She looked at the floor as if she wanted to afford me some privacy. There's a certain intimacy in wiping away blood, regardless of where it came from. When I was finished, a dark stain had bloomed on the towel and my hair smelled like lavender. I tried to speak again, wanting to explain, but she interrupted me—as if I were the tenth bloodied girl to appear on her doorstep that night, as if that's just what we do.

"Oh hey! Have I shown you my new record?"

I stopped and Dominique rushed over to her bookshelf, pulling out the familiar crate. She sat cross-legged on the carpet, narrowing her eyes at the titles until she pulled out a record; the cover had the black-and-white portrait of a ghostly pale man. Foxy wiggled under the piano bench and collapsed. It was her normal spot for music and affectionate toes.

"I found this at a flea market the other day." She removed the wide black disc from the sleeve and held it up to the light. "Can you believe it? One of the greatest concert pianists of all time, hanging out next to a lamp shaped like a turkey for two bucks." Dominique gestured at the unblemished surface of the record like a game show assistant. "This is when you say 'ooooooh.'" She rolled over onto her knees and put the record on. A symphony of notes danced on the air. She leaned back with her arms wrapped around her knees.

"Hang on." She pushed herself up and ran into the kitchen, returning a few moments later with a bottle of red wine and two glasses. "There's a right way to listen to classical music, and there's a wrong way. In this house, we do it the right way."

She placed the glasses on the coffee table in front of the couch and nearly filled them to the top with wine, carefully pushing one toward me with her neon-green fingernails. I sat down next to her, and she clinked her glass with mine. The sour liquid left a trail of heat down the back of my throat, forcing me to cough. Dominique laughed and leaned back on the couch, then nestled her toes, also neon green, between the cushions for warmth.

"If you're going to show up on a Friday night, then be prepared for a Friday-night lesson." She rested her head against her palm, and took me in. I didn't meet her gaze, keeping my eyes anchored to the glass in my hands. She was waiting for me to say something.

"I'm not twenty-one." I stared at the alcohol, unsure of what to do with it, not knowing how to taste or swallow it.

Dominique swallowed her laughter. I took a sip of wine to break the words caught in my throat into coherent sentences. I slouched over my knees to bring myself closer to the floor, tracing the stains in the carpet with my fingertips.

"Do you want to pick a record? I mean, you can." She chose her words carefully. "You look like you could loosen up a bit."

I wondered about the various interpretations that could be deduced by finding blood in a student's hair, and "loosen up" seemed just as legitimate as any other. Dominique waited for me to make a selection.

I slid down to the floor, breaking up a stubborn clump of carpet fibers matted with dark grit, listening to the piano and wanting to say something about it.

"Is he your favorite?" I finally whispered. "This composer?"

She regarded me from above, satisfied that I had finally spoken, then hmm'd at the ceiling.

"God, I don't know, Gabs, they're all so *tragic*." The shift in her tone surprised me, and I wanted to know if it matched her expression, but I was too exhausted to lift my gaze. So I looked from one thing to the next, gradually. First, the dark red wine stains on the table, then her neon-green toenails, the elbow resting on top of the couch, the hooked part of her nose. It stopped there.

"I mean, how do you pick your favorite kid when they're all psychopaths?"

I felt the pressure on my head soften when a choked laugh escaped my lips. She smiled at this, encouraged to continue.

"Take Ravel, for example. Brilliant composer. I still get whiplash every time I hear the opening of his Piano Concerto in G Major, but he lived in a human dollhouse and thought that mechanical objects had souls."

My eyes widened.

She nodded and lifted the wineglass to her lips, shifting her eyes and swallowing in ascent.

"You're kidding . . ."

"Oh, that's nothing!" She took another sip and pointed at me with her wineglass. "I mean, there's your average run-of-the-mill obsessive compulsives like Bruckner, who spent his free time counting windows, statues, and leaves. Sure, okay, impressive for amateur hour. Fine. But did you know that Erik Satie started his own church, and he was the *only* member in it?"

I smiled at the sound of her voice, at the way it filled with mirth.

"That's not even the weirdest part. He would only eat *white foods*! Eggs, sugar, scraped bones, fat from dead animals, coconuts, turnips . . . There's not even *a name* for that level of crazy. Everyone thinks that Mozart is the quintessential mad genius, but he was just a vulgar brat. He never had the commitment to be truly insane." Her tone became nostalgic. "I guess I kinda love them all . . . *except* Wagner. *Fuck* that Nazi."

She didn't notice that I had stopped smiling.

"And then there's Liszt . . . my bitch." We both burst out laughing. Wine spilled on the carpet.

"The original virtuoso. A master of experimentation and founder of the modern-day recital." She winked at me. "Who gave up a lucrative career as Chopin's greatest rival to join the clergy."

She approached the record player and lifted the needle. Then she dug around in the crate until she pulled out the right one and put the needle back down. The music didn't sound so difficult at first—earnest, amorous. I was suspicious of left-handed melodies, but at the end of what I envisioned to be the bottom of the second page, it switched hands—slipping off one sweet mask, and replacing it with another.

"This is my favorite piece. He was just something *else*."

It was beautiful. I wanted my mother to hear it, and that thought punched me in the gut.

Niyala poked her head through the swinging door briefly and, satisfied with what she saw, disappeared once again. I wiped my eyes with the back of my hand and pushed myself up, feeling the room tilt as I came vertical. The bookshelves lifted off the ground, and the floor fell away.

"In fact—stop the record. Lift the—lift the thing!" Dominique gesticulated, the words turning to slush in her mouth. I reached for the record player and lifted the needle. She climbed onto the piano stool, disturbing Foxy who raised her head only briefly. Dominique's fingers went to work.

"Everyone thinks Liszt is so difficult." Her head lolled from side to side as she played, and then she scooted over on the bench—a silent invitation for me to join her. "Well, he is." She snorted. "But he was a master of tempo. If you can master tempo, you can master Liszt." During our first few lessons, the distance between us had been pronounced and rigid. But at that moment, she was leaning toward me, her shoulder grazing mine.

My long thin fingers mimicked hers, and our hands danced across the keys—small, impudent representatives of their clumsy masters.

"Anyone can play Liszt. It's just a lot easier if you have large hands—or quick hands." She turned to me and held her tiny hand in front of her face and frowned. "I'm only quick." Then she reached over and grabbed my hand, holding it up— my palm placed against hers. "Liszt could palm a tenth." She squeezed her eyes shut. "Or was it a twelfth? I dunno. Maybe it's just an urban legend. Ask me when I'm sober."

I hadn't asked her in the first place, and if I had, I would have forgotten the moment the calluses at the top of her palm touched mine.

"You could play this one day. You have *much* bigger hands. And a certain grace." I bent the tips of my fingers over hers, and she filled the space, slipping inside my palm like she was its tendons. I didn't want her to touch me. I should have pulled away, laughed it off, or—or just left. I should have fought back. I should have said no. Stop. *Let me go. Please don't do this. I don't want it*—but I didn't. I froze. I panicked. And my body did what nobody else would—it defended me.

Right there, I passed into a creamy beige like cake batter on the piano stool, light enough so Dominique could note the shameful pink patches blooming at my cheeks. She pulled her hand away as if I had burned it. Heat licked at my fingertips. Dominique held her injured hand against her chest like a broken wing, and she kept her eyes on me. They were overrun.

22

NIYALA AND HER GUESTS LAUGHED FROM THE kitchen, and the sound cued my shame. I covered my mouth with my hands and squeezed my eyes shut so hard that the black behind the lids changed to indigo. Dominique jumped up and ran into the kitchen, disappearing for a small eternity before returning with a cold towel wrapped around her hand. I wasn't going to cry. I wasn't going to be hysterical.

Dominique stood in the corner of the room, one arm folded across her flat stomach, and the hand of the other clutching the Halloween-themed towel. A strange choking sound came from my throat, until a powerful hiccup replaced it. Dominique guffawed sharply—catching herself suddenly. She retrieved a box of tissues from the bookshelf and held it out to me with a steady arm. I retrieved one and snorted into it ungracefully, and that's when she lost it. The laughter that pulled her down to the floor, made her roll back and forth, utterly possessed. My color deepened once again like leather, and I propped my face on my elbows, watching her get it out of her system. When she sat back up, wiping tears from her eyes, she slid next to me on the piano bench, and we stayed like that for a long while, not speaking to each other—her staring at me, me staring at the floor, and silence writhing between us.

She moved closer by what seemed like mere millimeters. I cleared my throat, and raised my face and my voice, feeling the reddened burning skin around my eyes, where tears were meant to be.

It was the quietest she had ever been.

"This wasn't supposed to happen . . ." I trailed off, unable to explain the recent events. "You don't know what will happen to me if he finds out. You don't know what he'll do." I knew that I should stop talking; a plug had been pulled, and fears spilled out—tasting thick and foul. I told her about my mother. I told her about the bathtub. I told her about my father. I don't know how long I spoke, or the number of catastrophic scenarios I outlined before Dominique interrupted me, waving her hand for silence.

"Gabrielle . . ." Her sigh had the gravitational pull of a large cinder block.

"You. Can't. Tell. Anyone. If you tell anyone, it's all over. Everything will be all over, and they'll send me away." Dominique held her hand still, and I stopped. At first I was relieved, then annoyed at my compliance—and finally, calm.

"What do you think I am?" She looked aggravated—and this time it wasn't in jest. I panicked, sensing that I had said the wrong thing, and retraced my words in search of the offensive phrase, determined to try again.

"First of all . . . holy shit." She laughed, her voice turning into a harsh whisper. "Holy fucking shit! I mean you just changed the color of your skin in my living room. How the hell . . ." She laughed again, scratching at her chest from the sudden rush of adrenaline. "Do we really just *not* talk about that?" Her speech was loose and elastic from the wine.

I took my time before replying with a half-hearted shrug.

"Really?" She tilted her head and opened her palms expectantly.

I shrugged in exactly the same way again, unsure of how to share a revelation that was, for me, anything but—so I just waited for her to absorb it. She paced around the room, eventually slumping down onto the sofa with a sharp exhalation. She dropped her head between her knees, took a deep breath, and sat back up again as if pulled by string, staring at me with new resolve.

"First of all, I am *not* a monster," she said sharply, words carved like glass. "I've known monsters. *Lots* of them. But that's not who *I* am. Do you understand? And don't you *dare* shrug again—"

My shoulders froze.

"I get it. Your father is an asshole. He may be the only one *you* know, but for me—he's just par for the course." She waved him off with a flutter of her hand, banishing him from the conversation. I felt offended by this gesture, as if she knew a more talented villain than him, which seemed impossible. Then I briefly imagined what that villain would look like—to find his blue eyes looking right back at me. I shut the image away.

"Jesus." She exhaled breathlessly, and her eyes softened into a bemused expression. "I *knew* there was something different about you the moment I started teaching you, but I had no idea . . ."

I waited for the conversation to take a turn for the worse. They usually do.

"If I had known . . . but *of course*, it's not like you can just tell someone!" She threw up her hands and chuckled, losing track of me for a moment. I fiddled with my hands uncomfortably. She pushed herself toward the edge of the couch, folding her hands into her lap—another silent plea.

Come here, it said. I walked from the piano bench to sit next to her steady voice, her firm tone.

"I will never tell anyone about this. I swear."

I searched for a flicker of betrayal in her beautiful face, and she welcomed the analysis. I examined each word for duplicity—but I found none, and relaxed when I decided that she was telling the truth.

After all, I had no choice.

"You swear?"

"On my life, I swear it," she said, holding up her hand again.

I sat up a little straighter, and she smiled back at me.

I held my hand up, indicating that I wanted her to touch me again. This time, I wouldn't retreat. When she did, I passed my color into a shining black void. She didn't falter, but her eyes widened and inside them I saw something useful—fear.

"I swear it," she repeated.

I hoped she would never make me use it.

For the next hour, I told her everything I knew about passing, and she listened without interrupting. I told her about the white foods, and the white house, and this time she didn't laugh.

I told her about the afternoon at Kraig's house—omitting the gritty, shittier details of what had delivered me. She didn't push. She nodded her head. She raised her eyebrows. She shook her head. She ran her hands through her slicked-back ponytail until the edges hung sloppily around her face. My apprehension gave way to a feeling of abandon, more stimulating than any amount of wine, and I thought—*how exhilarating to rely on the unwavering loyalty of a near stranger.*

"This must be why," she said.

"Why what?"

"Why you're so . . . fevered." Dominique gesticulated toward the shiny vintage piano. "When you play, it's not like you don't make mistakes or anything—"

"Oh." My heart dropped.

"No no, let me finish." She placed a gentle hand on my knee. It burned bright red when she let go, and she stared at the color, shaped like her palms and fingers, as it slowly dissipated back to brown.

"But you play with such *urgency.* Like whatever you're playing, it's the most important thing in the world. Like if you don't play it the world will end."

This is what nobody told me when I began to play the piano. Music isn't some gift that delivers people from their demons. It's selfish, indiscriminate, and it had begun to chip away at me one piece at a time—possessing every scrap until I belonged as intimately to the practice as my secrets belonged to me. But I happily shed it all—there wasn't much I wanted to hold on to.

Dominique began to pace again, excitedly muttering to herself, before stopping with her back facing me, speaking in a lower, more measured tone.

"How is your mother doing now?"

I began to shrug, then stopped to clasp my hands in my lap again. Dominique sat back on the sofa next to me. Her constant moving about the room made me nervous, and it was nice to just have her next to me, being still.

"The doctor said that she will be okay . . ." I trailed off. "But I guess that's up for debate." I remembered my mother strapped up to a heart monitor and I rubbed my fingers against my temple as if to massage the image out of my skull, but it had already grown roots. "I dunno, maybe she will be fine."

"Hmm . . ."

I waited for Dominique to finish her thought, but she held on to her words for a long time while pressing the wrinkles out of her pajama pants, before picking up the empty wine bottle. "Well . . . I should drop by the hospital sometime. Bring her some flowers or something . . . Would that be okay? She sounds . . . lonely."

I nodded. She opened her mouth to say one thing but diverted to something else instead.

"You better get home before your dad does . . . something." She frowned, then left for the kitchen, disappearing behind the swinging door. I sat there, watching the last drops of red wine swirling in my glass. When she came back, she carried copies of new sheet music. "Don't freak out. This one is a bit out of your depth for the moment. But we'll get through it together—one page at a time." She rubbed a spot on the back of her neck, and the tone in her voice switched keys, stripped of levity. "In the meantime, try to see if you can figure out the fingering in a way that won't embarrass you."

Taking the record off the player, Dominique placed it in the thin paper sleeve and gripped it tightly in her hands. "My father gave this to me before he left our family to start a new one." Her words were flat as she extended her hand. "Perhaps it will bring you better luck." I took the record from her hand and placed it between my sheet music, still warm from the printer. Luck from a dead white man, gifted as a tribute to forgotten families and the crazed women who held them all together.

That's how desperate my situation had become.

23

WHEN I ARRIVED AT THE HOSPITAL THE FOLLOWING
Saturday, there was a large bouquet of wildflowers at my
mother's bedside with a note:

> *Thinking of you. Praying for you.*
> *Get better soon.*
>
> > *Love,*
> > *Dominique and Niyala.*

Dominique called me at home a few times to check in.

"She seemed in good spirits when I dropped by with the
flowers." I remained silent on the line until she had exhausted
her list of unnaturally optimistic observations. Then she asked
me how I was doing, and when I said that I was okay, she
waited on the line for *me* to say more. I sensed her disappointment whenever I didn't. I held on to those conversations while
watering the magnolias in the backyard, pulling up the weeds
by their thick, knotted roots, turning over the soil in the herb
garden to rid it of dead leaves and pests, then playing the piano
with filthy hands that smudged dirt all over the old ivory keys
until I felt weak.

When I did go back for lessons, Dominique seemed to restrain herself from asking too many questions, based on the urgency of the ones that she *did* ask.

"How many colors can you *do* exactly? Is *do* the right word for it? What do you call it again? Phasing?" She made it sound like an arsenal of weapons instead of the divine gift my mother had always packaged it as.

I slowly relaxed into our lessons, and my lessons were jealous of anything else that claimed my attention. Other distractions fell away to the worship of my practice. Every sonata, every orchestra, every prelude became a paradise of ritual.

I went to the hospital almost every day, and when I left, I cycled back to Dominique's house for lessons. But some days didn't involve lessons at all. My father became more scarce around the house; I didn't ask him to explain the absence I did not miss. I began to sit at Niyala's table more often, acclimating myself to the exotic conversations and smells that wafted out of their kitchen and stuck to my clothes. She could hold an entire conversation on her own, but she seemed most curious about my opinions on everything—which I didn't really have.

"Tell me, what do you want to study in college?"

"Mom . . ." Dominique warned.

"What? Can't I ask her about her education? Am I not allowed to take an interest in the future generation?" Niyala opened her palms and tilted her head. "Ignore my daughter, Gabrielle. She's so cynical about her dear mother. I'm just an old woman! I just want you two to sit with me and keep me company with your tales of youth."

I smirked, and she squinted to keep herself in character—but her smile was hard to disguise.

"So insensitive you are, my child. Laughing at a fragile old woman . . ." She placed her hand at her collar as if I had wounded her. My laughter deepened into a snicker and she pointed at me and turned to Dominique as if to say, *Can you believe this shit?*

I bit on my tongue and snorted, staring deep into the table.

"What's so funny?" she said, leaning in, making distorted faces, exaggerating her irritation. I shook my head, while Dominique just leaned back and smiled. "Go on, spit it out, Miss Gabrielle—what's so funny about me being old and fragile?"

I calmed myself and bit my lip. "It's just that, well, Miss Niyala—you're not *that* fragile."

Dominique hollered and pushed herself up from the table, leaning down into her mother's face swiftly to kiss her on the forehead. *"That's what you get!"* she proclaimed while clearing the table. Niyala stood with exaggerated movements.

"Well, I can tell when I'm not wanted," she announced through styled indignation. And then she placed her hand gently on my cheek and winked, before heading off through the swinging door.

"I know, I know—she's a handful," Dominique said once we were alone.

"It's okay, I really like her," I replied—meaning it.

"She hasn't always been like this . . ."

I approached Dominique at the sink where her hands were immersed in soapy sludge up to the soft curve of her elbows.

As I added dirty bowls and cutlery to the water, she began to peel back the layers of their story as if I had asked. Maybe there's some unspoken rule that women alone at the kitchen sink together have to pare back the outer skin of their lives, and I was standing in the corner of the initiated.

Dominique told me about how her parents made her take piano lessons from the age of three with the only Black classical instructor in Kingston, and she loved it, but always felt limited by the confines of classical music, which she described as an "interpretation" of someone else's genius, rather than an expression of her own. Niyala had been a jazz alto, and her father had been a composer with a deep baritone voice who slept with all his sopranos.

"Only sopranos," she said, rolling her eyes. "Anyone else was beneath him, like, you know what I mean." She frowned to herself.

When her father left to start a new family with a caramel-skinned soprano with green eyes, Niyala moved to America with her daughter to be closer to her sister. She helped them get their green cards when Dominique was only ten years old. Dominique reminisced on her anger and confusion, which seemed to reemerge while she aggressively scrubbed dishes. She developed a reputation for challenging boys of every color and shape to fights, which was an image that I enjoyed: Dominique the scrapper, returning home covered in fresh scratches like medals, reeking of dirt, sweat, and triumph.

"My accent made me a target. But even when people stopped calling me names, when I had beaten up everyone who spat at me sideways, there was still this look in their eyes when I told them where I was from, like, *What are you doing here?*" I remained next to her, listening, drying off dishes, and placing them on the rack.

"And then I heard *Vivid* for the first time when I was trying to lift some sheet music and . . . yeah, that was it. I didn't want to fight anymore. I wanted to be just like Will Calhoun instead." She laughed.

"He was just as dark as me—and *almost* as cool!" She nudged my shoulder with hers, imploring me to relax.

Her first drum kit had been a snare drum rehabilitated with masking tape, a bass drum, and two rusty cymbals. When Niyala got her first paycheck, she bought Dominique a new kit, paying it off in installments until Dominique beat that one to death too.

"Calhoun's just . . . perfect. He's the reason why I'm applying to Berklee College for next fall." She pulled the plug in the sink, and the water began to drain, revealing all the food pulp that had coagulated around the edge of the basin. There are a million ways to disguise disappointment. When she glanced sideways for a reaction, my face looked like it had been dropped against pavement. That was mine.

I pulled my hands out of the sink, brushing against hers in retreat, and wiped them on a dry dish towel. I walked over to the kitchen table to pick up my backpack and pulled out a music book. "I'd like to try these next." I held up the book in front of my face, blocking out hers.

"Sure."

I grimaced. Her disappointment wasn't subtle.

"I just really wanna give it a shot, you know? I've been thinking about it for a while."

"Sure, I understand," she said, her face washed free of expression.

It wasn't a complete lie. I had created a mixtape of the composers she had introduced me to over the months, rewinding some tracks a dozen times or more in my Walkman until the film from the cassette tangled in its reel. I learned that I loved Chopin, anything by Chopin. I was a fan of romantic tragedy. Up until that point, music had seemed like an expression of emotion that commanded its practitioner like a prisoner—but I never felt emotional when I played. I felt powerful, and the disconnect bothered me. Was I doing something wrong? When I expressed this to Dominique, she hmm'd to herself and sighed, pressing her fingers down onto the white keys first and then the black.

"Gabs, I can see why you'd think that, but *real* musicians have to be in complete control of their emotions. The music depends on it—it doesn't need us adding anything messy. An intelligent pianist"—she tapped her index finger to her temple for emphasis—"will make her emotions serve her, and not the other way around." I bit my lip, not as a response to what she was saying, but because I felt like I had been preparing myself for that conversation my entire life.

"You command the music; it does not command you."

———

My mother continued to request specific items from the house: a blouse or a piece of jewelry, even though she was only allowed to wear the thin paper gown that exposed the dimples of her bottom. All the items I brought with me stayed in their bags next to her bed as if she only wanted the comfort of their proximity. We sat alone in her room during my visits, watching television as she flicked through channels, clicking from talk show to talk show, until she found the men in suits slamming their fists onto the Bible. I slipped spices beneath her pillow when she hobbled to the bathroom. Little bags of cardamom and paprika. They seemed to lift her mood.

She asked about my lessons, but my answers rolled off her when she drifted. It wasn't a gradual transition. One minute the door was open; the next, it was shut, and I waited on the other side, flipping through the TV channels where she had left off.

I passed my color once when we were alone to show her that I was getting better at controlling it, hoping that she would join me. I missed feeling close to her, and the absence of her warmth at home unnerved me. But when I did this, she scowled with disapproval.

"You better pass before the doctor comes back."

I didn't try it again after that.

I STAYED LATE and filled out college applications while my mother slept. I bought food from the vending machine in the hallway and ate it quietly while she watched TV until the anchor of sleep forced her eyes closed. Other times, I retreated to the cafeteria to eat alone. Sometimes, I called Dominique from the pay phone near reception to give updates, but mostly I wanted to hear more stories about eccentric composers. She made a show of it. She checked out books from the library and dug up new facts to share about Mozart, Berlioz, and Scriabin. Satie became my favorite. She read me anecdotes on the phone where I curled the cord between my fingertips and listened to her eviscerate what she referred to as the world's most exclusive club of psychotic white prodigies.

I was putting my completed college applications in envelopes the night before my mother was supposed to be discharged from the hospital when a woman asked if she could sit with me in the cafeteria. I didn't recognize her straightaway, but when I saw the string of pearls around her neck, I realized that it was the woman from the waiting room. My tongue retracted from the sticky glue flaps and slithered back into my mouth.

"May I?"

It took me several attempts to actually nod my head, and when I did, it looked dislocated.

"I remember you," she said, sitting across from me—taking the lid off a Styrofoam cup of coffee, and pouring in two sticks of sugar, spilling some on the tabletop. "You were in the waiting room." She shoved the spilled sugar off the edge of the table, then dusted her hands. "I saw you."

"I remember," I replied, putting my pencil down, but then, realizing that I didn't know what to do with my hands, I picked it back up. Her skin was dark and rich up close. She had high cheekbones, and eyes that sat deep in her face like footprints.

She gave a slight laugh. "I bet you do. I bet everyone in that room remembers me." She used her plastic stirrer to draw a circle in the air.

"I'm Missy."

"Gabrielle," I replied.

"Gabrielle? I've always loved that name." She smiled. "Like the archangel who sounds his trumpet to herald the Lord's return."

"Well, that's *Gabriel*," I replied.

"So?" She raised her eyebrows. "Gabriel, Gabrielle—a woman can't be an archangel? Girl, you're too young to be so cynical about your own sex." I began to doodle in the margins of a notebook.

"I named my baby girl Mercy." Missy swirled the coffee cup in her hand. "Her father wanted to name her Abigail—said that it meant 'the father's joy,' but I told him that I carried her, I gave birth to her, and I was gonna nurse her, so his joy had nothing to do with it." We sat silently across one another for a few minutes before she continued speaking.

"She ripped me up." Missy laughed. "Her brother was easy. A few hours, and he just slid on out like an egg yolk, red, slippery, and ugly as sin." She added a third packet of sugar to her coffee. "But Mercy had to make a statement. I actually thought I was going to die before I held her." The more she spoke the more I noticed her accent. It wasn't quite Southern, nor was it Floridian. It sounded earthy, like it had been dug up from the dirt, stored there from a different time, waiting to be found.

"And you know what they did when they finally pulled her out of me, naked and screaming and covered in afterbirth? They handed her to her father. Not to me—*to him*. I'll never forget that."

The young doctor with the blond chin locked eyes with me from across the cafeteria and began to approach, but he changed his mind when he saw who I was sitting with, falling back on his heels and finding a table of nurses to chat with instead.

"I always wanted a girl. I'm blessed to have my son, but I always wanted a girl," she went on. "So much can go wrong with boys, especially if they don't have the right men in their lives. They need strength, but not too much, otherwise they become bullies. They need kindness, but not too much, otherwise they'll become burdens." She smiled at me. "But girls are elastic. They can know strength, kindness, cruelty, weakness—but they never forget how to love, no matter what you do to them." The words sounded different; the voice saying them was warmer, but they possessed a coldness that made me shudder.

"I guess you wouldn't know anything about that just yet." I smiled limply, because it seemed that she wanted me to, and I shook my head.

"I guess not."

The muscles in Missy's neck contracted. I froze in my seat, not knowing how to comfort her. A group of doctors walked past in heavily starched scrubs. They seemed like uniforms that people wear when their business is built on saying *I'm sorry, there was nothing we could do*—which felt worse than pity, because it was more useless.

"She was messing with that damned radio on the road. I told her a million times not to . . . she didn't listen. She never listened. And one day, bam! Out like a light. Doctors said there was nothing they could do."

"It was a car accident?" I asked. Her expression strayed around the cafeteria, narrowing at the scuff marks on the white floor. She nodded.

"The other person was fine. Barely a scratch. That's justice, I guess. Or maybe—Mercy?" She smiled bitterly and sipped her coffee.

"Now I come to these bereavement meetings here at the hospital where these doctors told me she died." She said *bereavement* as if it was a made-up word, using her fingers as quotation marks and rolling her eyes. "And I get to relive the worst day of my life all over again, in the same place where I come for healing." The last word of her comment had a curse on it.

People cleared out of the cafeteria, and janitors went from table to table to collect empty trays and cups. Without the hum of conversation and families, it was just another sterile hospital room where people went to die.

"Marriages can withstand a lot of things—losing a child ain't one of them." Missy stared into her empty cup, then met my eyes again and gave a strained smile.

"You remind me of her," she said. "Y'all must be around the same age. What are you? Sixteen? Seventeen?" I didn't reply.

Missy reached into her large bag and sifted through a number of items before lifting out a massive black billfold, the wallet of choice for moms, and removing a small, creased photo; then she handed it to me: a school portrait of Mercy. On the back it said eleventh grade.

"See? The skin color is different, but the features are similar." I saw a likeness in our high cheekbones, almond-shaped eyes, and small, flat noses. Her hair was pulled back tight into a high bun, and she smiled into the camera with a large gap between her two front teeth. She looked like the kind of girl who would give you half her sandwich even if she was starving. I could have easily slipped on her skin to complete the picture.

"Where are you from anyway?" she asked.

"Right here," I replied, and handed the photo back.

"Yeah, but where are your people from? You have an interesting face." Missy put the photo back into her wallet with her short, stubby fingers.

I felt my cheeks warm up. "I should . . . I have to go check on my mom."

"Oh, so that's why you're here all the time," she said. "Well, like I said, girls are the best." I gathered the envelopes and put them into my backpack. "She's lucky to have such a devoted daughter." Missy smiled at me as I gathered my dishes and tray, taking my hands to scrape the spilled salt from the table into my palm before scattering it over the empty plate.

"Thanks." I pressed my lips together and slung my bag over my shoulder. "It was nice talking to you." I genuinely meant it but knew the awkwardness of my expression indicated otherwise.

"Thanks for letting an old woman . . ."

I waited for her to finish her thought, but it evaporated. One minute the door was open. The next, it was shut.

I looked around the cafeteria, but it was empty. The clink of plates and trays sounded from the kitchen while dishes were cleaned. I ripped a piece of paper from my theory book and scribbled a message.

My name is Missy. I come here for bereavement meetings. Please call my family.

I slipped it next to her hand, still holding the photo of her smiling, gap-toothed daughter.

The hallway was normally packed with visitors, delivery men, therapy dogs, and small children screaming at the overstimulation that they all provided. In the early afternoon, I had to squeeze between families askew. But after sunset, the visitors with minor obligations or guilty consciences were replaced by the loved ones possessed by unshakable loyalty, and they curled up on tiny wooden cots next to hospital beds. I saw them when I walked past their rooms, clutching on to the unresponsive pinkie fingers of their loved ones.

My flesh was particularly sensitive in the hospital. It flexed instinctively to the tune of life and death. At first, my skin tightened to the loud rhythm of the ECG monitors beeping through the corridor, and then it expanded to the clamor of voices, and the feet running past me. As it contracted again, my skin pulled me down the corridor to follow the people rushing ahead, until I rounded the corner to my mother's room to see the floor covered in a reflective pool of blood. A nurse with small green eyes trampled through it and tried to push me back, but I resisted and shoved past her, searching for my mother, or a piece of her—just one piece.

Two doctors in soiled scrubs shouted at me over their shoulders without raising their heads.

"Get her out of here!"

It was an odd harmony of screams, machines, shoes scuffling on the floor, and commands—the most grisly orchestral arrangement. Two nurses pulled me back, lifting me off my feet as we slid out of the room in shoes that tracked dark red footprints into the hallway outside. We fell backward together, and I landed on them both collapsing onto the floor. The last thing I saw as I scrambled through the red slick on the floor was my mother lying in bed. She wore a silk blouse with silver jewelry—the stitches in her arm torn wide open; and from within, the bone smiled back.

24

THERE WERE TWO POSSIBILITIES: MY MOTHER WOULD die, or she would live. I tried to discuss both with my father, but he stopped speaking about her. That's what men do when they can't bring themselves to accept their part in the ruin of someone else. He came home from work, drank, fell asleep on the floor, and somehow woke up in bed the next morning— ready to do it all again.

"This is a place for peace and quiet, Gabrielle. Your mother made her bed," he relayed one evening while scooping the white rice and grilled chicken I had prepared onto his dinner plate. "*We* don't have to lie in it."

We sat at the kitchen table, and he continued this conversation with himself while I turned the rice over on my plate until it had formed a large, soft ball of mush. "That may sound mean, but I'm just being objective."

But I couldn't be objective. I could only obsess over her pending return. What if she tried to kill herself again, and failed? What if she tried again and succeeded? What if she decided life was worth living, but returned as a clone of her former self, with a new appetite for eating raw meat, bugs, or brains? Who could procure the ingredients for her new diet? Where would we hide the bodies?

But the scenario that frightened me the most was the one in which she didn't return at all.

The guilt I felt over my role in stripping her of her place in the church choir overwhelmed me. When my mind wandered back to that afternoon at home siding with my father, it quickly changed course and ventured to places I'd yet to visit, people I had yet to meet. I drifted off to a grand concert hall in Budapest with thick red velvet curtains that stretched from the floor to the ceiling where a stunning fresco of Greek gods danced around an elaborate chandelier. At night, I fell in love with a handsome young conductor with thick black hair and a French accent whose hands lacerated the air while negotiating complex fortissimos. I imagined kissing his soft lips and slipping my fingers through his hair while we listened to records in an apartment that was too small, and too expensive—but contained a bathtub that could fit two people, and a window right above a bakery that made fresh croissants every morning.

But I could never look him in the eye. When I focused on my imaginary lover as he hovered above me, his face was replaced with Sam's pallid squalor. First my body, then my skin—and yet, nothing prepared me for the betrayal of my own mind. Months had passed since the afternoon at Kraig's house, but I still couldn't forget the taste of sweat in my mouth, the agitation in my guts, and the blood spilling from Sam's ears.

My mother was moved to a psychiatric hospital across

town, and I wasn't allowed to visit, so my father went in the evenings after work, and I went back to Dominique's house after school.

"Take a deep breath." Dominique was trying to talk me through a prelude, but the notes blurred together. I was confusing my E's with my C's, mistakes of a less advanced student. During the last dissonant, my color erupted into multiple shades I had never adopted before. I balled my fists and bit my lip, but instead of yellowing, I chose my words carefully.

"I *know* this." I was emphatic.

"You *know* this," she replied.

Then she straightened her spine, pointed back at the music, and said, "Again."

When I had managed to make it through the piece without making a mistake and without passing, we took a break. Niyala came to sit in the parlor while we worked, grading papers at the coffee table while Dominique detailed the style of combining individual melodies and harmonies to create musical textures, switching between different sheets of music to show me the difference between a canon, a fugue, and an invention.

"The texture can have multiple melodies or just one," Dominique said, biting on the end of a pencil, circling notes in their individual stanzas to highlight similarities. "Whenever there's two or more melodies happening at the same time, the music becomes polyphonic."

"And that creates tension?" I asked, wondering what three different melodies would have to do with each other. She nodded enthusiastically, and smiled.

"Exactly. Beautiful, heart-wrenching, gut-punching tension. And that is what we want."

She edged me over on the piano bench slightly and began to play a piece that filled my mind with swaths of color that blushed into crimson events, and haunting indigo phrases. The melodies dropped off without reconciliation, and they negotiated back and forth in conversations of gold and silver: a man loves a woman, a woman loves a man, they have a child, then they chase a life that they can never have. My family was a three-voice polyphony screaming in a disturbing harmony that could not exist without one another. And there was a part of me that took comfort in being part of such an orchestral catastrophe.

"Can we record something for her?" I had been thinking about it for a while, some way to apologize. I couldn't sing, so I wanted to play for her, hoping that Chopin, Bach, and Shostakovich could say the things that always seemed to fall flat on my tongue.

Dominique perked up immediately, almost brightening.

"That's a fantastic idea!" She jumped up, went back to her plastic container of random gadgets, pulled out a chunky tape recorder and a pack of cassette tapes. She continued digging around until she pulled out a few batteries, sticking them into the back of the device. She blew over the top of the speakers, and a thin cloud of dust curled in the air. "Hey, take care of this for me, will ya?" She handed me the cassettes and I unwrapped the plastic, handing her back a blank tape. "She's gonna love this!" She smoothed a blanket over the closed lid of the piano and placed the recorder on top, then sat next to me again. Dominique looked over her shoulder to Niyala, who had been working quietly on the couch. She took the unspoken hint: stood up and left the room.

"Let's see . . ." Dominique tapped her finger to her chin and looked around. I mentally traced the edge her jawline. "What about the invention?"

I had mastered the two-page score, but the image of my mother's excited face when I came home with that first assignment stung. I shook my head and went back to the piece we had been practicing earlier.

"Shostakovich. Prelude Number Ten." I tapped my index finger on the paper, and let my hand slide down from it. I loved the curious melody of sharp black notes, the *moderato non troppo*, and the delicate trills of the last few stanzas that turned my arms into indigo stems. It was new, and I felt that's what my mother needed—to look forward, not back.

Dominique's thick lips curled up.

"Excellent choice."

I felt a fragile kind of hope. Dominique flipped the book open to the requisite pages.

"Remember—you know this." She winked at me. I took a deep breath, held it, and let it out so slowly I could feel my heartbeat drop.

"I do."

———

When I came home, my father was sitting at the kitchen table with a woman I had never seen before. Between them were a pair of wineglasses and soiled plates covered with disparate colorful stains.

"Gabrielle, come say hello to my friend."

My father's wineglass was still half full of red, while hers was drained to the stem. I walked closer.

"Hello."

The woman's eyes were wet, caking the makeup around them.

"Hi, I'm Stacey."

She extended a limp wrist toward me, and when I took her fingers into my hand, I squeezed them until I heard a knuckle crack. She pulled her hand back quickly and laughed, the necklace around her thick neck responding with a clinking melody.

"My, my, Robert! She has quite a handshake." Stacey rubbed her fingers into her chest and tilted her head to examine me.

"Well, good." My father took an inelegant sip from his wineglass, twirling the stem between his fingers. "It shows character."

"Robert tells me you play the piano. I would love a private concert." She was leaning too close toward me, and I inched away from her chair.

"She would love to," my father replied before I could make an excuse. I felt his glare on the side of my face and stepped away before it changed color. He was already pushing his chair back from the table, and Stacey followed, stumbling over on her heels to catch his arm as he guided her into the living room. I trailed behind, observing the way they moved around each other, touching and laughing.

"You're going to love this," he said, speaking only to her. "She practices all the time. She's *so* talented."

I arranged myself at the piano and stared at the keys until they began to blur, deciding on what to play. I could feel my back pass pale green beneath their gaze. I chose a waltz that I barely knew, hitting several dissonant notes within the first three bars. My father stopped giggling. I started over, and played them again—this time without the mistakes, but stumbled again on the second line of measures. Stacy kept whispering to my father, but I didn't hear him respond. I began again, each time getting further in the piece, but stumbling on a new note, chord, key, or change in time signature, finally apologizing before pulling my hands back into my lap.

"Sorry," I said half turned around. "I guess I'm not *that* good."

Stacey waved her hand, dismissing my apology. "Oh please, you're amazing! I could never play anything like that. Robert, she's a wonder. You must be so proud." I stared at the floor, waiting for him to respond—but he was stiff, unexpressive. Slowly, I elevated my gaze to meet his and found myself confronting an open fire that burned only for me.

It was the first time I had smiled at home in weeks.

*　*　*

My father traded in the bottle for women of different height, width, and shape—but each the same color. The only good part about their visits was that I didn't have to pass. My father said that it would have looked strange, being milky white with my dark-skinned father sitting at the table. But the moment they left, the rules fell back into place.

They all brought pasta casseroles and sat in my mother's chair, reworking the cushioning to accommodate the alien curves of their pale backsides as we ate. They asked me the same questions about school and piano lessons, each one eager to demonstrate her ability to relate, even though my father didn't care. I greeted them politely, shook their hands, listened to their stories, and ate their heavily salted food. When they left, I cleaned the dishes and guzzled water until my stomach bloated.

I replaced their real names with the ones they deserved, capturing the essence of their personalities as physical characteristics.

"I hear you're going to UF in the fall," said Crooked Teeth.

"It's such an exciting time in your life right now. Your father says it'll be pre-med, is that right?" asked Bearded Jaw. My father answered for me, bragging about the extra postage he had attached to my applications for tracking numbers, which he checked every morning from the kitchen phone before going to work.

"What I wouldn't give to be your age again, and have a do-over at life," said Hairy Mole.

I decided to call Stacey Thin Lips.

"You're going to have so much fun with the college boys," she said, leaning in close and winking at me as if we were in on some secret. "Gosh, what I wouldn't give to have your hair!" She reached over and sank her fingers into my curls, her diamond ring catching several loose strands as she pulled away. "You must drive them crazy." She untangled the hairs from the jewelry and let them float to the floor.

I decided that I hated Thin Lips the most.

The kitchen lighting caught in the powdered folds of her jaw as she leaned into my father's face and whispered something I couldn't hear. He chuckled, and the skin of my ankles burned into a light gray, while I fought back the urge to pass completely to butter white. I pictured Thin Lips screaming at the top of her lungs until even the scalp beneath her gray roots turned bright red as I transformed at the dinner table, continuing to eat her bland food. I swallowed a laugh, choking on it. My father scowled at me.

"Gabrielle, go to bed." Sunlight poured through the blinds, and I could still smell the scent of autumn. I cleared my plate from the table. As I rinsed it in the sink, Thin Lips and my father continued to whisper into each other's ears, smiling and laughing. I went to my bedroom, put on the cassette I had made at Dominique's house, and turned it up—loud. I knew that I was demanding too much from the music. It wasn't capable of disguising what was happening in my house, or the thoughts in my head. At best, it became a sophisticated soundtrack.

* * *

HER PERFUME STILL lingered in the bathroom when I woke up the next morning. Even when I opened all of the windows and swatted at the air with a broom, I couldn't get the smell of it out of the house.

The affairs never lasted long. Though the women accommodated him, they were too self-governing. They had lives they wanted to share, rather than surrender to him. Eventually, each one overstayed her welcome, leaving small tokens of cosmetics and clothing next to notes scrawled in smudged ink on torn pieces of paper sitting on the kitchen counter that my father rarely acknowledged.

I tore them up and tossed the trinkets over the fence in our backyard into the neighbor's property. This time, someone had seen and shouted, and I ran back inside. When my father came into the kitchen, dressed to visit the hospital, I had to stop myself from tackling him with the cassette tape. He smelled like dead flowers and the scent pushed me back farther.

"Can you give this to her?"

My father read the paper insert, on which I had written the title of the piece and a note:

Listen to the sound of my trumpet and follow it home. I love you, Gabrielle.

His face was expressionless as he turned it over.

"She's not allowed to have possessions."

"I read the information booklet that the doctor gave us, and it said that she wasn't allowed to have *certain* possessions." I used my fingers to repeat the list that I had memorized. "Pencils, pens, jewelry, razors, matches, lighters, alcohol—including alcoholic mouthwash, perfume, aerosols, glass containers, nail polish remover, and aftershave." My father blinked once, no longer looking at the cassette tape, but at me. "It said that music was okay, as long as it was checked in at the front desk. They can play it for her during her free time under nurse supervision, like when there are visitors. The brochure said it can help stimulate positive emotional responses to support reintegration after patients are released."

My father stuck the tape in his pocket and picked up his keys.

"Fine, but she's under a lot of medication, Gabrielle. You shouldn't expect too much of a reaction." He walked to the garage door and I followed him as he unlocked his car door.

"I just want her to listen. Can you please tell me what she thinks? I can try different pieces of music. If she doesn't like this one, I'll try another one."

He grunted as he climbed into the car and shut the door behind him. I felt myself trembling from excitement, certain that this was the way to get her back.

When I heard his car pull out of the driveway, I went back to the piano with a renewed sense of purpose. I wanted to learn another piece. And another one. And another one after that. I pulled out the book of mazurkas and studied the black lines, notes, and time signatures. I put my fingers on the keys and began, practicing the melody with my right hand and the accompaniment with my left. I dug into the composition, wanting to understand it, why it had formed the way it did, how it had become this way, trying to scrape at its nerves.

When I felt confident that both hands had some basic understanding of the composition, I began to play—slowly at first,
ignoring the time signature, wanting to hear the notes come
together, blurring them into a seamless stream. As I sped up, I
let my eyes stay on the music while my fingers played. I made a
mistake, I started over. I made a mistake, I started over. I made
a mistake, I started over. I wanted to expand my repertoire for
my mother. I wanted to see her in that beautiful purple choir
robe again, praising the Lord so beautifully that he opened the
sky to swallow her up.

25

I DECIDED TO PLAY SOMETHING THAT MY MOTHER hadn't heard before. When Dominique suggested that we try Chopin's second piano scherzo, I didn't hesitate. I snatched the book out of her hands and began to study the piece, tapping my foot impatiently, trying to intuit the time and key changes before I saw them on the page. B-Flat minor. Five flats. Opening with a solid presto, and then arpeggiated pianissimo chords. Notes piled on top of one another with naturals and flats that spread my fingers across the keys like tentacles. I stopped moving and looked up at her.

"This is harder." I didn't realize that I was smiling.

"Yes, it is." She looked very pleased with herself as she moved closer to me.

"Your technique is improving, but this will still be a jump." She paused. "A pretty big one too."

I leafed through the music. Crescendos. Decrescendos. Octave changes. Key changes to A major.

"How long is it?"

"Just under nine minutes." My eyes widened. Hers narrowed mischievously.

"If you're playing on tempo."

I winced. Dominique twirled a pencil in her hand then leaned into me. A smudge of oil shone beneath her ear that smelled like coconut. She began to circle dynamics on the page.

"Schumann described this piece as 'overflowing with love and contempt.' I have to be honest, Gabs—it's one of the most perfect pieces ever written, for any instrument. It made me fall in love with classical music." My cheeks flushed.

This tiny detail had its intended effect. Dominique wouldn't have it any other way.

"To really get to the heart of the piece, technique is key. These markings . . ." She used her pencil to point emphatically at a fortissimo and then a pianissimo. "Evoke the beating heart of the piece. You can just play a few sheets of paper, *or* you can actually transcend *with* the music."

I continued looking at the markings, then at the piano, tracing the black keys with my fingers. Transcending felt right, but I didn't want to do it alone. Gratitude flooded me, and my hands passed to a smooth, shiny copper color. Dominique smiled at this.

"Look, your mom's had a bit of a rough time. These tapes are probably the only thing she can look forward to in that place. The least you can do is play the damn thing right." It was an effective call to action. I arranged my hands over the B-flats. When I pressed down hard, we began a conversation without words.

As I tried to play from the sheet music instead of my in-tuition, the muscles in my neck strained. My shoulder blades tapped against each other to the rhythm. I wasn't even able to get through the first page, and I was sweating by the time I stopped. I was embarrassed by how little I was able to play. I pressed down on the keys in frustration. A loud dissonant chord hung in the air.

Dominique showed me how to play the scherzo in its completion. There wasn't any strain in her body, but her fingers shifted gears from note to note—one minute they were floating, barely licking the keys, the next they were locked into place, dominating all eighty-eight notes, even the ones she didn't touch. I closed my eyes and thought about being in the living room with my mother as we listened to records. Once again, the colors washed over me from note to note and I let them—from amethyst to aquamarine, violet and cerulean. The spectrum of pleasure.

When my skin subsided, I played the few bars of the scherzo that I could replicate, and then recorded a mazurka that I knew by heart instead. Dominique let me take the machine home. Since my father wasn't in the house, I decided to add a voice note at the end of my abbreviated performance. I rehearsed what I wanted to say, taking care not to mention anything about what was going on at home, just in case anyone else listened at the hospital.

Hey Mom. I'm learning a new piece now. It's a scherzo. I'm not too sure what a scherzo is, but Dominique says that it's one of the most beautiful pieces ever written. I just played a small part of it for you. The piece after that is a mazurka. A mazurka is a traditional Polish dance. Did you know that Chopin's heart is buried in a column in Warsaw? Apparently, his daughter brought it to Poland preserved in a bottle of cognac, and now you can visit it there. Maybe we can go someday. Anyway, the one I played for you is Number Seven. I hope you like it. If you want, you can record something for me on this tape and give it back to Dad so I can listen to it at home. It doesn't have to be much. Maybe a message to tell me how you're doing over there, and if you've made any friends. I miss you.

He smelled like mouthwash and cigarette smoke when he returned from the hospital.

"What did she say?"

"Like I said. She's heavily medicated and pretty out of it." He went to the kitchen for his plastic cup. I followed him around from a distance for a few minutes, waiting for more crumbs, but he said no more.

I tried again and decided it would be better to add the messages at the beginning of the recording.

Hey Mom. Have you ever heard of Erik Satie? He was a French composer who only ate white foods like rice, eggs, coconut, cream cheese, and sugar. Have you ever heard anything so strange before? Isn't that . . . um, interesting? Do you think he lived in a white house with white furniture? Anyway, he was a very talented composer. I really like playing his Gnossiennes. I'm going to play the first one for you now. It's not difficult, but it's gorgeous. I hope you enjoy it. Do you know if you'll be home soon? I really miss you.

"Anything?" I went into the living room where he fell onto the floor and turned on the television. He grunted and shook his head, then turned up the volume on the TV.

I tried again.

Hi Mom. Dad says you'll be home right before Christmas! That's wonderful news! I'm still learning the scherzo. I can play until the end of the second page now. Dominique and I have been working on a new nocturne by Chopin, in E minor, opus 72. She said that everyone and their mom knows how to play No. 2 in E-flat major, and it's not even that great compared to the others. It's not totally ready yet, but I can play the first page. By the time you come home, I hope that I will be able to play the whole thing for you. I hope you like it and I can't wait to see you again. I love you.

"Gabrielle, don't start. I already told you when she's coming home." My father had just closed the garage door and thrown his keys onto the kitchen counter. He began inspecting the items in the cupboard, and when he couldn't find what he was looking for, he took his keys and left. I heard his car pull out of the driveway. When he returned, he held a curvy bottle of brandy and went to the living room to enjoy it.

Some people preserved their hearts in cognac. My father buried his.

———

"Anything?"

I shook my head as I walked into Dominique's house. She was wearing a blue crop top and a loose pair of pants that bounced around her waist and hugged the hips beneath it. I sat on the couch instead of at the piano, and Foxy plopped down beneath my legs, licking my exposed ankle. Something felt wrong. I could sense it beneath my skin, but didn't know how to articulate it. A part of me could always feel my mother, even when she wasn't around. But since she had been moved to the new hospital, that feeling had been replaced with a numbness. Dominique read the contortion on my face and sat next to me, wrapping a pinkie finger around mine, as if we were children about to enter into a secret pact.

"Just keep going." Her voice was more tender than usual. "Just pick up where you left off and keep going." She made it sound so simple.

I had lost track of the number of tapes I had given my father. They ranged from preludes and études to simple fingering transpositions as I counted the fingering out loud to myself. I felt warm playing these pieces for my mother, like we were still in her bed and my father was still at work and we could stay there, knowing where we belonged. I sighed and pulled the recorder out of my backpack. Dominique excused herself.

"I'll be in the kitchen. Let me know when you're ready to play again." I watched her shoulders move as she left the room. Foxy stayed with me. I inserted a fresh tape and hit record.

Hey, Mom. This will be my last recording before you're back. I'm learning about Rachmaninoff. Apparently, he had the biggest hands of any classical composer—not Liszt. He could palm twelve whole keys, and that's why his music can't be played by most people. He actually went out of his way to make his music difficult for others! Dominique says that's a very Russian thing to do. He fled during the revolution on a sled with his wife and children and landed in Helsinki, before moving to America. Anyway, I already kinda know how to play one of his preludes, but Dominique says that learning by ear doesn't count. I just think he's interesting. I want to play his Prelude in G Minor. But for now, I'll play the first invention I learned. Remember? The first one I brought home? I've gotten much better. You'll see so for yourself when you're back. I love you.

D Major

(What man tells me)

26

"ARE YOU EXCITED, CHILD?"

The first day of winter break, Dominique and Niyala took me with them to pick out a Christmas tree. My father was spending his last day with Bearded Jaw before my mother returned home. He left a note on the kitchen table that smelled like cologne he never wore, scribbled aggressively in blue ink. As soon as I heard the garage door close behind him, I called Dominique.

"Or . . . are you nervous?"

"Leave her alone, Mom." Dominique stuck her hands into the needles of all the pine trees around us, searching for one that "felt like velvet." The sky was turned upside down and all its color had bled from the stars into the horizon. The trees held the pigment behind their branches like a paintbrush, backlit with an amber glow that had stopped rising above eye level in early December.

"What?" Niyala rolled her eyes. "My daughter, I love you. You're the best thing that's ever happened to me, but really— let me have a conversation with your friend, hm?" She sifted through trees twice her size and leaned into their scent, almost kissing their needles.

"I guess . . . a little of both?" I took my time replying, more scared than excited, but there was no reason to split hairs. Niyala was deeply invested in Christmas, and her enthusiasm held me back from my stockpile of cynical festive memories.

Niyala wore a red sweater dress even though it was still fifty degrees outside, gold jewelry, and long curved fingernails with snowmen painted on.

"It must have been very hard." She leaned sideways so that I caught her face aslant. "Being away from your mother for so long. I bet she misses you *a lot.*" Dominique glared at her mother, who held her hands up in surrender then went back to smelling trees.

In the end, Dominique decided on one with bald patches and a crooked base, because she felt like it had more character. We strapped the tree to the roof of Niyala's Buick. On the way back to their house, we drove past a shopping strip full of seafood restaurants with mermaids painted on their exteriors. Outside, boys in lobster and crab costumes held painted signs with dinner specials written in brightly colored chalk. Beside them was a sex toy shop where a mannequin in a naughty Mrs. Claus outfit held a pair of handcuffs in one hand and a stuffed elf in the other. At the far end of the strip was an antique discount store where my mother swore she had bought a real Fabergé egg that, when examined closely, said *Made in Indonesia* on the bottom. My father didn't let her forget it for a month.

Driving back, Niyala played patois renditions of Christmas carols in the car that made me laugh like a lunatic—though by the time we began to round into their neighborhood, I had adopted them as my own personal festive anthems, singing in a mutilated Jamaican accent that made Niyala and Dominique laugh.

We passed a corner shop with a neon sign advertising liquor specials that I didn't remember seeing before. Men sat outside the shop playing cards, checkers, and chess—scratching the graying stubble on their chins and taking long sips out of crumpled brown paper bags. Pulling up to their house, I noticed how the maroon stucco finish had faded considerably where it met the ground, covered with bright chalk drawings where the paint used to be. Two small fat girls with thick, shiny hair twists in brightly colored elastic bands were outside jumping double Dutch in matching acid-wash overalls, one wearing a neon-pink shirt underneath hers, and the other in neon green. Another pair of cousins.

"I'll go get the decorations," Niyala announced when we finished setting the tree up in the parlor. She wiped her hands against each other to get rid of the excess pine needles. Dominique and I plopped on the sofa, but something flimsy moved beneath me. I reached underneath to pull out a stack of pamphlets covered in colorful photographs of smiling people around my age. I flipped through them, reading the bold names: the Juilliard School, San Francisco Conservatory of Music, Berklee College of Music. Underneath, there were applications to schools in cities I had only fantasized about in my wildest dreams. Paris. London. Berlin. Vienna.

"Oh!" Dominique tried to sound surprised, sitting up and leaning in close while I pored over the forms. They had pictures of sprawling landscapes and campuses that took up whole city blocks, so big it was hard to believe anyone had managed to fit them to scale on one or two pages.

"I had these lying around in case I made mistakes on my applications. But I don't need them anymore." I nodded and set them on the coffee table, noting the red wine stains.

"So, you're really gonna go?" My voice was flat, stomped back into my throat.

"Go?" She tilted her head lower to catch my eyes. "Gabs, I was *always* gonna go. But . . ." She exhaled sharply, an indication that she was going to say something either kind or devastating. "I mean, don't you want to go too?"

I couldn't look at her. Dominique reached over to the coffee table and lifted the applications to place them back into my lap.

"Haven't you thought about it? Because I have." I had learned to recognize the hint of patois that flirted with her adopted American accent when she was excited. "I gotta be honest, since I saw you, um, pass, it's the only thing I've been able to think about—getting you the fuck out of there."

I rose from the couch and let the applications slide onto the floor in a pattern of glossy photographs. She stayed seated, waiting for me to say something. And when I didn't, she hooked her index finger into the belt loop on the back of my jeans and gently tugged me back into place, next to her on the sofa.

"It's so easy for you, isn't it?" I began without a hint of anger, only awe. "To just do what you want. To just say whatever you're thinking." My words came out flat, pressed into the back of my throat, crushing my spine. "I can't just leave."

"Why not?" She was quick to counter; she was prepared. "Seriously, why not? I need to know." She leaned over and picked up the applications, smoothing out their creased pages.

My mind began to stutter and the words broke in my mouth.

"I already applied." I swallowed more spit. "I'm gonna study medicine." Dominique clucked her tongue.

"You're still gonna let him tell you what to do even after you move out?" She moved her head toward mine, a nervous directive. "What's the point of even leaving?"

I opened my mouth to say something, but nothing came. I wanted to tell her that I fantasized regularly about disappearing. Not dying, and not being abducted—a scientific anomaly that erased the past, present, and future and left people wondering if I had ever actually existed.

"You gonna let him tell you who to marry too? What about how many kids you're gonna pop out? Why stop there?" She opened her palms to the ceiling and sighed. "I can't wait to see what he names them. Todd. Karen. Chad. I mean, Gabs—hey." She reached for my chin and tried to turn it toward her. I wanted to resist, but couldn't. "Is that really what you want?"

I smelled grass and plantain, and felt a sickness creep through me, spreading rapidly to my stomach. I was nauseated and trapped, and it leaked from my stomach as a wave of lime green that crept down my arms and pooled in the palms of my hands as they began to shake. I yanked my head away before it could spread.

"So, he tells me what to do. And you don't?"

I didn't recognize the sound of my own voice. It felt alien but good. If I doubled down within this new timbre, maybe it would change other parts of me and harden them.

"I thought that's what you liked about me."

Dominique's hand dropped and she leaned back. A smell like caramel began wafting from the kitchen, an indication that Niyala was preparing lunch and something sweet, which she always did when I stayed for the afternoon.

"You're mad at me." Dominique's tone was flat.

I lifted my shoulders then let them collapse, tears stinging behind my eyes. I felt my color roiling inside my belly, but I pulled it back and held it firm as steel, compressing the urge to pass into something sharp and pointy. I passed back to my natural state. I shook my head too quickly, not ready to speak again. I swallowed hard and flinched.

"No—I'm not."

"Yes, you are."

Her face washed over with concern. A slow exhalation pulled her back from the attack. She reached for my bag, and inserted the applications, zipping it back up again. I sank into the cushions beside her and she pushed the bag beneath my knees, an egg to protect until it hatched.

"Just think about it. Please." Her head dropped along with her voice, sensing that she had already pushed me to the edge. "For what it's worth, I think you stand a real chance with music.

There's this program in Berlin, it's superprogressive, for people with varied experience. The program lasts five years instead of four, but they're putting some of the best concert pianists out there right now. It's like a whole new model."

She caught her breath and then gave me the softest smile I'd ever seen.

"Like Liszt."

Niyala came back into the parlor carrying a cardboard box of decorations and wearing a Santa hat that balanced meekly on her thick curly hair, full of the youthful glow reserved for children.

"Found it!" She set the box next to the tree and began to untangle lights from ornaments of reindeer, snowmen, and elves. She squatted on the floor with her skirt hiked up like a child.

Dominique left my side and crouched next to the crate of records, pulling out one by a Swiss conductor whom she described as having "the warmest phrasing," before putting it back. She lay on her side, using her hand to balance her head while she made her selection. The curve of her hip bone protruded from her baggy sweatpants.

"Put on something good!" Niyala shouted as she began to wrap herself in sparkling garlands and tinsel. I reached beneath me and lifted one of the applications out of my bag, flipping through until I found a page asking for basic information. On line five, there was a prompt about my race or ethnicity, and I broke out into a cold sweat. I slipped it back into my backpack, then looked up at Dominique who was still sorting through the collection. She narrowed her black eyes and withdrew a thin sleeve. On the cover was a barefoot Black woman with a lazy eye and a loose white dress, with a painful smile. Dominique placed the disc on the record player. I watched as she approached me, then extended her hand.

Enough of that, then . . . she said with her eyes, with her fingers, with the corner of her lips that curved up into a dimple. Niyala squealed when the music began, and she ran over to her daughter to snatch her hand away from me, skirting Dominique away to dance. Dominique laughed too much to be truly annoyed. Niyala dipped her daughter low then twirled her around, humming to the melody as smoke filtered in from the kitchen.

"Wait!" I said, just a second before Niyala caught the smell.

"Shit!" She took off through the swinging door, leaving a trail of curses behind her that made Dominique burst into hysterics, bending over and clutching her knees for support while we listened to her mother open and slam doors, pour cold water on things, cough at the steam, shout at the ceiling. Niyala meekly poked her head back in, biting her bottom lip, before suggesting that we order out.

Dominique's smile was tight, holding back additional laughter. "My love, you choose. I'll sort this out." She headed back to the kitchen. Dominique saluted her, then once Niyala disappeared again, let the laughter roll through her body. I watched her in awe, how she could maneuver so seamlessly between upending my entire world and retreating to the safety of her own. She didn't even break a sweat. A slower song began to play, and Dominique stood next to the piano, regarding the new Christmas tree, the box of glittering ornaments, the smell of burnt sugar from the kitchen, and the thin cloud of black smoke hovering above the door.

"Right," she announced, weighing something carefully to herself. Dominique strolled over to me, extending her hand again with the silent invitation. I slipped my fingers into hers. They wrapped around my palm.

"I'm going to place my hand here, okay?" she asked, hovering at my hip, waiting. Her eyes were soft, rounded from their usual sharpness. I nodded, and she pulled me close, her heat radiating onto the coldest parts of me. I placed my hand around her shoulder, my fingertips tracing the tiny curls through the coconut oil slick on her neck.

She pulled me from side to side, as if she were in dialogue with the song and I just happened to be in the room. She held me close, and we breathed in harmony with the tempo. When it ended, she stepped backward, peeling herself away from me—first hips, then torso, then the soft resting place between her neck and shoulder. She went to the record player and removed the needle, her back turned to me as she did so, and I stared at the muscles that flinched in her shoulder.

27

MY FATHER THREW FESTIVE ADORNMENTS AROUND the cold, sanitized walls of our house without considering a theme or aesthetic. Thick scented candles filled the rooms with a smell torn between a crisp winter scent and the stale warmth of a retirement village. Floral arrangements with mismatched leaves and snow globes with pilgrims and turkeys instead of reindeer and elves appeared around the house like fat red pimples. This was all meant to make the house seem less incarcerating; they in fact had the opposite effect.

Decorating was something that came naturally to my mother—even though she was only allowed to do so during the holidays. She had meticulous eyes that twitched when fussing over charm. But the beating heart of home had fallen off time in her absence, thumping a half second behind the rest of the neighborhood, which welcomed the Christmas season with colorful displays and dinner parties we were not invited to. Our house could be spotted by the black hole it became at night, flanked on either side by twinkling lights.

In anticipation of my mother's return, I scrubbed the house clean. I decorated the tree to my father's conservative tastes. But I filled my pockets when his back was turned, and I added extra ornaments and tinsel in small bursts. With Christmas Day only a week away, the white plastic tree had begun to tilt, made of more Christmas than plant.

"WHAT ARE YOU doing?" The keys jingled in his hand as he prepared to leave for the hospital.

"Nothing."

I rummaged through boxes of gold garlands and red baubles, stringing them around the living room, tying them into a dozen different types of glittering wings. The light they caught reflected off my skin, the color of warm custard—muted, unthreatening, meaningless.

"That's enough. It looks cheap." He pulled the box of decorations from my lap and took it into the garage with him, but instead of getting into his car, he went to the garbage bin and tossed it inside.

I watched him drive away, then I reached into the can and retrieved one more silver garland, dusting off the grass clippings and dirt. I wrapped it around my waist and went back inside to dance without music.

The sun was set low over the horizon, hovering there through the morning and afternoon, unable to decide whether to share its warmth with the rest of us. When the garage opened, I stood in the hallway waiting to embrace my mother, but someone else walked through the door.

Though tied down and weak, my mother had been elastic the last time I saw her, cushioned within herself by fat, still young with a voice like jam. But the woman holding on to my father's arm was none of those things. She was bent crooked by the disproportionate amount of weight she carried from her torso upward. Her lips cracked at the corners, lined in a thin white film. The flesh of her face had receded, emphasizing the sharp bones underneath. But it was her hardened skin that shocked me the most. It wasn't white, or black, nor any of the vibrant hues I had seen her adopt over the years. It was the absence of color, bled to a dry, flaky shell. When she saw me, she reached out, said my name, and I walked into her wiry frame. Her grip was weak, her eyes glazed over, the very color of her blood had washed away.

"It's so good to see you again," she whispered.

"Welcome home." I breathed into her neck, inhaling the lingering scent of disinfectant.

"Did you cook?" She pulled back and smiled at me. The whites of her eyes were yellow and coppery.

I took her hand in mine, slowly leading her to the kitchen, where I had set the table with the holiday white linens and white porcelain dinnerware. I had added some of her secret spices to the chicken. Because I had prepared it in the slow cooker instead of the oven, the skin had retained its sickly white color so my father would have little room to protest. I'd also placed some sage and rosemary beneath her pillow.

"Your mother needs to rest," my father interjected, setting her bag down in the hallway and taking her hand to pull her in the opposite direction.

"Yes, I suppose I should lay down for a bit?" Her tone had a subtle uptick of reluctance, presenting her words as a question rather than a statement. She looked at my father for confirmation of her own state of mind. "I *am* exhausted?"

The sound of her hand slipping out of mine scraped like sandpaper. Wobbling to the end of the hallway, she kept one hand to her head, perhaps struggling to keep the contents inside. Each step was slow and judicious. Her body was a series of metal parts trying to outmaneuver the rust. When she reached her bedroom, she gripped the doorknob tightly before shutting herself inside.

My father and I ate dinner in silence.

28

MY MOTHER SLEPT THROUGH MOST OF THE DAYS
that followed, and I saw her only three times as a result. The
first time, I was at the piano. She emerged from the bedroom
completely naked, bent over with her hair loose and wild. "I
can't hear myself think with all that noise!" Dry coughs punctuated her words. "Not now, not now, not now." She shook her
head slowly and sucked air through her teeth and I recognized
in her fright how the sound of music must have burned her in
some invisible place.

"I'm sorry . . ." I shut the lid and rested my hands on the
cover. Her eyes remained screwed shut.

"It's okay, it's okay." Her lips were tight, her nostrils flared,
and her hands dismissed my apology as she disappeared back
into the bedroom.

The second time I saw her, she was examining my father's
selection of Christmas decorations around the house. She handled the makeshift nativity scene at the fireplace, examining
the outfits of the Virgin Mary, baby Jesus, and the three Wise
Men. She removed their clothes, rubbed the material between
her fingers, then put them back on the figurines. She lifted up
the snow globes, turning them in the light, this way and that,

perhaps hoping to catch some hidden flaw in the perfect snow, or the crystal-clear glass. She moved around the house like a ghost, appearing in one room, then in another, without ever appearing in the hallway that joined them.

When I lost track of her, I assumed she had gone back to bed. But as I rounded the corner of the narrow hallway that led to my bedroom, I saw that my door was cracked open. Using my right hand to slowly push through, I discovered my mother in the far-right corner with her back to me. Between my dressing table mirror and the bed, she held the college applications I had hidden there, kept in the old journal that I had once shared with Kraig. Flipping wide-eyed through the pages of the pamphlets, she looked at the maps, at the course offerings, at the smiling white faces staring back at her, and she didn't stop until I spoke.

"What are you doing?" The question seemed ridiculous.

She turned to face me with large eyes and an open mouth. "Just looking, I just saw this lying around . . ." She trailed off.

"No, you didn't." My response was flat, neither accusatory nor contrite. She put the applications back into the journal and closed it, laying it on my bed so that the cover with a sticker that said DO NOT ENTER stared back at her.

"I'm beat." She rubbed her neck and chuckled. "I think I'll head back to bed." Inching cautiously past me, her gaze cast downward, she muttered to herself over and over again about how she needed her rest. I moved my body sideways to give way before shutting the door behind me.

I opened the journal and let the applications slide out from between the drawings. Their faces, their hopeful testimonials about the campus, promises of a better life to come. Glossy secrets. Kneeling onto the carpet, my hands spread the brochures out on my bed into a semicircle. I pulled a black pen out of a dresser drawer and opened the first application—opening the page wide open so that my writing didn't bleed into the spine. The pen hovered over the fifth question that asked for my ethnicity—the distinct options listed before me, separated by line breaks and spaces and agency. I put the cap back on my pen and let it roll to the side. Then I turned back to my drawer to retrieve a red pen, letting my hand circle over the options several times before making my mark. The color of teenage compunction. A fervor shot through my blood, followed by guilt as thick as honey. It shaped itself into a rusty knife that plunged right through the heart. Betrayal was multidimensional.

Which the brochures had conveniently left out.

———

Dominique called me on the darkest day of the year. I realized it was her as soon as my father picked up the phone and his voice changed from a gentle inebriation to a hardened one. Standing anxiously next to him, I heard his questions, but was unable to hear her responses—though I imagined them to be quite clever. He shoved the phone into my chest, nearly poking me in the eye with the long metal antenna. "She's a real piece of work." I avoided his gaze while his heavy footsteps made their way back to the silver glow of the television.

"Hello?"

"Wow, he's a real piece of work."

I retreated into the hallway that led to my bedroom, taking care not to wander too far for fear of losing the call to static. My father's eyes followed me.

"Well, he just made it easier for me to say what's next." She paused, shifting her focus. "So, feeling the Christmas spirit?"

"Yeah, I guess." The words were unconvincing. She waited for me to say more about my mother, about her return, but it wasn't safe. Remaining silent, the distant echo of Christmas carols on the other end filled the empty space on the line.

"Is he still there?"

"Mm-hmm." A finger scratched at a nervous itch behind my ear.

"Ahhh . . . okay." She took a moment to recalibrate her words. "Well, what are you doing tonight?"

"Nothing, really."

"Well, do you *want* to be up to something, like, tonight?"

In the background I heard Niyala chide Dominique, and Dominique hiss back before they both went quiet. I silently wondered if I had been the subject of that brief exchange.

"Sorry, my family is driving me absolutely *insane*." She emphasized the last word, and I knew that she had said that more to Niyala than to me. Somewhere in the distance, I heard a bedroom door open and I guessed that my mother had woken up. I hadn't seen much of her since she discovered the applications in my bedroom.

"Oh wow, you're really gonna make this awkward for me?

Okay. A-a-ahem . . . To the esteemed household of Lady Gabrielle O'Hara . . . Gabs for short . . ." I widened my eyes at
the exaggerated British ponce, and laughed, releasing the tension in my shoulders. "You are cordially invited to the house
of Lady Dominique St. James of Kingston for winter solstice
dinner this evening, to engage with her nosy family, eat your
weight in fried plantains, and to jam on our respective instruments. I will be your chauffeur. I will pick you up, you can stay
the night, and I will drop you off again tomorrow."

She spoke as if I had never been to her house before, never
eaten at her dinner table, never played her piano.

"The challenge, should you choose to accept it: to prevent
me from dying of boredom." I laughed again at her mixed ref-
erences. I felt the color warm beneath my sweater, and the skin
darken slightly.

I hesitated. "I don't know . . ."

"Oh come on, after all that? You're making me work for it.
Look. It's a bunch of my mom's friends who converge on our
house every year. They're all academics, and it could be good for
you to meet them." She took a deep breath over the phone line.
"Look . . . I have a feeling that things are kind of intense there.
And I kind of feel bad for pushing those applications on you
before. Let me apologize with food. I'm no good with words."

I wasn't sure if I understood. Nobody had ever apologized
to me for anything—not with words, or food. I wasn't even
angry, though her tone made me think I should have been. But
even if I wanted to be—it was no use. I held my breath while

imagining the feast Niyala would prepare. When I exhaled, I was salivating.

"Well, it's not *me* you need to convince."

"Ah, the gatekeeper," she divined. "Hmm, I guess I didn't help the situation by sassing him before . . ." I nodded on the phone. "So I have to apologize twice in the same day? Yeesh, I thought this was the season for giving." I laughed, and I heard the soft muffle that her lips made against the receiver, curling up into what I hoped was a smile.

"Look, just hold on a minute," I said, putting the phone down. There was a very short list of ways to appeal to my father. I walked over to where he lay on the floor, propping himself up on a large pillow and holding his white plastic cup while he suckled on an ice cube.

"Dad . . . Dominique's mom invited me over for dinner tonight to meet some of her friends. They're doctors and they teach at UF and FSU. Maybe I should start networking early? Dominique can pick me up, but I'd have to spend the night." It wasn't a complete lie. Niyala was a doctor . . . of music theory. I assumed her friends were too, but even these minor embellishments made the lie sound infinitely more absurd. I never asked him for anything, because the answer was always no.

My father tossed the ice cube around in his mouth, a sound like fingernails on glass. "What does her mother do?"

"She's a doctor too." I held still, thinking that any minor twitch might give me away. He fancied himself an expert on deception, but his confidence was misplaced. My mother and I were the ones who pretended to be other people every day.

"Leave their number and address next to the phone." He turned the volume up on the television. He added something else, but I missed it over the screech of cop cars pulling someone over. I withdrew into the hallway, nearly tripping over my feet. My stomach twisted as I picked up the phone.

"Well?" Dominique nearly spat out. I relished her agitation, sighing deeply to dramatize the moment, and she went stiff on the other side of the line.

"So . . . what time are you picking me up?"

"What?" she blurted out. "He agreed?" Disbelief made her louder. "Cool. I'll pick you up in an hour. Don't forget your toothbrush!"

There was a brief silence before the line clicked, as if she had been waiting for me to respond to that specific command. But it was only me. In the distance, I heard a door close slowly, creaking shut like bones snapping back into alignment.

29

I TRIED TO HIDE MY SURPRISE AT THE RECEIPTS, food wrappers, and empty water bottles filling Dominique's car. It was as if a tropical storm had just blown through the driver's-side window and left through the other side. Kicking the detritus aside to make some space, I uncovered the book I had seen in her backpack the first time we met. I traced the cover broken by vulgar cracks, flipping through heavily underlined pages with illegible notes scribbled in the margins. There was a quote about tools and masters and houses that Dominique, or perhaps someone else, had circled repeatedly in aggressive pencil. She took it from my hands and tossed it in the back seat. It slid between the seats and I couldn't reach it once we began to swerve through the streets like a brewing wind.

Dominique was a genuine contradiction. She liked reggae and metal. She didn't want anyone's help, but she was a legal adult living at home with her mother, because she "couldn't imagine living in a house that didn't smell like fried plantains." She was a fanatic about seat belt safety, but she only ever had one hand on the steering wheel at any given time, even when honking at an old man who pulled out of his driveway without checking his rearview mirror—nearly running us off the road.

"You know that my mom is a doctor of music theory, right?" She propped her free elbow out the open window to balance her head, while I clutched my armrest and forced words out between narrow escapes from rear-end collisions.

"I know that. But he doesn't."

Dominique clucked her tongue in surprise.

"I'll have to loop Mom in, just in case he calls." I raised my eyebrows. Dominique's skin was darker in the daylight.

"What? I kinda *have to* have your back now, otherwise, I'm basically saying that you have to be honest all the time, and I'm not gonna do that. Sometimes, that shit is necessary—you know?"

I did know.

We pulled into her driveway and she yanked on the parking brake, before hopping out of the car, her long black pony-tail whipping behind her.

Two girls ran up to us, each one with conflicting accounts of who had acquired the higher double Dutch score. I recognized them from the day we had brought home the Christmas tree. "This one," Dominique said, pointing with her index finger directly above the head of the girl with the yellow shirt, "is Kamilah, and this one"—she moved her finger above the girl with the neon-blue shirt—"is Tanisha. They're the twins." At that introduction, they turned their attention from Dominique to me, and started asking a series of questions at breakneck speed, occasionally shoving each other when one interrupted before I could answer.

I lifted my bag high above their heads as we made our

way into the house, wading through a friendly flood of questions. Looking behind me, I saw that Dominique had run to the end of the driveway to check the mailbox, and as she removed several thick white envelopes, a skinny man in stained gray sweats approached her from across the street. He held his baggy pants up with a scarred hand, and I saw that his thin fingers were covered in dark scabs. His skin was also dark, but dipped in the sheen of hunger. I couldn't hear what they were saying, but I saw Dominique reach into her bag and give him some crumpled dollar bills that he squeezed in his hand before patting her on the arm and shuffling away.

It was the first time I had entered her house through the front door, instead of the one next to the garage. The rest of the house was different. The living room had a more intense style, crammed with artifacts, books, and collectibles that poked you from every direction if you shifted too much. This side of the house smelled of cinnamon and cloves; it was adorned with muted abstract paintings—with paint so thick and tactile that you could see the imprint of the individual brush hairs. But I was most captivated by the walls—covered from hip to ceiling with framed pictures. School portraits of children in bright matte colors; faded war conscription photographs in black and white; sepia-toned wedding portraits with large, crooked creases running through the middle, cutting plain, round faces into misaligned, discolored halves. Some were as dark as the inside of a tunnel, and others were as white as the light at the end of it. But there were others—people who didn't fit either binary. They were different shades of red, brown, yellow, and everything in between—some with blue eyes, others with brown, some with freckles, and some with scars, filling the white space on the wall like wood grain. On an old dresser with an oval mirror hanging above it sat a color photograph in a silver frame of a little girl with dark skin and black plaited hair, smiling up at the camera through large teeth and round cheeks while a skinny puppy nestled on her lap. It took me a moment to realize it was a photograph of Dominique and Foxy. Her face was softer in the photograph, more affectionate but just as precocious.

"You found me." She walked up beside me while I lifted the portrait in my hands. Even though our age difference was negligible, Dominique only came up to my shoulder. "I think I was seven or eight in that picture."

"Foxy looks so young." It was the only comment I could muster.

As if she had heard her own name, the dog entered from another room I hadn't seen before and hobbled from side to side, shifting weight and momentum from paw to paw. Dominique knelt down to meet her, reaching out to rub her softly behind one of her ears. Foxy began to pant, leaning into her hand to increase the pressure.

Dominique let out a series of shrill calls around the house, alerting everyone as to our arrival. They were returned with curt replies of acknowledgment from the kitchen, the living room, some dark room with blue light tucked away to the side.

Unlike her car, Dominique's room was organized with militant precision. On her walls were large vintage posters of people who stared back at us with flowers in their hair, or through horn-rimmed glasses. Books were strewn around her room, spilling out from a bookcase behind the door and onto the floor, the nightstand, and the dresser with her makeup brushes.

Dominique lit several black candles, which she said were meant to "absorb negative energy." I wondered if she meant me.

———

I tried to help Niyala in the kitchen, but I was intimidated by the spices stocked in the cupboard. I knew spices the same way I knew myself—by color, not by name. One shelf was dedicated solely to different types of chilies from remote corners of the earth, including whole Honduran peppers in a vacuum-sealed jar that she said had to be touched with latex gloves lest a skin rash was sure to follow. When I accidentally dumped a tablespoon of cayenne pepper into the stew instead of paprika, Niyala put me on door duty.

The guests came in an endless procession of outfits, faces, and side dishes wrapped in steaming aluminum foil. The plates piled onto a long dining room table that had appeared out of nowhere. Every time I closed the door, it seemed that the bell announced someone else. None of them looked or spoke like one another, with accents and names that quickly became jumbled in my head like words spoken in a language that I couldn't understand. I gave them wineglasses that I filled dutifully from a stockpile on the kitchen counter. By six o'clock, the small house was packed with inebriated people from Jamaica,

London, Brazil, Colombia, Nigeria, Germany, and Japan, who pointed at one another in disagreement before embracing in a fit of sloppy laughter. The air was thick with the hot breath of their arguments, a symphony of affectionate conversation.

Niyala navigated all her guests with ease, swerving her round hips with a seduction that synthesized conflict into mirth. Wherever she was, people wanted to be—and they found their way to her in the kitchen, breaking ice in the cooler in the garage, or stacking logs in the backyard for the campfire. She seemed to feed off the attention, growing more amiable with each interaction, evolving from the single mother of a grown woman into the beguiling adjunct professor who could defuse a heated argument about Serbia with the tip of a champagne bottle, or weigh in on the Australian Reparations Treaty while flipping salmon patties in a pan of sizzling coconut oil with one hand. If Dominique was blunt, her mother was even more so, and the severity of her comments were underscored by the jovial atmosphere she had created.

"I hear your father's a real bastard," she said to me while I rushed past the open kitchen door with an armload of coats to the guest bedroom. She checked the temperature on a turkey in the oven, its skin brown, curling, and pulling away from the charred bones.

"Mine was too." She winked at me, then went back to humoring a man from Lagos. He described himself as "a mediocre novelist who had become a drunken one when his book didn't sell."

Olabisi's polished demeanor unraveled quickly after his

second drink. His dark bald head began to sweat profusely as he stumbled through a rant that fell off his jagged tongue with drunken fanaticism. "If monogamy was so natural, then why do our fucking balls hang out of our bodies like chimps'? *Chimps!* They'd fuck a hole in the ground if it was warm enough!" His words were slow and thick.

"Well, if you didn't like the person you married, then why did you marry her?" Niyala chopped a cucumber and threw the pieces into a large salad bowl. He slumped against the pantry door, rattling the spices it contained.

"All I'm saying is . . . I am entitled to change my mind. Why should I have to suffer for the rest of my life because of a decision I made two years ago? You know what that's called, little queen?" He sauntered over, lowering himself to meet me at eye level, close enough to smell the red wine on his breath.

"Olabisi . . ." Niyala dropped the knife. He ignored the warning of the thin metal blade clinging against the countertop.

"That's called *prison*, and y'all wanna put a Black man in, *one way or another!*"

"*Will you shut the fuck up?*" Niyala whipped her head around. "Get out of my kitchen. Lena! Come get your husband out of my kitchen!"

A short woman in a stern pantsuit entered as if she knew exactly what the problem was and exactly who had caused it. She strode over to her husband, grabbed his hand, and pulled him through the door.

Several guests asked me about how I knew Dominique, and when I told them that I was her student, they made me promise to perform for them before the evening ended. I looked forward to it, if only to curb the excitement eating away inside me. A poet from London with a smooth scalp named Dembe wore a velvet jacket of turquoise-and-black paisley patterns, folding over his body like a cape. When he caught me staring at it, he took it off and handed it to me.

"Every great performer needs a great performer's jacket," he said. His voice was throaty and rich, finely aged like whiskey. The rest of the guests made remarks about how much better the coat looked on me, and Dembe nodded enthusiastically.

"How often do you get to style an up-and-coming virtu-oso?" he asked.

Nobody argued.

Niyala entered the living room with a tall man who had skin like warm embers. James had long black hair plaited into a single braid down his back and round, dark eyes that sat high upon his chiseled face, surveying the layout in front of him. He towered over Niyala, holding the roast pan in a pair of floral oven mitts while the turkey sizzled and spat. Everyone gathered around the table. Dominique sat to my left. Dembe sat across from me, squinting his eyes, rubbing his fingers on his chin thoughtfully, and then he mouthed the words, *Definitely better. Much better on you.* Niyala took her place at the head of the table, and the man situated himself in the empty chair to her right.

"James and I want to thank everyone for attending another winter solstice party in our home." James winked at her. "This time of year can be hard for many reasons, but with such good friends from all over the world"—she motioned toward each person at the table and finished with Dembe, who replied with a warm smile and moist eyes—"life is *full*." I glanced toward Dominique, but she kept her eyes fixed on her mother, the soft lighting painting the curls on her head.

Everyone else stared at Niyala with reverence and elastic smiles, as if it were a day that existed to celebrate her. Olabisi was the farthest away—slumped in his chair with half-open eyelids. The flickering candles cast a dark shadow on his face, and Lena sat by his side, glaring at him.

"As you may have noticed already, we have a new guest at the table this year—and that's a real blessing." Niyala locked eyes with me and I felt my cheeks heat up. "Gabrielle, child, I want you to know that you are welcome in my home anytime. The world needs more radical Black friendships." Everyone rapped their knuckles. I hesitated, but allowed myself to join in the gesture. Dominique scanned me briefly and a smile blossomed across my face.

"That's enough of that," she continued, wiping a tear from the corner of her dark eyes with a swift gesture. "You're all my family, and I love you. Thank you for coming to my home, eating my food, and for being such brilliant pains in my ass." Soft laughter rose from the table. A man from Rome filled my wineglass, then slipped it into my hand with a wink. "Raise your glasses." Chairs scraped against the floor and Foxy, who had been sleeping soundly next to the fireplace, jerked her head up at the commotion. She yawned and stretched out on her side. I held my glass high.

"Happy solstice, my loves." Our glasses were a chorus of wind chimes. Dominique and I toasted last, and when we all sat down again, I felt her hand reach under the tablecloth to grab mine, and squeeze.

30

THOUGHTS DISLODGED IN MY BRAIN, PLUCKED LOOSE until they slipped—untethered and liquid. After the first glass of wine, I began to smile at Lena, who had begun to fight with her husband in plain view of everyone else. After the second, I swear that Lena began to smile back at me. After the third, I began to laugh at Dembe's corny jokes. And after that, I accepted Juan's hand for a dance, allowing him to turn me around until the floor and the ceiling churned in an ethereal haze. The skin pulled away from my bones. I became fluid, disconnected from the fears that held me together like glue. I floated freely inside my body, above my body, above everybody, and I enjoyed a moment shaped by something other than hopelessness.

———

The wood burned red and orange beneath the black sky, licking through the air toward the stars. Dominique's arm wrapped around my waist beneath a blanket that smelled like singed hair. James held a small pine tree in his hand, casting the bottom four branches into the fire, causing the flames to roar and brighten. He lit a tight wad of dried sage leaves at the base of the fire and walked around us, blowing the smoke into our faces. Niyala and Dominique pulled wisps into their hair and onto their skin. Others positioned themselves around the fire, wineglasses in hand. The flames from the fire separated our faces while the smoke—and the wine—changed James's eyes from black to mirrors wreathed in red and gold that looked right through me.

I was engrossed in a different sensory plane, where I smelled, tasted, and felt things that I shouldn't have been able to—the affection between Dembe and Juan, the nostalgia in James's voice as he spoke, the flavor of the wine as it surged inside me. I pushed myself from the ground and stumbled toward the house. Dominique appeared at my side, and together we teetered on wobbly earth as we approached the sliding glass door.

"Keep going!" she shouted behind us.

I put my lips beneath the kitchen faucet and let cold water stream into my mouth.

"You're a cheap date." Dominique leaned against the kitchen sink with her arms crossed over her chest. I didn't feel drunk. I felt light. I couldn't tell if it was the wine, the feeling of Dominique sitting next to me, the stiff goose bumps on my skin that responded to her, or the smell of wine on her breath. A dark water stain bloomed on my sweater. It felt cool and welcome against my skin.

"I need to change."

Dominique's head pointed tenderly. There was a small part of me that knew when her head finished moving, it would face her bedroom, knew she would follow me when I stumbled into it, and this confidence grew with each assured step echoing behind mine.

I had thought a lot about the different ways to say no since that afternoon at Kraig's house. With screams. With tears. I said it with the trail of waste, and space-black skin, but I kept wondering if they might have listened to something else. I didn't say yes to Dominique, but when I took off my sweater and lifted my gaze, I passed into the color of rusty earth just as her fingers reached the curve of my shoulder.

It was abstract first. A pattern of words, sounds, and body parts. But it was the curved nose that pushed into my cheek when she put her mouth on mine, the warmth that pulled me from a deep winter hibernation into a room—into a moment— where spring was alive and well.

She slipped her hands in my pockets and pulled me closer, but the curve in my spine held me back. My eyes fluttered open as our lips moved, and I watched her without her knowing, which seemed to make the moment even more intimate. She moved her lips down to my neck, and I squeezed my eyes shut to squirm around in the dark.

I told myself to stand so I could keep my legs shut. I distracted myself with the objects in her room—a pair of dirty socks, the cracked spine of a book splayed on her dresser, a dark stain on the ceiling shaped like curling fingertips. I refused to speak. The success of the evening would hinge on guesswork, and we would walk away from each other awkwardly, feeling insecure and unfulfilled. I wouldn't have it any other way.

"Is this okay?" she whispered into my ear. I nodded, and

pulled back, finding the corner of her dresser and gripping it hard. My knees buckled as Dominique pulled me to the floor. I kept one hand attached to the dresser.

"What are you doing?" Her voice was husky. She tried pulling my hand down, but it wouldn't let go. I was anxious to quicken the process, to stay in control. I pursued the end. I cut her off with another kiss, and she laughed. Dominique sank her fingers through my hair and inhaled me, filling her lungs with the smell of wine and fire. I used one hand to explore her body, while the other explored the blemished wood grain, as my nails dug into its finish. It felt cheap. I searched the lines of her neck and collarbone with my nose and my mouth, but I kept imagining the moment we could say to each other, *Wasn't that amazing?* without knowing specifically what we were referring to.

"Hang on." Dominique reached for the hem of her dress and pulled it up over her head, then pulled my top over my head, catching on the wrist still connected to the dresser. My body was limp. She wrapped an arm around my bare waist. I could feel the slight protrusion in her stomach from dinner, a tiny bulge of joy. She blew on my belly and a litany of goose bumps replied. She marveled at the way they glowed bright and golden like fireflies. My senses were consumed with appetite and fear—the push and pull of desire.

I touched the pieces of her I could reach—a shoulder, an elbow. She maneuvered around my inexperienced fingers, placing them where she wanted. Fascinated with the folds of flesh around my stomach and arms, there were giggles when a new color dimpled my flesh in response to her own. "Amazing." Her voice was a whisper.

Dominique kissed gently. She squeezed gently. But such tenderness allowed for too much space in our choreography. And things crept in.

I watched myself from above—imagining being roused to orgasm in a slow montage by the magical stroke of a cock that I couldn't see. I called out silently for this convenient fiction. I summoned all the confidence I had seen in men on-screen who seemed to know exactly what they were doing, and in exactly the right way, driven to success solely by the confidence a penis affords.

"Does it feel good?" she asked, stroking the back of my neck with her hand. I tried to roll on top of Dominique, but she rolled me back.

We were interrupted by a laugh from the backyard, and I searched for the sound. Dominique grabbed me by my hips and pulled me closer, bringing me back into focus. The friction from the carpet underneath my back sent shocks of dark blue electricity down my spine. This was how I saw her in my mind when I was alone. Not someone drilling me to learn my scales. But someone who spread her legs wide on the piano. Someone whose body was top heavy with muscle that added an off-beat rhythm to her gait. Someone who walked into a room with the quiet assurance of belonging there, whether anyone else believed it or not. She didn't give a fuck. She'd carve out a place for herself wherever she went, and she'd pick and choose the people who came with her.

My hips were eager as she removed my jeans. She hovered for a moment with her fingers inserted at the edges of my underwear. I flinched, surprising us both. Her eyes softened with concern.

"Do you . . . want me to keep going?"

I licked my lips that felt both dry and wet.

But I was at a mechanical loss. I looked up at the ceiling, but there were no answers there. Only the dust piled thick on the blades of the ceiling fan. It was cruel, putting my body in that situation without its permission. I reasoned that as long as I didn't enjoy it, I was remaining loyal. She brought her face to mine, and kissed my cheeks, making her way to my ear.

Mine's the biggest . . . we all agreed . . .

I jerked. I blinked, and when I did, my skin was a different color every time. First black. Then red. Then metal.

I dropped my hand, turned away, and rolled to the side, passing into white—feeling numb and callous as I did. I lay like that for a while, staring at the crust of things gathered beneath her bed, holding all the sounds of a bleeding heart in my mouth. Dominique waited for me to roll back. She sat there, the sound of her fingernail scratching a patch of skin, and then shifted her body to lie behind me, rolling into my backside. She jumped at the initial chill of my skin, but remained undeterred. Snot dripped from my nose, and my eyes burned. She buried her nose between my shoulder and neck so that I could count the spaces between her breaths by how they warmed that small cave. Her arms wrapped around my waist, pulling herself into me, and we watched the things beneath her bed until we both fell asleep, when the heat from her body absorbed into mine.

I LEFT HER side to pee, and I returned to find her on the bed, engaged in some dreamy altercation with the blankets, a light blue sheen coating her dark, charcoal skin. A living, breathing, snoring version of some marble Romanesque work of art, framed by cheap pillows and expensive Indian hair weave, instead of gold. I crawled into bed beside her and into a calm sleep without nightmares, without dreams, without the stuttered waking and drifting of insomnia—nothing but heat and darkness.

————

The clock next to her bed read 12:10 when I woke up and, as if on cue, a clamor came from the kitchen. I thought I was dreaming until I heard Niyala's stern voice, but Foxy's barking made me sit up.

"You're going to have to wait, Mr. O'Hara. I'll let her know you're here."

I threw the blanket aside and jumped out of bed, with Dominique reaching idly for the warm empty space I had left behind. My legs were loose, and I felt as if I were sinking into the carpet, while my joints popped uncomfortably in and out of place.

So, that's what alcohol does, I thought—understanding my father a little bit better.

I cracked open the bedroom door and saw him standing

uncomfortably among so much color while Niyala stared him down, backing away slowly to keep her eyes on him while he approached. Only the evening before, she had been the amenable host, but in that moment she was someone who had been up all night waiting—hoping—for a fight. Christmas isn't complete without at least one. My father saw the sliver of light through the cracked door and narrowed his eyes.

"You were supposed to be home already." His voice was filled with venom.

"It's only 12:10."

"Only 12:10?" His voice was flat, and it trailed off.

Niyala's face was as rigid as her posture approaching Dominique's bedroom door, but it softened with sympathy when she saw me. Her height could not compare to his, but she wielded her words with the confidence of someone twelve inches taller—just like her daughter.

"Well, it was fun while it lasted, hey?" she whispered, before closing the door and standing guard outside.

"I told you before you left—be back by twelve." His voice was low and measured on the other side of the door. I responded to his lie with one of my own.

"I . . . I didn't hear you," I shouted while scrambling. I imagined a shadow passing over his face.

I should've seen that moment coming. I tried to pull my sweater on, but the wine sank heavily in my limbs, defiant and stiff. Dominique sat up on her bed, rubbing sleep from her eyes—watching me curiously.

I just wanted it to be over, desperate to turn the humiliation of the moment into an instant memory so that Dominique and I could laugh and say, *Remember that time my father nearly gave me a heart attack the morning after I was too scared to fuck you because I was sexually assaulted by a group of boys who are all now presumably suffering from some sort of deafness? Wasn't that* hilarious?

I fished for my shoe under the bed, but couldn't grip it. When I gave up, she was pacing in front of the bed with her arms angled like chicken wings, arching her back to round out her stomach, her cheeks puffed out. She circled around on the carpet, jutting her head in and out, mocking everything my father said on the other side of the door.

"It's time to go."

Dominique narrowed her eyes, shook her finger, and mumbled a string of incoherent noises that sounded like ground glass.

She ducked down then scooped herself back up, tilted her head, and opened her mouth to begin pantomiming, swallowing at air and clucking around. She turned her head to the poster of Nina Simone and shook her finger vigorously. I felt a chuckle kick at the back of my throat. I knew that monsters, whether they're hiding in the closet or in the structure of your DNA, must never be laughed at. When monsters become funny, they become small and frightened.

I opened the door and walked out wearing only one shoe, nearly choking on the laughter. My father's gaze burned into me like hot coals.

That's when I decided that I would try again—for her.

31

I CLUNG ON TO MY MOST VISCERAL MEMORIES FROM the party as we drove home. Dominique's dress, the way she looked at me as I guzzled water from her kitchen tap. The fire's smoke forming a halo around her hair. The way her back arched before pressing her chest into mine. By the time we arrived home, fevered hallucinations circled through my head. Come Christmas Eve, the best parts of the night had become a script of all the things I had done wrong. The awkward fit of my underwear. Biting her lip too hard. Being too clumsy with my tongue. Drooling too much on her ear. I wanted to shed my skin and evaporate.

I woke up on Christmas morning in a mild depression, staring at the ceiling until my father thundered through the house to announce that Christmas had officially begun. As I uncurled myself from the bed, I pictured our neighbors sitting patiently at their trees, balancing unopened presents in their hands, waiting for my father to initiate their Christmas mornings as well. After joining my parents in the living room, I was as amenable to the Christmas spirit as I was to the barren white walls of the house itself.

I began to play something at the piano that I hoped my

mother would like. In the past, she had enjoyed singing Christmas carols, which she used to perform with the local operatic choir in churches around town. About halfway through my first one, I caught the sound of heavy breathing and turned around to see her weeping. Her head was bent forward, and the vertebrae in her spine rippled through her paper-thin skin. I rushed over to kneel at her feet and took her hands in mine. The blinking white lights of the white plastic Christmas tree glowed behind us.

"What's wrong, Mom?" A useless question. The mismatched festive items around the room seemed to mock my efforts to connect with her.

"Nothing, it's nothing." She shook her head and took in large, vocal gulps of air. My father leaned away from us both at the end of the sofa. He was invested in the idea of a festive performance, happy to treat the events of the last few months as if a distant memory, behaving like a man blessed with little memory while my mother and I were cursed with too much. My hands passed to a warm cerulean blue that I used to rub hers, but the rest of me was a hard cold white.

"Let's start with the presents." My father pulled me toward the tree by my arm. My eyes stayed on my mother, who began rocking back and forth with her eyes closed and arms crossed.

"This one's for you, Tallulah." My father passed her a small golden box tied with red ribbon.

"What is it?" she said slowly, rolling her eyes up to meet my father's.

"Why don't you *open* it, and find out?" Irritation bit through his vowels.

She lifted the lid off the tiny box, revealing a pair of diamond earrings in a white-gold inlay, as beautiful as they were bland. She examined the jewels beneath the light, two tiny rainbows dancing across her face.

My father reclined on the floor with his stomach heaving beneath his thin white shirt. "My turn now," he said with a self-satisfied smile. I handed him a box wrapped in snowmen and reindeer.

"A rifle bag." I broke out in a sweat at the sound of his flat tone.

"It's waterproof." I spoke quickly, trying to defend my choice. "Suitable for hunting anytime of the year. Randy said it was one of the best." Randy had also taken nearly an hour to explain the selection to me.

My father turned the box over in his hand, examining the writing on the back, then tossed it to his side. "I guess you're next then." His movements were labored as he reached under the tree, but something hit him in the face and fell into his drink with a splash.

"You son of a bitch." The words slithered out of my mother as he retrieved an earring from his cup.

"These are *fake*!" She threw the other one, but it landed somewhere in the thicket of the Christmas tree, which rustled with the new offering. Displaying hidden reserves of strength, she stood and grabbed plastic pieces of white tree, silver tinsel, and ornaments to hurl at her husband. My father tried to shield himself. The trinkets bounced off his ashen forearms.

"They're fake! They're *FAKE*!" she shouted as if she were

trying to convince him, as if she were trying to convince us all. After she ran out of ornaments, my mother grabbed a snow globe with Puritans and Indians and held it high above her head with a shaking hand.

"What have I done to deserve such an animal? I've given up everything for you, and you put me in that awful place! You don't want me to live, but you couldn't even let me die."

"Tallulah." My father held up his finger and pointed it toward the patch of skin between her eyebrows. Nowhere else, only that spot. She stopped to consider the warning.

"Throw it and see what happens."

My father's voice cut her open. Even in a manic state, one word could pull us out and remind us that there were worse things to fear than cuts and bruises. And it was enough to restore a calm and terrible balance.

"Mom—" It felt strange to call her that. I walked around the sofa and reached for her shoulder with a shaking hand. "Put it down, please." My fingers wrapped around bone. Her hand slowly fell, unsure of what to do with the anger she had summoned so quickly. The snow globe's iridescent confetti caught the light from above and held it softly. My mother turned and smacked me hard against the cheek with the back of her hand. The slap pushed through me, spreading across the right side of my body.

"You just—just—" I pressed my hand into my cheek, waiting for her to finish.

"You and your stupid tapes."

A fat welt began to blossom over my cheekbone as I took

in her distorted face—stripped of both color and affection, reduced to little more than a frame of bones. I weighed the possible responses, but couldn't decide whether to cry or scream, too shocked to make either convincing.

All I could do was laugh.

F Major

(What the angels tell me)

32

I WOKE UP ON NEW YEAR'S EVE WITH MULBERRY skin, and slithered around inside it indulgently, the way it felt like wet earth and dreaming all at once. My father was working. My mother was praying, alone in her bedroom, only faint murmurs slipping beneath the closed door in the twisted language that she believed brought her closer to God. She stayed like that all day, and all night, and the murmurs became louder and louder, until they became echoes heard and felt in my bedroom.

I closed myself off in my father's study and called Dominique.

"About time."

"I was hoping you'd . . ." I let my sentence trail off, knowing that she'd finish it for me.

"Nope! I've been waiting for *you*. It's already perfectly clear what *I* want."

I nodded on the phone, and the mulberry turned to wine. I had convinced myself that my embarrassing exit had changed things, that attraction was a fleeting concept that hinged upon doing everything right.

"I was thinking . . ."

The faint muffle on the other end of the line told me she was smiling.

"I have an idea," I finished. And this time I smiled back.

When I was a little girl, I loved watching the fireworks. My mother and I would drive down to the Everglades and run between the mangrove trees covered in Spanish moss, beneath the lights exploding in the sky. She would pass her skin to match the glittering displays, and I passed mine to look like hers. And we ran, and ran, and ran, chasing each other and laughing, like two firecrackers on earth that would burn forever.

I caught the number six bus downtown, passing all the cars in long lines that snaked up and down the interstate. Dominique picked me up at the bus stop. As she drove us to Lake Eola, the glow of the sparklers on passing streets lit up her face. The lakeside was filled with pickup trucks and SUVs, people in thick downy jackets stretched out on their hoods with picnic baskets and bottles of champagne by their sides. Others looked on from hotel balconies, in plastic tiaras. We edged away from the most congested area, into a side street lined with tourism offices and novelty shops, parking next to a cluster of buildings with long thin windows like awestruck faces—and we sat, waiting. An orchestra came on over the radio, but Dominique quickly switched it off.

"You don't listen to Mahler's Third on the radio. That's something that should only be experienced in person." This thought lingered. I hoped we could hear it together one day. I was already eager to get her analysis on everything the conductor had done wrong.

We sat in silence, our hands in our laps like embarrassed children. I tried to figure out what to say. Finally, I pulled up my leg and twisted toward her, forcing myself to find her face in the dark. Someone waved a sparkler outside and the reflection from its flicker illuminated the bruise on my cheek. She leaned in and twisted my chin to get a better look, pulling herself close enough for me to smell the mint she had licked down.

"Jesus, Gabs! When did this happen? Did he do that to you?"

Her fingertips began to shake in anger, and my first instinct was to calm her down. I took her hand from my face and held it between my hands, passing them into the color of warm tree sap.

"No," I replied. "*He* didn't."

Her eyes widened, and I flinched at her pained expression. She dropped back against her seat and ran her free hand through the long thick twists that hung down her back. She compressed her nose and her mouth as if reacting to an awful smell.

"I don't understand." She stared off through the window. We were both quiet, looking at a couple walking with their arms wrapped around each other. They laughed together, stumbling over the pavement so they could lean into each other even more. "How can you still go home every day?" She tilted her head to look at me. "Aren't you angry?"

But I wasn't. I would have liked to be. My anger was easy to lock up somewhere and throw into a dark place like old moving boxes that I couldn't be bothered to unpack. It was always choked out by the anger of my father or my mother, far more robust, far more dominating, leaving only space for exhaustion.

"No, I'm not."

Dominique removed her hand from my grip and it joined the other hand in her hair, confusion distorting her beautiful face. "I could never forgive someone for that."

I possessed an inherent distaste for the concept. Forgiveness walked on the backs of memories until they turned into amnesia. Only then did forgiveness seem possible, and I didn't think it was real otherwise.

I shook my head.

"You have to leave."

I held my breath for a few moments, followed by the most inconspicuous nod. I knew she was right. I reached into my bag and pulled out a stack of envelopes.

"I can't send these." I averted my eyes to the armrest between us, obscuring my bruise in shadow. "I mean, I can't get to the post office without explaining why."

Dominique placed a hand on top of mine and pulled the applications toward her. I sat back up in my seat and stared ahead, rubbing my thumbs over each other.

"I still need letters of recommendation for them."

"I'll take care of it," she replied instinctively, dismissively. Her resolve felt soothing, necessary.

Dominique put them in the back seat and reached for my hands again. Our palms warmed each other just as the first fireworks began to explode, filling the sky with smoke. She leaned in close and my lips found the satin curve of her cheek.

Her hands released mine and found my neck, then my arms, then my waist, and I allowed her to lift me out of my seat and into her lap, my feet draped over the passenger seat. I kissed her, trying to get that one thing right. I took my time memorizing the details of her face with my mouth, trying to understand it—how something could be so open.

Her cold hands thawed against the lower part of my back, letting me take my time, knowing that it was important for me to move slow. Nothing would happen unless I wanted it to. The car groaned as we moved, and the fireworks intensified, lighting up our limbs in red, orange, violet, green, blue, gold, and white—a reel of color that flickered and faded over and over again. I took off my sweater, and let her take off hers. I pressed myself into her, and allowed the curved parts of me to fill in the flattened parts of her, where soft flesh met hard, and the courage to try again became redemptive.

——

Dominique only had two rules after we started sleeping together. The first was that I start calling her Dom, which I almost couldn't believe I hadn't done before. The second was that our lessons continue unchanged. Mailing my applications renewed her plan to get me away from home. She tightened time frames for mastering new pieces of music and began to randomly drill me on scales, their progressions, their diminished variations, their major sevenths.

Niyala never asked us about our longer lessons, but she began leaving out an extra plate for dinner. She became invested in my schooling as well and started quizzing me on composition structures at the kitchen table. Dinners were mostly spent watching them argue back and forth about politics, religion, and art. Their opinions were comparable, but Niyala delighted in the heated discourse, provoking Dom to respond—whether it was prison privatization or the appropriation of reggae music. The more impassioned the debate, the more their American accents undressed to reveal the Caribbean lurking just beneath. They raised their voices like they were trying to raise the dead. But at the end of every debate and their half-eaten plates of food, someone cleaned the dishes, someone else packaged the leftovers, and both left the kitchen with the conviction that comes from knowing that you are fiercely, undeniably loved.

Being home and watching my parents aggressively scrape their plates with knives and forks became more difficult. It was the way they fought with everything around them. It was how the air rushed out from beneath their bodies when they collapsed onto different pieces of furniture. It was a monophonic melody of violence.

"DINNER'S READY." MY mother was passing by when I walked through the front door. I placed my bag down on the floor, heavy with new books.

"I'm not really hungry." I pulled a dark red apple out of my bag, pinched from Niyala's fruit bowl. I rinsed it off in the sink, and for a moment considered the strangeness of the apple's color against the smooth white porcelain. My mother had stopped scooping mashed potatoes into a serving bowl and watched with wide eyes as I bit into the skin, spitting a mushy part out into the trash can. Mash fell off the spoon in a steaming heap, and I walked out of the kitchen to practice Chopin's second scherzo, writing notations beneath the Italian dynamics while I held on to the apple with my teeth. Fully immersed in the first key change, I didn't even hear my mother approach. I felt the apple yanked out of my mouth, only a small chunk left on my tongue.

The apple shook in her hand as her eyes moved between the piano and me, both shirking in her shadow. Wet and sticky fascination coated my face.

"Dinner is ready," she said with more breath than words. I slowly stood to follow her. But she continued past the kitchen, through the sliding glass door and into the backyard, throwing the half-eaten apple over the wooden fence. Our neighbor's dogs enthusiastically finished it off just as my father walked in through the garage door.

I passed my color, as instinctive as blinking, before he rounded the corner to see us. My mother remained the same shade of peeling snakeskin. She took his coat and briefcase, and I presented him with his white plastic cup.

When she passed around the mashed potatoes, I handed them to my father without taking a serving, and my parents looked at me as if they had caught the fresh scent of dog shit. After serving himself, he placed the bowl back in front of me. The glass of the tabletop rattled. He picked up the serving spoon and added heap after heap after heap of potato to my plate.

"I'm not hungry." I felt my stomach falling away from my body. I pushed the plate away very gently, declining a second time. Quiet fury turned my father's face blue.

"Eat your food!"

I took my time picking up my fork. I sank it deep into the potatoes bringing a serving to my mouth that was almost too big to fit. I chewed even while the melted butter in the food burned the flesh on the inside of my cheeks, and I chewed while staring at my father with some level of bemusement, relishing in the discomfort of this familiar dance.

I shoveled the rest of my food in the garbage can when he went to drink in his study, passing back into the color of tree bark. My mother studied me with an expression that seemed to question how I had walked into her house, sat at her dinner table, eaten her food—come from her body.

33

WHEN DOM AND I WEREN'T TOGETHER, MY MIND would race with questions. And my mother's trips to the grocery store became opportunities for me to browse teen magazines for answers. I was drawn to their cover stories about decoding the elusive behavior of inattentive boys, and I tried to apply this checkout-line logic to Dom. I was determined to overanalyze "our relationship" to death. Everything about her became some codified message that I had to interpret, too afraid to take her at her word. Dom and I didn't discuss our future in any certain terms, so I inferred its parameters by other means. I inferred that she kept me inundated with assignments so that I wouldn't have the time to pursue dating others. I inferred that her love for me meant pushing me to apply to music schools so that she could rescue me from that house and its people. I inferred that the grease that splattered me when she fried plantains in the kitchen was meant to brand me as her property. I was excited to assign meaning to these mundane things.

I began to notice the way that men stared at Dom—the way the clerk at the music store gave her an employee discount even though she had never worked there. I saw the way that women looked at her too—all kinds of women. Women with shaved heads, women in wheelchairs, even some women with husbands and children in tow. Each admirer sparked an unfamiliar response which threw my thinking into malignant hues. I wasn't sure if what I saw was real or just the slanted perspective of someone falling in love for the first time.

One afternoon, with a baby drinking from her breast, a woman with long blond hair reached for a music book at the same time as Dom—so that they had no choice but to acknowledge each other. While they spoke, I went quiet and cold, disappearing to the other side of the music store to pretend I had an interest in bassoons.

"What's the matter with you?" she spat out as we approached the car. "You were acting like that lady is my girlfriend."

"She seemed into the idea," I mumbled, counting palm trees through the window.

"Don't be silly. I'm not really into white women—except you." She pushed me gently from the driver's seat, and the combined effects of her words with this gesture acted as a soothing balm over my insecurities—for a little while.

We went to her bedroom when we got back to her place. Niyala wasn't home. We listened to cassettes, and she drew on me with a selection of artisanal pens I had given her—remnants from my infatuation with Kraig. Their tiny nibs carved intricate jazz compositions onto my skin. She tapped her free hand while she drew, writing music in real time, using my skin as the most convenient canvas.

I was lying on my back on the top of her bed with my arm

extended outward, and she lay on her belly, propped up on her elbows. I caught sight of the fake ring on her nightstand. It had never occurred to me that she would continue to wear it, and yet the sight of it made me think of all the men it was meant to fend off.

"Go on."

"What?"

She stopped drawing and tilted her head to look over at me.

"Say what you wanna say. You've been moody all day."

I reached out toward the nightstand and brushed the ring with my pinkie finger, barely turning it so that the fake diamond glinted at me.

"You still wear that?"

She seemed surprised, as if she had only just noticed it was there. Her eyebrows sat up, a bemused expression that bordered on sympathy.

"Really, Gabs? You're jealous of all the middle-aged dads I can't stand?" She bit back a laugh. "I mean, until they come up with a more effective repellent, this is the best I can do."

"Never mind." I pulled my arm away and sat up on the bed. I was positioned in a pool of sunlight pouring in through the window and allowed my skin to pass to a similar hue. Looking through the barred glass, I saw the old man with the bad foot limping down the street. Dom sighed and hung her head, then she rolled over to me and slapped me on the back as she sat up, drinking in the sunshine alongside me.

"I'm sorry. I can't help myself," she whispered in my ear.

"I just . . ." I sighed and began looking for the words to

describe a problem that didn't require further articulation. I knew that my jealousy was ridiculous, just as I knew that if a fake ring was real enough to ward off aggressive fathers, it was real enough to inspire envy.

She fluttered her lips. I leaned my head against her muscular shoulder, and she reciprocated by resting her head on top of mine.

"That color makes you warmer."

She wrapped her arm through mine and I marveled at the smooth reflective quality of her dark skin. Lifting my hand and rolling the ring in her fingertips, she slowly pushed it onto mine. Her fingers were shorter and thicker than mine, calloused by the drumsticks she beat in her hands until they chipped and splintered. She often joked that others could tell that I was the pianist and she was the drummer simply by looking at our hands.

Bringing my hand close to her lips, she began to gently blow on my skin to set the ink—disarming me with affection.

"Okay, but I still need their money. And if I end up kneeing some bastard in the balls because the ring disappeared, and he stops paying me to teach his kid, it'll be your fault."

The thought made me smile even more than I was already. "Is that a promise . . . ?"

She threw a pillow at me and grabbed her car keys.

———

My mother spent more time in the living room when I sat down to practice, not speaking or singing the way she used to—just observing. Watching, as I carried joy with me from one page of music to the next.

I was playing one of the more difficult Polish dances. A chill broke through the skin of my arms as I reached its sentimental end, turning them light blue. I dropped my shoulders as the rest of my skin passed into a variety of colors, analogous and tertiary pinks and blues across my face, arms, and legs. As I released my foot from the damper pedal, repetitive clapping interrupted my bliss. I turned to see my mother on the sofa, repeatedly slapping herself in the thigh. I ran to her, nearly turning the bench over.

"What are you doing?" I cried out. "Stop!"

I tried to take her hands into mine, but she withdrew them and proceeded to pinch, poke, and prod herself. She balled her hands up into bony little fists and began driving them into her legs.

"Why won't it change again?"

The hair around her face was stiff and matted against her head.

"Why can't I pass anymore?"

Tears pricked at my eyes. My mother continued to beat herself, and I didn't try to stop her.

I WOKE UP that night staring at my closed bedroom door, catching the faint sound of a single note being pressed down on the piano, over and over again. C-sharp. I slipped through my bedroom door in my white woolen socks and walked as lightly as I could down the narrow hallway, peering around the corner to see my mother standing still at the piano in her nightgown. The outside light illuminated her body through the thin material, as slight as a crescent moon. Her right hand pushing down on the note over and over again. I went back to my bedroom, locking the door behind me.

———

My father skipped breakfast and left for work early. As soon as the garage door closed behind his car, my mother focused on me from across the kitchen table with a determination in her eyes that I hadn't seen for months.

"Do you love it more than you love me?"

Chewing a mouthful of oatmeal, I suddenly bit down on my tongue, wincing. Her expression was earnest, desperate.

"What?"

She cleared her throat and asked again, this time squaring her shoulders, the posture of someone ready to witness.

"Do you love that instrument more than you love me?"

I considered how best to comfort her. Reverend Jeremiah knocked people onto the ground with a flip of his suit jacket. They tumbled to the floor in trembling fits, claiming that the power of the Holy Ghost had compelled them, rather than the scent of expensive Italian silk. I wished I could give her that kind of peace.

"No, I don't."

Her face softened with relief as she attended to her untouched food, releasing a sharp breath.

"Do you love her more than you love me?"

I froze. Her expression was hopeful. She knew me like the trees know the leaves on their branches—all my colors, all my seasons. And no longer being able to pass, she retained her other senses—smell, touch, and most of all—sight. I had been smiling more, sleeping better, losing weight as the Savannah hollies shook off the sleepy cirrus of winter.

"Who?"

Her face fell, and whatever devices that held her together before buckled. She collected the dishes from the table to wash in the sink. She had seen through me straight to the place where the truth sat and waved from its comfortable perch.

34

SHE WAS HOLDING UP A LETTER WHEN I CAME HOME from Dom's house, twisting it in the sunshine, examining the envelope's shape as she turned it in the light. It was four in the afternoon, but she was still in her nightgown, now practically worn through at the armpits so that you could see the flicker of curly black hair on the other side. She didn't hear me enter, and didn't respond when I kicked off my shoes, or put my key on the kitchen counter. She faced the sliding glass door, tracing the addresses with her fingers.

"What are you doing?"

Her fingers stopped, and the knot in the front of her throat bobbed as she swallowed. Her arms dropped and she turned toward me, the letter in both hands.

"It's for you." She extended her hand slightly so that I had to get close to her body to retrieve the envelope. The return address said *Hochschule für Musik Hanns Eisler*, and I felt a sharp pain in my chest that nearly caused me to fall over.

I wanted to speak, but the words wedged in my throat. My fingers worked the edges of the envelope nervously, my sweat eating through the paper. My mother didn't often check the mail. She only removed it from the mailbox and placed it on the kitchen counter until my father came home to sort it into junk for her, and bills for him. But I had never received mail of my own, and I imagine it was strange for her to see someone else acknowledge my name, my address, my very existence in print—no longer a secret kept from the world. I wanted to explain, even though nothing would put her mind at ease.

She already knew.

Under an embossed letterhead was an invitation from the admissions board asking me to audition in front of a panel of delegates at the local university concert hall in one month. I was to confirm by calling the university directly and, in what felt like a final mocking note that also offered a rare glimmer of hope, the university's chancellor wished me luck in one of the most competitive audition processes known to man. I read and reread the letter a hundred times. Its awkward English phrasing and the formal tone told me that it had been translated. I spilled a single drop of water on the chancellor's signature just to watch the ink run and ensure that it was indeed handwritten.

When I showed Dom the letter later that day, she was slow and methodical, holding it in front of her face with both hands. She read the letter through just once, discerning both its implied and explicit meanings.

"Well," she said in an unaffected voice. "Now the real work begins."

I balanced my elbows on the piano's hood, hoping for a more revealing analysis, but details didn't matter to Dom unless they said something new.

"You need to prepare a baroque piece, a classical piece, and a romantic piece. We will have to scrub out the pencil markings, because you'll need to present the original sheet music." She sucked on her bottom lip.

"And we need to make sure that you memorize every piece down to the last presto." She stopped short with a sudden intake of air, sizing me up. "You need a black outfit too, a dress. These people tend to be conservative." She gestured toward the tight kinky curls on my head, already thick with humidity. "And we have to pull your hair away from your face somehow."

Presumably so that the panel can see how much I suffer for my art, I thought.

"It's a process of elimination, Gabs." Dom rubbed anxiously at the part of her throat where my lips lived after every lesson. "They're not looking for who they should accept. They're looking for people they can reject. We have to show them that you're better than everyone else. Ten times better than everyone else! That way they have to let you in."

"But . . ."

Dom paused, waiting for me to finish interrupting her master plan.

"What's the point? What's the point of being ten times better than people who are ten times worse than me?"

She clucked her tongue against her teeth. That was her reply, and it was the only one she could give to a question without an acceptable answer.

——

Several days went by, and I waited for my mother to ask me about the letter, for her to wake up at a reasonable hour, to get dressed in a clean outfit, to become lucid, and walk into my bedroom to demand an explanation.

But it never happened.

I received responses from my pre-med university applications. Orlando, Tallahassee, Gainesville, and Miami were all enthusiastic to welcome me, and followed up with information about the cleanliness of their labs, the quality of their cadavers, which were ethically procured from people who had donated their bodies to science, rather than criminals on death row who had been electrocuted in Bradford County. My father was thrilled, but he had already decided on his alma mater in Gainesville. He wanted me to go farther in life than he had, but not so far that he couldn't reach out with one hand and pull me back into the hell he had built for us.

I received two more responses about my music applications, which were left on the kitchen table examined, but unopened.

They were both rejections with the specifics of their decision laid out, commenting on my "tremendous talent" while highlighting the competitive nature of the application process, encouraging me to apply again in a year or two.

"Or never," I told Dom over the phone, my voice crumbling into the phone.

"Fuck 'em," she said. "You only need one, and half of the people on the admissions panels are just bitter teachers who never had a career in music."

Dom also received a rejection letter from Berlin, but mentioned it only in passing, as if she had expected it.

"I'm sure they didn't make it past line five of my application," she scoffed over the phone before adding, "Have you heard from Berklee yet?"

"Not yet." I hesitated, holding in my breath. "What about you?"

"Nope. Nothing yet."

I exhaled and reread the particularly French repudiation from the Conservatoire de Paris, which listed all the unacceptable qualities of my application and audition cassette in caustic English.

35

"WHERE ARE YOU GOING?"

My mother woke before dawn to make breakfast, which sat in the kitchen until the ceremonial hum of daybreak forced us out of our beds. The rest of the day she slept, and in the evenings, her presence became a ghostly backdrop. Her skin undulated in and out of beige tones like a flickering light bulb, but never passed—and never glowed. My father insisted she was only pretending to be feeble for attention. I helped her anyway, feeding her at dinner, watching the food fall out of her mouth in chunks that I wiped away with a napkin. I shut the blinds as she slept throughout the afternoon. I closed the curtains around the house so the shadows could keep her company. I knew her mind in a way that he never could, because he only saw what came out of it—and I had inherited its jagged design.

"Dom invited all of her students over for dinner, to celebrate the summer break." My lie was well-rehearsed.

The weather couldn't decide if it wanted to be cold or hot, so it vacillated between the two as a frantic pendulum confused by daylight savings. By lunchtime, I discarded the sweater I needed at eight in the morning, baring the shoulders that burned by four in the afternoon. My mother sat at the kitchen table fanning herself. She hadn't left the space since the evening before; insomnia coated her eyes. My father was passed out on the living room floor, with his empty white plastic cup tipped over onto the carpet.

I wore a white sundress—the only white dress I owned, made of cotton and decorated with pearl buttons up the back that itched in the humidity that touches all corners of the peninsula. My hands shook while searching my body for flaws in the mirror—stains, loose threads, rogue drops of sweat.

"I'll only be gone a few hours."

My mother nodded. I brought a glass of water over to the table, then kissed her forehead. Her hand shook as it took hold of the glass, and I walked out of the kitchen slowly, just in case she wanted to say something else before I left.

———

Dom's expression was critical when she opened the door, reaching for the tangled halo of hair on top of my head, which had exploded in the humidity.

"I think we gotta do something about that hair before—"

I stopped in the doorway and waited for her to continue.

She smirked and let me inside.

"Before?"

"Dinner." The word was clumsy. She kissed the suspicion wrinkling my forehead with a loud smack that filled my cheeks with blood. "Come on." She took my hand and we went into her bedroom, where she made me sit on the floor while positioning herself on the edge of the bed behind me, between her spread legs. I wrapped my hands around her ankles and stroked the bony protrusions with my thumbs. Next to her were tubs of oils and creams, a spray bottle, and a comb with enormous, sharp teeth.

"Tilt your head back." She surveyed the dimensions of swirling curls across my scalp. She smoothed my edges to gather them in the back before spraying water everywhere and coating me with a thick pomade that smelled like coconut. I braced myself for the yanking, the pulling, the grunting, the familiar puffs of broken curls to float down around my body like ashes. But it never happened. In the mirror, I watched Dom work with a clip in her mouth as she contorted her hands and burrowed her knuckles deep so that everything above the wrists vanished in a cloud of hair.

After dividing my hair up into sections, she began to manipulate the coils in a way that sent shivers of relaxation down my spine. My toes glowed orange like a soft fire and she watched me rub them over one another. Flashing only the faintest hint of a smile, she slowed her pace, and I found that when my hair wasn't being burnt with a hot comb it could be loved instead. I rolled a braid in my fingertips. She stopped working the second section halfway through and peered down at me.

"Hasn't anyone ever braided your hair before?"

I thought about my mother's hot oil treatments and home-made shea butter mixtures that smelled like decaying leaves. The way she retrieved a half-rusted hot comb from her bedside drawer, heavily caked in residue, the way it hissed and crackled when it hit my scalp, melting hair and flesh until it turned oily, black tufts into fine strands of silk that reflected beneath the kitchen lights—when she said I looked like a "real Indian."

I closed my eyes and leaned back, shaking my head.

My mother liked to reference our indigeneity when she did my hair, but only in regards to making it as straight as possible. That's all it was to her in the end: a silhouette of a story of a memory of a family I never knew, so forgotten and shadowed that the only thing we remember about them is their hair.

Dom smoothed down my edges with a toothbrush when she was finished. She stroked that tender spot with her fingers until I opened my eyes and caught hers peering back at me in the mirror—eyes as full as ticks.

We heard a knock at the door, and Niyala cracked it when nobody protested. "Okay you two, time to eat." She turned to leave, but not before I caught the grin on her face—familiar because I had seen it on Dominique so many times before.

I STOPPED SHORT when I saw the large cake on the kitchen table, decorated and shaped like the black and white keys of a piano. Balloons hovered near the ceiling in a rainbow of colors with silver ribbon that I instinctively swatted away before I had a chance to absorb the moment. Niyala ran up to me, pulling me into her chest with a fat embrace.

"Happy birthday! Are you surprised? Oh *please* say you're surprised. I've been planning this all week!"

I laughed and hugged her back. She smelled like cardamom, and when I sank into her arms and neck, I found that
they were a perfect fit.

"I'm very surprised." Dom leaned against the doorway, trying her best to appear unaffected. With everything that had
transpired since my mother's return, I had completely forgotten that it was my nineteenth birthday. And given how I had
left the house, it seemed as if my parents had done the same.

"I didn't really have much say in this," Dom said. "When
Mom got the idea in her head that was pretty much the end
of the conversation." She walked up behind me and placed her
hand at the small of my back, then pulled out a chair. Foxy was
already beneath the table, waiting for crumbs of cake.

"Yes. It. Was." Niyala's punctuated breaths emphasized
her pride. She pulled a disposable camera out of her apron.
We both stared at her for different reasons, and she paused.
"What? We have to celebrate. It's your birthday! This is our
moment to bask in the glow of the next great concert pianist
before she's selling out Carnegie Hall. Squeeze together you
two, and smile!"

This time Dom really did look embarrassed, and whatever
clever retort she may have lined up in response seemed to dissi-
pate on her tongue. A grin split across my face, and as I moved
my chair closer to Dom, I felt my ankles pass to a burning red
beneath the table. I had never seen Dom blush before, but I
felt certain that she was just then, and I placed my hand on
her knee to let her know that she had been found out. Niyala pressed the shutter and wound the camera several times,

making sure to get us from several different angles—with the cake, and without it—before she was satisfied.

"Okay, okay, I think I have enough for future blackmail. You know, in case you decide to forget all about us when you're rich and famous." This time I rolled my eyes, but I couldn't keep the smile off my face. Niyala lifted her finger and shook it. "Okay, miss, I'll remember that. Just send us postcards from all of your adventures or I'm releasing these photos to the highest bidder of the trashiest tabloid. Nothing sells quite like teenage humiliation." She giggled to herself and slipped the camera back into her apron.

Niyala had prepared a feast. She wanted to know everything: how my mother was doing, which schools I was most interested in, if I would miss Florida at all, how excited I was about my audition. She asked me about which pieces I planned to play, and why, using my musical preferences to paint a picture of the concert pianist I would go on to become. Then she began to reminisce about her own years as a young college student studying music. She applied so much artistic license that I wanted her to one day tell the story of my life with similar enthusiasm and fondness—happy for it to be rewritten with her unique luster.

"I bet it's hard to watch your peers go off to school while you stay behind," she said. "But I think it's smart to take a year off before beginning another demanding curriculum. I think Europeans call it a gap year. If they can have one, why shouldn't you be able to?"

"That doesn't feel like the most accurate comparison." I

tried to choose my words strategically. Europeans took gap years to travel Europe, Asia, and Africa, where they could take photos with dark-skinned children. "My gap year was in my living room."

Niyala shrugged and smirked.

"Bah, you're destined for better things. Anyone can become an administrator, but you are an artist. A musician! There is no higher calling in life."

I could see that Dom wanted to interject with something sarcastic, but she didn't contradict her mother.

I felt drained and wide awake all at once, having run on pure adrenaline since Christmas. I barely remembered a single moment. My brain had been compassionate enough to wipe the past few months from my memory, but it had left just enough room for me to retain every detail of every second of that dinner at Dom's house, swathed in light and laughter—even with exhaustion tugging behind my eyes. But the smell of rice and peas, jerk chicken, and spicy patties seduced me from the edge of slumber to the middle of hunger. My appetite was a fever. Niyala clucked her tongue approvingly as she continued to spoon leftovers onto my plate. Dom ate a little, but mostly kept her eyes on me.

"Slow down, Gabs." She chuckled, but didn't try to stop me—ready to jump into action if I started to choke on a bone.

The phone rang, and Niyala excused herself after removing the plantain tarts from the fridge. I tore one open with my fingers, sucking the sweet violet goo that leaked from the seam of the parcel, then licking the buttery residue off my fingertips.

"Pssst."

I looked up mid-chew and Dom swooped in close to kiss me, holding my face in her hands. I dropped the tart on my plate and placed my greasy fingers on Dom's face, pushing my lips into hers. When I pulled back she gasped, and I laughed with my mouth still full of pastry. She kicked me beneath the table, and I kicked her back with a joy too full to stand still.

Niyala came back into the kitchen. Dom caught her first, and I caught the reflection of her face in Dom's eyes.

"What is it, Mom?"

Niyala composed herself, with the phone still in hand, and turned toward me.

"Gabrielle, child, you need to go home."

"Where is she?" I felt the joy bleed from my heart. I stood up ready to move quickly, imagining the problem to be right there in her house and not on the other side of town.

Niyala took a deep breath and exhaled.

"He won't wake up. That's all she said. He . . . he won't wake up."

36

I AM NOT A GOOD PERSON.

On the outside, I am my mother's reflection. On the inside, I am its distortion—with the swallowed thoughts, weakened stomach, flattened feet, and nervous impulse to bite my lip because I secretly ache to hurt the people I'm supposed to love, but secretly hate.

I am not a good person.

There are many different ways to die and I'm certain, when it came to my father, I had fantasized about them all. I borrowed deaths from the footnotes of history. A mathematician so paranoid about being poisoned that he only ate food if it was prepared by his wife who, after being hospitalized, left her husband to starve to death. Or the first Chinese emperor, who died after ingesting the mercury pills he thought would make him immortal. The hubris of it all was that it wasn't bitterness that ended my father, but the piano that he drunkenly passed out on after attempting to stand up from his afternoon nap.

When I was five years old, I liked to curl into the shape of my mother every day after preschool until every curve of my body fit into every crevice of hers, and I stayed there with her until my father came home to remind us that I belonged to him. As my mother imparted me with kisses, my father yanked me away by the shoulder and told me that my kisses were his. That was the first time I thought about killing him.

I am not a good person.

I didn't want to torture him. I didn't want to humiliate him. I didn't want to do anything to him that he had done to me. I just wanted him to expire, so that my mother and I could lick our wounds without carving out new ones. This seemed an act of mercy in my eyes.

I am not a good person.

I didn't clean the blood from the white carpet around the piano. Dom waited with me at home until my mother returned, and we sat on the sofa watching the blood stains turn from red to black. When Dom began to search for spray and rags, I asked her to stop. I had never seen color that bright left undisturbed in the house before. It was so out of place, and I felt it had earned its time to shine.

My father's blood alcohol was three times the legal limit when he fell. He lost his balance and came crashing down before his brain had sent the proper signals alerting him to the danger that waited below. It was supposedly an extraordinarily painful fall—one that crushed his spinal cord and broke his neck. It seemed too simple to be true, and I considered a number of external factors: a strong gust of wind through a cracked window, a bad piece of shellfish, a misplaced shoe with an evil agenda. I was convinced that some secret power had turned my wish into a reality, and I wondered if my father had fallen—or if I had been pushing him through pure mental will that had been manifesting for years. My father couldn't be ended through ordinary means.

I am not a good person.

All my father's girlfriends came to the funeral. Thin Lips. Crooked Teeth. Bearded Jaw. Hairy Mole—the Weird Mistresses whose very presence whispered tragedy and bloodshed. Their movement was a stiff breeze cloaked in matching black dresses. They avoided getting too close to my mother. The skin beneath my dress flushed white from the chill that kissed my neck every time they walked past. Each one individually expressed her sympathy to me, listing all the glowing attributes in my father they would miss: his warmth, his generosity, his compassion. They wrung their hands together and blew into snotty handkerchiefs lined with the smudged mascara that had caked around their blue eyes. I knew that they were four different people, but I couldn't tell them apart.

The left side of the church was occupied by expensive tailored suits, expensive watches, and exasperated sighs. The right side was me, her, and the ghosts of people who welcomed him home. My mother was quiet during the service, with her hands folded in her lap. Reverend Jeremiah's benediction was framed by the church chorus. Gospel hymns transposed to pop tempos filled the church.

"Jesus has come to welcome home his beloved son." The Reverend stood at a wooden pulpit in a dark pin-striped suit with a white rose on his lapel. My mother's eyes were large pools when he spoke, swallowing him up.

"We can't always understand his master plan, but we must

trust in it nonetheless—especially when the days seem their darkest." He paused to drink in the attention. "And we ask the Lord, and all his sheep here today, to care for Tallulah and Gabrielle while they grieve the loss of their loving, faithful, honest, devoted husband and father."

When the casket procession began, my mother changed suddenly. She wailed as if she had just discovered her own lungs, surprised to find that they weren't just a pair of organs that let her breathe, but an alarm that she could sound at will. She collapsed into my arms. The light fell on the skin of her throat as she cried, her voice scraped raw from trying to reach the floors of heaven. My father's colleagues, having finally realized that they were at a funeral and not a protracted board meeting, stopped checking their watches and stared at their feet instead—heads hung with the weight of shame, and I luxuriated in their guilt.

The casket was large enough to contain a few average-size people, or one very large one, the lid left open to display the velvet-lined interior. I tried to look at his body without running away. I wondered how he had continued to age since the day he had died. It gave me an opportunity to really see him for the very first time: the constellation of pockmarks on his face that marked the journey from little boy to sadistic tyrant; the little knot of cartilage jutting out of his throat; his stout belly brushing up against the roof of the casket. It was the first time I had ever seen my father with groomed eyebrows. I was anxious for the undertaker to close the lid, as concerned as I was that he wouldn't stay dead.

I wanted the others to see everything—especially the Weird Mistresses. My mother's response, my father's presence, and how I absorbed it all, allowing it to ferment. The grief of my father's death didn't belong to them. It belonged to the people who grieved the lives they had given up for him. The moment my mother and I sat back down on the right side of the church, she stopped crying. She went silent, lifted her head, and swallowed any remaining anguish until her belly was full.

37

RUMOR OF MY FAMILY'S MISFORTUNE SPREAD AROUND our small designer neighborhood. Wherever we went, people offered sympathetic goods in place of sympathetic words— homemade casseroles, freshly caught catfish, jambalaya and pound cakes that smelled delicious and tasted like nothing. I left them on the counter for my mother, who licked the plates clean every night. "At least she's gotten her appetite back," Dom said.

My mother began to leave the house again, waking up early to buy various adornments to fill up the space a man once occupied. But she was sloppy. She had stopped caring about her dulled skin color, and let people stare. The church set up a hotline for us where the public was encouraged to call in with prayers and donations for my family's resilience, but it was quickly taken over by psychics who claimed to have been visited by my father in their sleep. They were the same ones who appeared on television in bright blue eyeshadow and pink lipstick, with wrists weighed down by gold jewelry. The freckled skin of their forearms dangled as they touched their temples and clutched the pendants around their sagging necks—drawing upon the strength of some dead relative who had been a witch or a shaman or some other iteration of "spiritual but not religious." One woman called our house directly and said that she had seen a vision of my father in her soup, and when I asked her what he looked like, she said "cold."

The only person who didn't try to make things better and, therefore, didn't make things worse—was Dom. Not long after the funeral, she began to pick me up for lessons. Her car bothered my mother much less than it had bothered my father, though the neighbors found it fascinating. One day it was just a "convenient stop" on her way home from the music store, the next she was "just in the neighborhood," and the day after that, it was "raining too hard" for me to take the bus or ride my bicycle. Eventually, I stopped asking. She wanted to be there, and I didn't want to be alone.

If I wasn't at the house when my mother came home from searching for bargains, she'd call Dom's to mumble into the phone at Niyala, Dom, and myself—becoming angrier and angrier as the phone passed from one ear to the other. Though she often threatened to, my mother never picked me up. I arrived home, prepared to atone for my offense, but she was always shut away in her bedroom with the door closed. I only heard the dull incantations of a preacher blaring from the television.

Sometimes, I heard my mother stumble into the living room in the middle of the night. I heard her crying softly to herself. Other nights, I heard a sound like clapping, and when I met her at the breakfast table, I found fresh bruises budding on her calves and wrists, as dark and bitter as unsweetened coffee. When I asked her what had happened, she only shrugged.

My mother's need for new dysfunction intensified. In me, she found a source of enduring resentment. But as long as people kept dropping by to express their condolences and offer their support, she managed herself with polite conversations that only lasted a few minutes.

Then one morning I woke up and found my mother watching television in her nightgown. She leaned forward from the sofa with her palms pressed together in front of her face. It was difficult to make sense out of what was on the screen until I rubbed the sleep from my eyes. People were caked in dust and debris, disoriented and wandering around with severed limbs and bloodied faces, ashen and gray. Policemen and firefighters clawed at the rubble of a federal building then ran in every direction as another level came tumbling down, and bodies toppled down over layers of brick and live wires. The camera switched to a helicopter view of a building that had been leveled by a two-ton car bomb. Inside the structure, there were desks, chairs, children's toys, wiring, and ceiling fans— inanimate objects as mangled as the people spilling out into the street.

People stopped asking about how we were doing after that, and my mother stopped leaving the house.

———

Dom and I drove past the men who usually played checkers. They were huddled around the silver glow of a small television that had been dragged out of the liquor store so that everyone could watch the aftermath of the bombing.

Inside her home, Niyala was watching the news from a TV on the kitchen counter. One hand was balanced on her hips and the other held a knife. The room smelled like onions and burnt garlic and vegetables lay partially chopped on the counter. We called out to her when we entered, and took turns hugging her, before the mug shot flashed on the screen again and again. We stared at it together, unmoving.

Niyala returned to the cutting board, slicing some peppers, removing the seeds with small jerking movements. The tips of her fingers had turned angry from the spice. She didn't respond to any of our questions or chide us for sneaking into the bag of kiss cakes in the pantry. As we turned to exit into the living room, Niyala pointed the knife at the TV, shaking it repeatedly. Her voice strained, cracked from the inside out.

"And they *say* that they're afraid of *us*."

38

WHEN I WAS YOUNGER, I SAW THE EARTH MOVE FOR
the first time. My mother took me outside to look up at the
sky, the color of alligator skin.

"See?" she said, bending over to smooth back my hair from
my eyes. "We're not the only ones."

The wind picked up and I heard the rustling anticipation
of leaves. When the lightning flickered behind the clouds, the
air around us became a twitching network of veins. The dogs
circled on their chains, growling like old men at the sky. The
Great Dane that occasionally nuzzled my mother for a pinch
of nutmeg broke loose, then ran down the street barking at the
shuttered windows that shivered as she passed.

My father was nailing plywood to ours but accidentally hit
his thumb with the hammer. He retreated indoors, and the
half-exposed window winked while we watched him fill his
plastic cup.

The ground writhed like skin, opening up small pockets
from which snakes slithered out as crooked as scars. The holes
became mouths that swallowed up the surface. Houses, mini-
vans, people, dogs, whole highways with restless traffic—one
minute, barely able to exist beside one another, the next—not

existing at all. Life became an abstraction, once rooted in a cross-stitch of buildings and streets, turned inside out by an angry cloud that tipped the world on its edge until everything spilled out. The storm stripped the trees of their pretty green leaves, exposing the naked, ugly roots buried underground, that resented us for pretending that they weren't there. Now, with them replanted, I pass their stalks in reverence.

My mother and I made a game of it. We ran around the backyard in our nightgowns, howling at the wind like a pair of wolves, mocking the storm with our skin. When the clouds turned black, so did we. When the sky turned violet, so did we. When the storm turned *violent*, so did we—throwing up our arms, convulsing, and kicking with our legs like we were possessed. It was the first time I remember being in awe of my mother. She was utterly fearless when it came to the disorder that circled in on our unbent piece of earth.

When the rain began to pour, we passed our skin into the color of blood to keep us warm through the chill. But then my father screamed at us from his drunken perch to come inside, and when we finally did, he hid behind the couch while the house shook, whimpering into his cup, while my mother and I prowled the house, too excited to calm down. Furloughed from our usual roles, we edged the furniture with our shoulders, and we danced in the living room like twisters all the way through the eye of the storm.

Through the window, I watched the large oak tree in our front yard begin to sway, stretching and cracking the earth around it. With a single painful groan, it was torn from the ground and collapsed onto the house across the street, pulling the power lines down with it.

Then it was dark. And so were we.

We were woken up the next morning by the Great Dane's barking. And upon surveying the damage to the street, we found one of our neighbors in the hole created by the oak tree's demise—eyes dead, palms turned up as if asking to be beckoned home. He was tied between the roots like rope, an intricate network of slipknots around his arms, legs, and neck.

It was as if they had been waiting for him.

———

I heard her feet slapping against the hard white floorboards on her way to my room. She slipped through, even though there was no one left to hide from. My mother's bedroom visits came off the backs of weird dreams, with bowls of magnolias swimming in water as offerings to soothe the nightmares. She placed them on my dresser, and climbed into bed with me, clutching on to my arms to tell me she was afraid.

"Afraid of what?"

Afraid of the news, and the world, and ghosts, and empty spaces, crowded corners, and men—the way that men can rip the faces off buildings, while hiding behind their own masks for years. I tried being gentle and coaxed her with soft-spoken assurances.

"Nobody will hurt us. We're safe here."

But her grip strengthened until the skinny fingers bit into my muscle. She needed to hear those things from me because her own mind warped the same words into a lie that she couldn't trust. I untangled myself from her grip, uttering soft rebukes that cut her face with anguish.

"It just feels weird."

"I have to pee."

"I'm ready to get up now."

The meaning of even my mother's innocent touches changed in the aftermath of the real physical intimacy I shared with Dom. The affection I shared with my mother was either welcome or disagreeable—but it could never be ambiguous again. I wanted to embrace her, but my bed seemed like the worst place to do that. Rejecting her had chipped away at the last remaining drops of glue holding us together.

"What are you up to today?" I was careful to remove myself from the question. I edged into my closet to change, emerging as she sat up on the bed.

"Maybe you should think of singing again. I would really love to see that."

She didn't speak, kneading her threadbare nightgown between her hands. I had an idea and ran out of my bedroom across the house into hers, opening up her closet, searching. When I came back, I held up her purple choir robe.

"You look so beautiful in this." I laid it on the white bedspread, fanning out its velvet sleeves so the embroidered gold dove on the breast shone brightly. The only thing missing was a silver tinsel halo.

She lay back in my bed, pulling the sheets over herself, pushing the robe toward the end of the bed with her feet until it fell on the floor. There was a brief sigh, and then she was asleep again.

I watched the outline of her body rise and fall beneath the covers for a few minutes, then I marched over toward the window and drew the blinds, welcoming in bright sunlight. Her eyes remained closed, unaffected.

I slammed the bathroom door behind me—and locked it.

All my life I had looked forward to my father's business trips so that my mother and I could be left alone, to eat, and play, to love each other. But when we buried him, we buried the parts of ourselves that knew how to exist without him.

In the end, he took everything.

"Are you going to the firing range?"

My mother was awake when I finished, but still in my bed. Her face was garish, ominous like the storm rapidly barreling toward us. The hurricane reached from Key West to Leon County.

"Firing range?" I ate a white peach for breakfast, offering one to her. She was slow to acknowledge the gesture. Her eyes were thoughtful, laced with sleep.

"With your father."

I paused, feeling the peach's flesh sour on my tongue.

"With Dad?" My words were slow, pointed.

Gifted from the trenches of the Atlantic, Hurricane Harriet had become a category-five-level storm the night before. A traditional start to Floridian summer.

She pinched a piece of lint from the bedspread and hmm'd affirmatively.

"What time will you two be home?"

My stomach clenched.

"Mom."

"This storm is going to be nasty."

I swallowed hard, and felt the peach cut my throat.

"I'm making his favorite tonight."

I nodded slowly, feeling each click in my neck, unable to bring myself to believe what she was saying. I strained to remember his body in the casket. His groomed eyebrows. His reedy legs. His belly pushing against the lid. I looked into the living room. The piano was still there.

"Do you mind if I hang out with a friend tonight?"

Her hands snaked around the peach in her lap.

"Is it Dominique?"

I nodded.

"Sure."

She pulled the sheets back up around her, clutching the peach in her hands.

SERVICE STATIONS AND discount supermarkets across the county sold out of gas, batteries, and toilet paper the week before. There was an odd comfort in knowing that, though the state could detach and drift out to sea any moment, it'd be done on a bedrock of clean assholes whistling harmoniously together into oblivion. I took the path through the woods, passing into white beneath their empty branches, and scoured the empty supermarket in search of last-minute scraps for the hurricane party Dom was throwing. Wind had already started contracting around the neighborhood, twisting itself through the trees. They sang to me as I bowed to them. The only items in the store were a family-size bag of 3D Doritos, a six-pack of Hi-C coolers, and a lone box of Little Debbie oatmeal cream pies, abandoned on the shelf—the only snack food that nobody wanted to evacuate. In Florida, survival is a season.

An old woman with red hair graying at the roots was the only other person in the store. She looked like the dog-eared pages of a used book that tells the story of a dozen hurricanes that had come before, and all the things she had lost to them. Laboring over every item, her raspy breath a soundtrack that guided each product from one side of the scanner to the other. The remaining last-minute confection by the checkout was a Berry Blast Ring Pop. When I put it on the conveyor belt for her to include, she surveyed the empty market.

"You might as well take it before the looters come." She released a wet hiccup, and I caught the scent of sour cream and onion.

"Are you staying?" I tilted my head, emphasizing the creamy white skin on my throat. She lit a cigarette in her yellowing fingernails and leaned across the counter so that her nose dove into the cloud of smoke.

"Darlin', I don't get out of bed for anything below a category four."

"But this one's a category five." I put the Ring Pop in my pocket. She took another long drag from her cigarette, swallowing the smoke.

"Well, I'm outta bed, ain't I?"

I passed back in the woods on my way home and threw the Ring Pop into a puddle of mud, where it joined a torn condom wrapper. Horny, chaotic Floridians.

My mother had pulled up a chair on the front porch where she sat in her nightgown. Neighbors loaded bicycles and strollers on the roofs of their cars, shouting at each other, and she observed the curious panic.

"Hey there, Tallulah!" Our neighbor Diane waved while nailing plywood against her windows with her husband. I had walked past multiple houses being shuttered up with plywood, but ours remained open, gawking at the small caravans of cars as they peeled down the street. *Cowards,* it said.

My mother waved back, and crossed her legs, allowing a current of ants to pass beneath her heels unscathed. Diane held a large bottle of water as she spoke to my mother, sipping from it occasionally and nodding.

"You sticking around?"

My mother rocked back and forth in her chair calmly. It was still bright outside, though the wind had picked up speed. I could see the outline of her breasts drooping slightly; the line of her bony hips stuck out sharply. A few people stopped to stare as she drank up the sunlight while the rain bands closed in from the east and the birds began to shriek.

"Sure that's a good idea? They say this one is gonna be the one." Diane's voice was accented with concern. "We got some room in the van, if you and Gabrielle wanna join us? We're heading to the arena."

"We have plans for dinner tonight, Diane." My mother's tone was even. "So you better get going. Don't wanna hit the interstate during peak traffic." Diane pursed her face, shrugged, and walked back across the adjoining lawn with both hands at the small of her back. She had tried. It was more than anyone else would do. As they pulled out of the driveway, I caught Matthew's face through a tinted window, covered in pale sweat and sunscreen as they joined the cavalcade of people rushing to the far end of the city for shelter.

I walked inside and I saw something on the kitchen table, laid out on the glass, torn into incoherent fragments. I picked up a piece and let it float back down to the tabletop. Then I picked up another.

It was a letter. I sifted through the ripped pieces until I found two scraps with the letters *Ber* and *klee* in cursive.

I scrabbled with both hands, working the pile of scraps like puzzle pieces, trying to construct a cohesive message, or a call to action, or even a single sentence. That's when I found the pieces *Jui* and *lliard*. It wasn't *a* letter. It was many.

The spiky leaf of a neighboring palm tree tapped on the sliding glass door. My mother was still sitting on the front porch, her back turned toward me. It would have satisfied most people to tear a piece of paper two or three times, but she had mangled them.

The names of places I had assumed rejected me slowly came together, reaching out instead with open arms. I made out dates, some of which had already passed, and the horror of this realization made my stomach crash. The shakes set in, and pieces of paper fell from my fingers all over the table, just as the first pellets of rain began to tap on the roof, ahead of schedule, excited to raze the land around us. My skin passed into the color of chili, and it burned as I pushed it back.

I repeated the words aloud several more times to convince my mind of what I had read. There were still approaching deadlines, but I had no way of telling which one applied to which school. She had made it impossible to form a full picture. I piled the pieces together and scooped them into my hands, stuffing them into my pockets. The thunderclaps moved closer together.

All the windows in the house had been opened with the thick white curtains pulled back into pale smiles. Small droplets began to slap against the house, and into the living room, the kitchen, the bedrooms, girdled by a wind that pushed down the narrow hallway connecting the kitchen to my bedroom. I grabbed what I could. The dress was marred in dust balls beneath the bed, but I shoved it into my backpack nonetheless. My journal. Pens. A broken crystal music box. That was everything. That was all of me.

She was on the porch, swaying from side to side like a tree about to collapse, stripped of all her pretty leaves. Reverend Jeremiah's face lit up the TV in the living room. Though the sound was muted, I read the familiar rebukes from his lips, as unchanging as the Old Testament itself.

My mother's skin contracted as I approached. She had looked tired for a long time—pale, thin, wrung out like a flimsy rag—but never old. Yet real age had snuck up on her all the same—the kind that sinks into eyes, noses, and mouths until all that's left is skull. I tried to remember when it had happened and thought of the day we buried my father, realizing that she must have truly loved him, because she had spent nearly thirty years and her entire youth waiting for him to die. That was no small commitment.

"What time will you come back from the range?" She placed her elbows on the open windowsill, leaning backward into the house as rain trickled down her face.

I didn't answer, and she finally looked at me. With a firm voice, she repeated her question.

"A couple of hours," I replied, feeling that this was somehow the answer she wanted. I went to close the door, but she interjected.

"Leave it," she said. "The breeze is nice."

I slowly dropped my hand, and walked down the porch—stepping over the ants moving frantically as the wind picked up and began to bend the palm trees around us. The smell of algae from the neighborhood drainage ditch mixed with the sound of crickets and whimpering dogs. A clap of thunder pierced through the wet night as I limped down the driveway and into the chaotic darkness. Thick green clouds swirled overhead, blanketing the neighborhood, and heavy rain began to slant down in every direction. When I looked back, our once bright white house had been reduced to large gaping holes being cut into shards by the slanting rain. The brick and paneling were blurred by the chaos of the storm, and in the middle of it all—a woman with a vacant smile on her face. As

I ran, her silhouette was drowned behind me until it was only a dull light that too disappeared. One minute the door was open, and the next it was shut.

I tried to laugh. I tried.

D Major

(What love tells me)

39

THE RAIN HAD RIPPED THE FLIP-FLOPS OFF MY FEET. A streetlight exploded overhead, the broken glass falling around me and tearing into my heels as I hobbled to a nearby 7-Eleven. I called Dom from a pay phone shortly before a transformer blew up behind a neighboring fence, knocking out power throughout the block. I hardly recognized her car through the sheets of rain that tossed it across the lanes. The road was obscured by rain, but I made her out when she began to flick her lights on and off. She pulled in front of a gas pump long bereft of gas, and we turned around just as a gust of wind nearly tilted the car off its axis, twisting the chassis like a washcloth. Her expert swerving showed me it wasn't the first time she had driven in a hurricane, and she navigated the toppled power lines and trees with precision.

I hobbled to their front door on bloody feet. While Niyala paced the living room floor, I tried and failed and then stopped explaining what had happened. When Niyala went to the kitchen and returned with a bowl of warm water and bandages, it was Dom who took them from her, sinking to her knees to clean the cuts on my feet, gripping them tightly in her hands to numb the sting.

"I'll try calling the house," Niyala said flatly. "Maybe she's still there." Dom looked up with a severe expression and shook her head, but even then she didn't try to stop her mother. Niyala glanced over her shoulder to make sure we were still there before disappearing behind the swinging door that led to the kitchen.

Dom removed the small bits of gravel and glass from my feet, her blue fingernails turning brown with blood. She didn't stop until it was done—not even when my color passed from brown to red to black in the clutch of her palms. She bandaged my feet and I slept in her bed for only the second time, finding that the sheets prickled against my skin, even though I sank into them like a corpse, finally and mercifully entombed.

A spirit came to me that night. She knocked on the coffers of my dream until I woke, and when I opened my eyes there was a tall woman with red skin and scar-shaped lips that bled when she smiled. I wanted to scream, but I couldn't open my mouth. She slapped me hard with hands that felt like paddles expressing her disappointment. "I'm a ghost," she said, as if what she really meant was, *Dummy, can't you scream? That's the point.*

I squeezed my eyes shut, and when they opened again she was still there, with a face painted in black and white and a halo of eagle feathers. She knelt beside my bed, looking into me with the dark holes where her eyes should have been. Taking my head into her hands, she leaned forward and sang in my ear, her voice hissing like a rattlesnake. I blinked, and she became an old woman with a puckered expression that came to a point at her mouth, shriveled like the pedicel of a lemon. She collapsed on the floor and writhed until her skin peeled away and all that was left was dust.

That was when I screamed.

Dom shook me awake, rocking me in her arms as I sobbed into the bedsheets, clawing at myself. She forced my hands into my lap and whispered soft comforts into my neck until I had nothing left. She waited for me to speak.

"I didn't even have the courage to say goodbye."

———

The day after the storm had passed, we went looking for my mother. The roof of the house had collapsed, and all the white things it had once contained were smeared in mud and leaves. I went into the bathroom, where I had found her body once before, and an alligator hissed from the tub. Its claws scratched against the porcelain basin as it tried to extract itself. It knew the curse that had been placed there.

We held a small service when the debris was cleared from the land, but nobody came, because we didn't have a body— and so many others waited for graves. The Reverend promised to show, but we waited for an hour before carrying on without him. Niyala said a few words instead.

"Life isn't easy. Lord knows it isn't."

The tone of a person who had said words like these too many times before.

"But Tallulah O'Hara gave it her best and brought into the world a beautiful daughter that I—that we—will look after from here on out. Rest in peace, dear angel." She laid a blanket flower on the ground and stepped back, motioning for me to continue. I stepped backward instead.

"Gabs, it's bad luck not to speak at your mother's service." Dominique was adamant. Both of them implored me with superstitious expressions. I shuffled forward. My feet were heavy, and my fingers fidgeted.

"My mother was special." I waited for more to come to me. "There was something in her blood that made her special." I lowered another blanket flower onto the ground, then stepped back. I didn't acknowledge the concern on Niyala's or Dom's faces. I didn't know how to explain to them that I had already said goodbye on my own, and that it didn't involve any words they would find comforting.

We planted a magnolia tree where my house used to be, and it blooms every spring. The dogs from around the block take turns keeping her company, nestling in her shadow, ripping up her weeds, adoring the broken twigs that fall to the ground, smelling of cinnamon and nutmeg. With every storm, her roots shift in the ground to claim something new, and now she rests on a pile of dead, broken things—a tomb of her own unique creation.

40

THE MORNING OF MY BERLIN AUDITION, I PULLED
the black-and-gold dress out of my backpack and presented it
to Niyala.

"This thing looks like it's been through a hurricane." She
winked at me, then reached into the cupboard for the ironing board. "You go on and get ready, child. I'll take care of
this." She took it from one hand, while Dom held on to the
other. She hadn't let me go since the night of Harriet, when
the strength of the wind nearly forced me into her car, and she
slipped her fingers through mine to make sure I didn't blow
away. Leading me into her bedroom and sitting me on the
floor in front of her bed, she gently pressed my head back so
that her face hovered above mine.

"You ready?" She smiled down at me. I smiled back, letting
my shoulders drop and easing into the space between her legs.

"You'll be fine." She began to smooth my edges with her
hands, dividing the curls into sections again before remem-
bering that she didn't have the coconut oil by her side. "Shit—
hang on." She flipped a leg over my head and jogged out of
the room. I leaned against her bed, and the green book I had
inspected in her car once fell down from the edge. A serious

woman with a freckled face and a short Afro posed on the inside back cover. I flipped through the pages once again, and two pieces of paper fell out: the rejection letter from Berlin, and another letter from Berklee College. I read it twice before I heard Dom's heavy steps approaching.

"Found it!"

She waved a small tub of oil and collapsed onto the bed—moving the book behind her with a swift gesture. I closed my eyes and leaned my head back to keep the swirling thoughts from tumbling out. She slowly inserted the long end of a comb through my hair and began to grease my scalp. I swallowed several times to keep my voice even.

"Did you ever hear back from Berklee?"

"Nope, not yet." Dom sighed. "But maybe the hurricane delayed the mail? I'll give it some time. And anyway . . ." She tilted my chin up to face her, that familiar assertion. "Today is about you. Don't worry about Berklee. You need to keep Berlin on the brain." I forced my lips to curl into a smile, but it didn't reach the corners of my eyes.

"I'm so excited for you," she continued. "A fresh start in Berlin. I'm so proud!"

She rubbed the coconut oil between her hands and ran them through my hair, massaging my scalp, working the strands from root to tip. I nodded while she talked, and laughed when I couldn't—anything to keep my eyes dry, burning until they were rimmed with thin red cracks where tears should have been.

"This is a delegation—not the teachers you'd be studying

under directly, just their representatives based here. But if you don't impress them, you don't get in, so . . ."

"So I should impress them." My tone was flat.

She clucked her tongue affirmatively.

"What—what exactly do they know about me?"

Dominique paused briefly, holding the paddle brush. Several hairpins hung out of her mouth like toothpicks.

"Pretty much just what was on your application, and in the recommendation letter.

"Just remember that I'll be with you every step of the way," she repeated several times.

"Actually, I was thinking . . ." I tried to disguise my pause as scalp pain. "I'd like to go into the audition alone."

She looked at me in the mirror.

"Oh, okay." She moved her hands again and then stopped. "Are you sure?"

I felt my teeth grind as the lips parted into a smile.

If she was hurt, she didn't let it show. I wondered if she had learned that from me.

"Okay, I can wait in the café." Dom's eyes darted almost imperceptibly to the book by her side, then back to my scalp, smoothing back the edges until my hair was pulled into a smooth bun that lifted the skin of my cheeks, sharpening the bones underneath into arrowheads.

"Just remember—when you walk into that auditorium, you walk in there like you own everything and everyone in it. Got it?"

She worked on my hair silently, and I wrapped my hands around her ankles, trying to memorize their shape, their texture, how the bone of the left foot was slightly smaller than the bone of the right.

WE SAT IN the car. Dom traced the thick dark lines in my palm with her fingers as if they were a million tiny cuts that she could smooth away. I thought about all the scores she had drawn on my arms. My hands. My finger that sparkled with the fake ring she had slipped on. I watched others come and go with their music books and raw emotions, soothed by the instructors and parents gathered around them.

The clock on the dashboard said I was twenty minutes out from my audition, and I decided to head inside. I gently pulled my hand away from Dom and turned to the door, but my fingers hovered on the lever. We were both afraid to speak.

"I'll be here when you get back." Her voice was thick. "You got this."

I left without acknowledging this. The walk to the auditorium was painful—each step its own kind of end.

The building was freezing inside. The sound of distant notes drew me closer to the audition hall where I listened as one girl made several errors on her baroque score, stopping each time to apologize with high-pitched excuses. When she left the auditorium with a trembling bottom lip, a hive of people swarmed around her before the tears had a chance to hit the collar of her dress.

A cellist sitting across from me motioned with her chin toward the girl being escorted through the exit, held up by loved ones who repeated in harmony that her performance had not been "that bad."

"Another one bites the dust." The cellist shared her smug declaration with a violinist sitting next to her.

Once the hallway had emptied out, I was alone with all the things I hadn't said in the car to Dom. I was the last musician for the afternoon. I went into the bathroom across the hall, the click of my knockoff designer shoes echoing on the hard floor beneath me. I steadied myself in an empty toilet stall, waiting for my hands to stop shaking. The lingering smell of vomit sat firmly in the air, a parting gift from the pianist who had suffered a case of debilitating performance anxiety before butchering her étude. My eyes searched the stall, and I noticed a tiny line of white powder on the toilet lid, smeared into an ashy residue that faded into the porcelain finish. The cold in my hands flooded the rest of my body, and the chill stiffened my posture like a plank of wood.

I was as white as hate.

As I exited, the auditorium opened and a pear-shaped woman called my name. I gave her my books and walked past her into the concert hall, down the stairs to the large black grand piano in the middle of the platform. The seats rose up around me and I sank into the stage. As I descended, the judges' gazes consumed me as if they were observing me with their mouths instead of their eyes.

There were three of them, sitting in ascending order of

sour disposition, each one with a facial expression more caustic than the last; all of them woven together to form a single wrinkled scowl. My music was laid out before them, naked and shrinking beneath their flaccid stares.

"Whenever you're ready," said the man with a pointed, ashen face.

I placed my hands on the piano keys, and when my fingers began to move, I played as if the music, the piano, the stage, the auditorium, and the ground beneath were mine. I called them by a name that wasn't their own, and said that they belonged to me.

Just the way she taught me to.

Acknowledgments

I AM FOREVER GRATEFUL TO MY OUTSTANDING AGENT, Milly Reilly, for believing in this story (and in me) from the very beginning and being a tireless champion for Gabrielle and Tallulah; to Andrea Joyce for making sure it found a place back in my first home, where it belongs.

To the brilliant team at Catapult, especially my publicist, Selihah White, and my editor, Alicia Kroell, whose razor-sharp editorial eye challenged me to bring this story to a level I couldn't previously imagine; Radhiah Chowdhury and Meredith Curnow at Penguin Random House Australia, for embracing this story down under. My ANZ family thanks you too.

Thank you to Nikki, who gave me access to the kind of reading that taught me the history never covered in any public school curriculum; to Cousin Joe and Cousin-in-love Kellie, for coming into my life at precisely the right moment; Claire, my sister in all but name, and your parents, Jude and Michael, who are family in the only ways that matter.

It would be impossible to thank all my friends, but I do want to highlight a few women and genderqueer people who have pushed me to this point with their tireless support and invaluable perspectives on gender, race, motherhood, mental health, music, magic, accessibility, and family over many, many years. Their wisdom is interwoven throughout this book and is now also a part of me—body and soul.

They are Shannon T. Lewis, Verónica Soledad Zaragovia, Dr. Jessica J. Lee, Dr. Cassandra Thiesen, Jen Bell, Dr. Uchenna Ikediobi-Jukić, Danielle Smith, Sorcha Breen, Karamea Grant, Vicky Kershaw, and Kellie Robertson. Y'all are truly unfuckwitable.

To my blurb writers who made time and space to write deeply kind words about this story: Rebecca Rukeyser, Tom Drury, Gene Kwak, Sami Shah, and Ruby Hamad.

Amy and Tom from the Berlin Writers' Workshop for making me think critically about love and violence on the written page. Everyone at the MacDowell Artist Residency program for supporting artists like me (and keeping us well-fed in the process).

Archana, for taking such care in helping me get here.

Given that music played such a significant role in this project, I want to share a playlist of albums that shadowed me while writing, scrapping, writing, editing, selling, and reediting this book. I wrote this story to an exclusive playlist of classical and jazz music (much of which is referenced in the story itself). But that doesn't account for the hours spent walking around my local park while meditating on plot holes. These artistic productions have been my lifeblood for the past six years. I can't promise that listening to any of these albums will add some color and shape to the story for anyone who reads it, but I can't promise that it won't either:

Ohms (and *Gore*) by Deftones
Crosses (and *Permanent.Radiant*) by Crosses
Distorted Lullabies (and *Mercy*) by Ours (Jimmy Gnecco)
Blame My Body by Little May
Coloring Book (and *Material Control*) by Glassjaw
Bosnian Rainbows by Bosnian Rainbows
Honeyblood by Honeyblood

To Pimp a Butterfly by Kendrick Lamar

Good News by Megan Thee Stallion

Fossora (and *Utopia*) by Björk

Everybody Is F.O.O.D. 3 by Conway

AIM (and *MATA*) by M.I.A.

We Got It From Here… Thank You 4 Your Service by A Tribe Called Quest

Dawn by Yebba

Ctrl (and *SOS*) by SZA

Over It by Summer Walker

Cuz I Love You by Lizzo

Cool It Down by Yeah Yeah Yeahs

Blackstar by David Bowie

DiCaprio 2 (and *The Forever Story*) by JID

The EP trilogy by Nine Inch Nails

Lianne La Havas by Lianne La Havas

99 Cents (and *Spirituals*) by Santigold

Ego Death by The Internet

Mountain Moves by Deerhoof

Swimming by Mac Miller

JP3 by Junglepussy

Fetch the Bolt Cutters by Fiona Apple

Prima Donna EP by Vince Staples

Remind Me Tomorrow by Sharon Van Etten

American Love Song by Ryan Bingham

Sound & Color by Alabama Shakes

Room 25 by Noname

RTJ4 by Run the Jewels

Caprisongs by FKA Twigs

Leave the Light On by Pillow Queens

Ritual Spirit EP (and *The Spoils*) by Massive Attack

Trapsoul (and *Anniversary*) by Bryson Tiller
Wasteland, Baby! by Hozier
Kingfish by Christone "Kingfish" Ingram
Skin Deep (and *Sweet Tea*) by Buddy Guy
1–4 EP by Jelani Blackman

Vielen Dank to the Philharmonie Berlin for comping me a ticket to see a performance of Mahler's Symphony no. 3, which provided me with the inspiration to completely restructure the book.

To Natasha Lomboy, my best friend, and my center of gravity, who has been pulling me back to Planet Earth (sometimes kicking and screaming) for nearly twenty years. I love you forever-ever ("Forever-ever?") Yes, jerk, forever-ever.

This story would have looked very different had it not been for my upbringing in the great state of Florida, whose swamp water runs through these veins and whose natural beauty acts as a tertiary character in this book. The story is fiction, but the magic of Florida is very much real. To the activists and ordinary citizens trying to preserve its beauty and integrity, I salute you, and I look forward to the day when the corrupt oligarchs who are doing their best to turn Florida into an authoritarian regime are either dead or in federal prison (whichever comes first).

Thank you to librarians and booksellers everywhere who are doing their best in a collapsing global economy—for creating spaces where children are safe to daydream, as I did (and still do) so very often.

And finally, to everyone who spent their hard-earned cash on a copy of this book and/or took the time to check it out of a library—I hope you enjoyed the ride. As long as people read, hope remains. From the bottom of my heart—thank you.

JENNIFER NEAL is an American Australian author, artist, and occasional stand-up comedian. Her work has been published in NPR, *Playboy*, *Gay Magazine*, *The Root*, *The Cut*, and many other publications. She is a MacDowell Fellow and a Pushcart Prize–nominated essayist. She is also the author of *My Pisces Heart*.